DUCHESS OF F

"Simply delightful. It has a cha_____
Lady but with a panache all of its own . . . It's a story that
will linger with you long after you read the charming
epilogue."   —*The Columbia (SC) State*

"I laughed, cried, and cheered in triumph right along with
spunky immigrant Lana and her Prince Charming, lov-
able scoundrel Jesse . . . The book grabs hold of your
heartstrings and will not let go! If you are a devotee of
the movies *Pretty Woman* and *My Fair Lady* or still choke
up at Disney's *Cinderella*, then you must read *Duchess of
Fifth Avenue!*"   —*A Romance Review*

"A very romantic read . . . A strong heroine, a caring
hero, compelling story, and a gorgeous setting—what
more can you ask for? When I'm lucky enough to read a
terrific romance like *Duchess of Fifth Avenue*, 'life,' as
Lana would say, 'is grand.' "   —*All About Romance*

"A delightful romance . . . has all of the elements to make
this a treat to devour."   —*Romance Reviews Today*

"A delightful story that is full of emotion . . . A read that
will reach into the reader's heart and this reviewer had a
lump in her throat at its ending . . . Four hearts!"
                                     —*Love Romances and More*

"Terrific . . . a powerfully descriptive historical romance."
                                     —*The Best Reviews*

"A lot of fun."   —*Curled Up with a Good Book*

continued . . .

"Simply marvellous . . . sure to leave many readers sighing contentedly with the last word . . . It is this reader's opinion that *Duchess of Fifth Avenue* is among [her] very best so far."   —*The Romance Reader's Connection*

"A sweet story . . . the abundant niceness is refreshing."
    —*Huntress Reviews*

ASHES OF DREAMS

"Delightful in its flashes of humor, poignant in its depiction of human characters, *Ashes of Dreams* makes for a good rainy afternoon read."   —*Crescent Blues*

"A pleasure to read . . . For sheer entertainment value, *Ashes of Dreams* is a treat. The fact that Langan is a skilled writer certainly doesn't hurt either."
    —*The Romance Reader*

"Tender and romantic . . . Ms. Langan will continue to be a must-buy for this reviewer and for any reader who enjoys heartwarming historical romances as well."
    —*Love Romances and More*

PARADISE FALLS

"Characters so incredibly human the reader will expect them to come over for tea."   —*Affaire de Coeur*

"Langan's historical romance provides a vivid look at the unpleasant realities of life for a single young woman without family protection in class-conscious, rural 1890s America."   —*Booklist*

"Nicely detailed descriptions, a straightforward plot, and sympathetic, beautifully depicted characters add up to a powerful, rewarding historical. Langan is a popular writer of heartwarming, emotionally involving romances."
      —*Library Journal*

"Ruth Ryan Langan tells a story that's as warm as a quilt on a snowy evening and tender as love's first kiss. *Paradise Falls* is a book that touches the heart and comforts the soul."   —*Nora Roberts*

HEART'S DELIGHT

RUTH RYAN LANGAN

BERKLEY SENSATION, NEW YORK

THE BERKLEY PUBLISHING GROUP
Published by the Penguin Group
Penguin Group (USA) Inc.
375 Hudson Street, New York, New York 10014, USA
Penguin Group (Canada), 90 Eglinton Avenue East, Suite 700, Toronto, Ontario M4P 2Y3, Canada
(a division of Pearson Penguin Canada Inc.)
Penguin Books Ltd., 80 Strand, London WC2R 0RL, England
Penguin Group Ireland, 25 St. Stephen's Green, Dublin 2, Ireland (a division of Penguin Books Ltd.)
Penguin Group (Australia), 250 Camberwell Road, Camberwell, Victoria 3124, Australia
(a division of Pearson Australia Group Pty. Ltd.)
Penguin Books India Pvt. Ltd., 11 Community Centre, Panchsheel Park, New Delhi—110 017, India
Penguin Group (NZ), 67 Apollo Drive, Rosedale, North Shore 0745, Auckland, New Zealand
(a division of Pearson New Zealand Ltd.)
Penguin Books (South Africa) (Pty.) Ltd., 24 Sturdee Avenue, Rosebank, Johannesburg 2196, South
Africa

Penguin Books Ltd., Registered Offices: 80 Strand, London WC2R 0RL, England

This is a work of fiction. Names, characters, places, and incidents either are the product of the author's imagination or are used fictitiously, and any resemblance to actual persons, living or dead, business establishments, events, or locales is entirely coincidental. The publisher does not have any control over and does not assume any responsibility for author or third-party websites or their content.

HEART'S DELIGHT

A Berkley Sensation Book / published by arrangement with the author

PRINTING HISTORY
Berkley Sensation mass-market edition / July 2007

Copyright © 2007 by Ruth Ryan Langan.
Cover art by Leslie Peck.
Cover design by Annette Fiore.
Handlettering by Ron Zinn.
Interior text design by Laura K. Corless.

ISBN: 978-0-425-21633-0

BERKLEY SENSATION®
Berkley Sensation Books are published by The Berkley Publishing Group,
a division of Penguin Group (USA) Inc.,
375 Hudson Street, New York, New York 10014.
BERKLEY SENSATION is a registered trademark of Penguin Group (USA) Inc.
The "B" design is a trademark belonging to Penguin Group (USA) Inc.

PRINTED IN THE UNITED STATES OF AMERICA

10 9 8 7 6 5 4 3 2 1

*For all those generous souls who take in the lonely,
the unwanted, society's castoffs, and create family.
There's a special place in heaven for you.*

And for Tom, my heaven on earth.

PROLOGUE

———◆✦◆———

Chicago, Illinois—1890

HODGE EGAN PICKED up the cards dealt to him and eyed the pair of aces without expression. About time, he thought as he lifted the tumbler of whiskey to his mouth and drank. He'd been donating to Jasper Sullivan's wallet for two hours. He was long overdue to win a jackpot.

The overhead chandelier, aglow with dozens of candles, was reflected in the U.S. marshal badge pinned to the lapel of his black coat. When he picked up the expensive cigar and bit the end, a pretty woman with yellow dyed hair and a gown that revealed a great deal of pale, firm flesh reached over his shoulder to hold a flame to the tip. He puffed, adding to the pall of smoke that hung over the table. As soon as his glass was empty, the woman poured another drink from a crystal decanter. When she glided away, her perfume lingered.

"I'm in." Jasper, the chief of police and cousin to the mayor, tossed a gold piece in the center of the table.

"I'll see you." Maxwell Body, who owned a nearby stockyard, flipped his coin and watched it bobble before settling.

"Me, too." Emmet Harding, who owned one of Chicago's finest restaurants, took a coin from his neat pile and leaned forward to add it to the pot, all the while holding his cards close to his chest.

"Marshal?" Cyrus, the bartender at the Beal Street Hotel and Gentleman's Club, who was filling in for the regular dealer, looked over.

"May as well." Hodge kept his tone casual as he added his gold piece to the pile. "Been losing the whole night. Why stop now?"

The men around the table shared wolfish grins, each one waiting as Cyrus dealt the next of their cards.

"I hear you're thinking about retiring, Hodge." Jasper picked up his whiskey.

"How does a man retire from the law?" Emmet grinned.

"He turns in his badge and lives the good life." Hodge eyed the cards as they were dealt.

"You're too young to retire. What would you do with the rest of your life?" Jasper downed his drink in one long swallow.

"I'm thirty-six. That's old for a U.S. marshal. Most are dead by that time, killed in the line of fire." Hodge sat back. "Been thinking about going to San Francisco. Went there once to deliver a prisoner and spent the best week of my life visiting some fine gentlemen's clubs. I figure I'll grow old playing cards, drinking good whiskey, and enjoying pretty women."

Maxwell sighed. "Doesn't get much better'n that. I

envy you, Hodge. With no wife or kids holding you back, why not?"

"That's what I figure." Hodge watched their eyes as each man studied his hand. Over the years as a lawman he'd learned to read a lot in a man's eyes. His own were steely, unblinking, and guaranteed to put the fear of death in a man. He'd learned to use his eyes, his voice, like extensions of his weapons.

Jasper blinked hard, and Hodge knew the man wasn't happy with the outcome. Maxwell kept his gaze fixed on his cards, refusing to glance around, which only confirmed that he had what he hoped was a winning hand. Emmet glanced left, then right, as though trying to assess his chances against the others.

Only after he'd studied the others at the table did Hodge look at his own card. He fought to keep his composure as he saw the third ace. He was going to thoroughly enjoy raking in all that money. Not that he needed it. His pay as a U.S. marshal was generous, and his lifestyle simple. But the win would guarantee him bragging rights among his cronies for weeks.

"Jasper?" Cyrus nodded toward the man on his left.

"I'll call."

"Maxwell?"

The man's bushy beard twitched with humor. "You'll have to pay to see mine, Jasper." He glanced around the table before tossing another gold piece and accepting his last card. "You'll all have to pay to see these little darlings."

Emmet tossed down his cards. "Too rich for my blood."

Cyrus turned to Hodge. "Marshal?"

"I'll pay to see them. In fact, Maxwell, I believe I'll

just fatten the pot." He tossed two gold pieces and had the satisfaction of seeing Maxwell's eyes go wide.

"Thanks. I'll be happy to relieve you of all that . . ."

"Marshal!" A breathless voice was shouting hoarsely from the doorway.

Hodge glanced over with a twinge of annoyance when he recognized Will Stout, the kid who worked at the train station and ran the telegraph.

"Marshal!" With the air of one who had the attention of everyone in the room, the boy hurried over and announced loudly, "There's been a bank robbery in Madison."

"That's in Wisconsin, boy."

"Yes, sir." Will took a moment to catch his breath. "The robber shot a clerk working at the bank, then shot the bank president, before taking off with all the money. Before he left town he shot the police chief."

"How badly are they wounded?"

"They're all dead."

Hodge's eyes narrowed to slits. "Anybody on the case?"

The boy shrugged. "Don't know. With the police chief dead, they said they want you there as fast as you can ride."

Hodge swore, low under his breath. Damn the timing! He tossed down his cards.

Seeing them, Maxwell whistled. "Too bad you couldn't have toyed with us a while longer, Hodge. I figured my hand for a winner. Doubt I'd've quit until you ran me up a couple hundred more."

Hodge snarled. "Cash me out fast, Cyrus. I'll use it to buy my train ticket and bill the government later."

As he pocketed the gold and strode out the door, he swore again. The train would take him only as far as

Milwaukee. If the thief decided to make his escape into the back country, he could be weeks on horseback in some godforsaken wilderness before he'd know the luxury of a gentleman's club again.

He hoped this wasn't a sign that his luck was about to desert him.

ONE

———◆———

Delight, Wisconsin—1890

"Aunt Molly!" A chorus of children's voices had Molly O'Brien glancing over her shoulder in alarm. "Flora's hanging behind the wagon by her knees."

"Flora." Molly drew back on the reins, slowing their horse to a walk. "Get up at once and sit in back with the rest of your sisters. Right now."

"Yes'm."

A cursory glance showed that the fearless four-year-old had done as she'd been told.

"Don't try that again."

"I just wanted to see how the ground would look while we raced over it, Mama Molly."

Her comments caused no more than a sigh from the woman up front. Molly had gradually learned that this child would constantly test the boundaries of any rule. It was, quite simply, part of her nature.

"Why couldn't we stay in town another night, Aunt

Molly?" Ten-year-old Delia O'Brien sat astride a bulging flour sack in the back of the wagon, nibbling an apple from the bushel that her aunt had bartered at the Schroeder farm.

" 'Cause she didn't want to have to spend any more time with Mr. Monroe." Flora grabbed Delia's hand and managed a bite of her apple before the little girl snatched it away. "Isn't that right, Mama Molly?"

"That may have been part of it." It wasn't possible for Molly to lie, even about something as awkward as a farmer determined to court her. "But it was time to go. I just didn't have anything left to barter for another day at the boardinghouse, luv." Molly O'Brien carefully guided the team of horses around a stand of trees.

"Mrs. Teasdale would have let us stay another night for free," the little girl persisted. "She said she likes having us visit."

"It wouldn't be right to ask." Molly wiped a hand across her brow. "We always pay our way."

Flora looked up. "How come every time we go to town, Mrs. Teasdale introduces you to all those farmers?"

Sarah, the oldest, was quick to respond. "Because she thinks Aunt Molly should be married."

"I didn't like Mr. Monroe. He had mean eyes."

Molly sighed and fought for patience. "Flora, Milton Monroe is a nice man."

"He doesn't like little kids."

"Did he say that?"

Flora gave a quick shake of her head, sending dark curls dancing. "I could tell by the way he looked at us. He has mean eyes."

Molly let the remark pass without comment. Little

8

Flora's mother had called herself a gypsy, and though Flora couldn't remember her mother, she seemed to have inherited her gift for reading others.

The back of the wagon was loaded with sacks of flour and sugar, tins of lard and tea and coffee that Molly had bartered at the mercantile in town. The people of Delight were always happy to see her, because the milk and cheese from her dairy farm were the finest in the area.

"Good thing you had that basket of eggs left." Flora tapped a finger on the basket now filled with Annabelle Whitney's strawberry preserves.

"Had to save something to barter if I was going to fill that sweet tooth of yours, Flora."

"I have a sweet tooth?" The little girl started moving her tongue around her teeth, searching for the sweetest one.

"Aunt Molly means that you have a fondness for sweets." Sarah gave a sigh of exasperation at the little girl's ignorance. In light of her advanced age of fourteen, she considered it her duty to impart some of her wisdom on the three younger girls.

Though Sarah would never admit it, she'd also yearned for one more day in town, whether they could afford it or not.

Their rare trip to Delight took better than a day each way by horse and wagon, if they pushed the team to the limit, which was why they made the trip so infrequently. As always, Molly had arranged to extend their visit for several days, so that the girls could attend Sunday services with the townspeople and spend some time doing the things the children in town took for granted. They'd picked apples with the Schroeder clan. Had gone swimming in a nearby pond with Reverend Dowd's daughters after Sunday services. Had attended a barn dance on the Cramer farm, where they'd been entertained by both a fiddler and a lad who played the mouth organ. To top it all off, Carleton Chalmers at the mercantile, after loading their wagon with their long list of supplies before dawn, had invited each girl to choose a candy stick from the jar on his counter. Molly had watched with pride as each of her four girls thanked him before accepting his generosity.

Molly knew that these precious days spent in the company of others was especially sweet to her niece Sarah. The girl was midway between child and woman, and Molly had watched the shy interaction between Sarah and the boys and girls in town. One boy in particular, sixteen-year-old Samuel Schroeder, already as tall as a man and muscular from his years of farm work, had gone to great lengths to appear disinterested whenever Sarah was around. But Molly had seen the flush on his cheeks when Sarah had helped him carry a heavy bushel of apples to the barn. With the bushel between them, the boy and girl kept their gazes averted, except for a few hesitant glances. But those were enough to alert Molly that Sarah was suffering the first fleeting stirrings of womanhood.

Not that she'd had much experience with such things herself, Molly thought with a sigh. At her brother Daniel's urging, she and her parents had left their home in Ireland when she was just fourteen, to join Daniel and his bride Kathleen on their wilderness farm in Wisconsin. Within the past fifteen years, Molly had witnessed the birth of two adorable nieces, the long illness and death of both her parents, and then, without warning, the sudden deaths of her brother and his wife, leaving her alone to struggle with the demands of two little girls and a hundred head of dairy cattle.

"When will we be home, Aunt Molly?" Ten-year-old Delia's voice was just short of a whine.

Home. The mere thought of it had Molly's brogue thickening. She loved the farm that was now hers. Loved her life, despite the endless chores that kept her working from dawn to dusk. " 'Twon't be long now, luv."

The first part of their journey home had been made in companionable silence, as the little girls enjoyed the fine weather and their special treat. Now, after a long day in the crowded wagon, they were growing impatient.

Delia, who, like her sister and their aunt, had inherited the O'Brien red hair and pale white skin, glanced at Flora. "What's that you're eating?"

The little scamp didn't bother to reply.

"Is that a candy stick?" Delia's tone was one of outrage. "Aunt Molly, Flora has another candy stick. She took two."

"Flora. Mr. Chalmers offered each of you only one. How could you take two?"

"I didn't cheat. It's the same one as before." Flora's words were spoken around the confection in her mouth.

Delia wasn't about to let that go. "I saw you eat that one this morning."

"I broke it in half and saved some for later."

"Why'd you save it 'til now?"

"So I could eat it in front of you." The little girl gave one of her sly, pixie grins.

"You shouldn't tease Delia like that." Six-year-old

Ruth Ryan Langan

Charity, the most tenderhearted of the four, was quick to rush to Delia's defense.

Charity's parents had been traveling missionaries killed in a runaway carriage accident. When no relatives could be located, Molly agreed to take in the infant, who had grown into a sweet child. Though older than Flora by two years, Charity was as shy and timid as four-year-old Flora was bold and reckless.

Flora's gypsy mother had boasted of traveling the length and width of the country before settling in Delight. But after only a few months she'd abandoned her baby on Molly's farm, with a note saying she was confident that Molly would find enough love in her heart to care for one more stray. It took but a single look at that sad little face and Molly knew there was no way she would turn the child away.

Molly and her diverse brood were considered an odd little group by the people in the town of Delight. Being nearly thirty and unmarried was bad enough, especially since many farmers in the territory had tried to court the pretty little Irish immigrant and had been rebuffed. It wasn't that she didn't want a man in her life, but the demands of farm and family left her little time to think about courtship. Besides, Molly reasoned, most of the farmers who sought her company were only interested in someone willing to share their chores as well as their bed, and she had enough chores of her own, thank you very much, without taking on those of an overburdened farmer, as well.

It occurred to Molly that she was probably lacking in some basic female instinct. But shouldn't a man cause a woman's heart to flutter before she consented to share his bed?

Her own heart was no doubt too hardened by the loss of so many good people in her life, and the role that fate had thrust upon her. Whatever the reason, she chose to live without a man, rather than accept one who might prove to be just another mouth to feed.

A spinster who chose to work her farm without the help of a husband was bad enough. The addition of four children, two of whom weren't even kin, just had the gossips' tongues wagging faster. Though most of the folks in Delight admired Molly's spunk, not to mention her kindness and generosity, she knew that they saw her as a kindhearted but odd little misfit. Perhaps she was.

She knew, too, that some of the gossip arose from the fact that she allowed a former slave to help out with her farm chores. Addison lived in a little shack in the woods near her farm. She'd offered him the opportunity to sleep in her barn, but he'd refused, saying he needed to be alone. She suspected that his refusal might have had something to do with preserving her reputation, as well.

Whenever she needed to go to town, the old man was willing to milk the cows and watch out for her farm in her absence. In return, she always brought him tobacco and whiskey and supplies from town, knowing he would do without before ever making the journey to Delight. Whatever had happened in his past had been too painful to allow him to interact with people. The fact that he never thought of Molly and her children as being like other people didn't occur to her. It was just the way it was.

"It isn't fair that Flora's eating candy in front of us."

"It's my candy," Flora jeered. "You could have saved some of yours. Now you'll just have to eat an apple."

"I don't want another apple." Delia was almost in tears. "I want a bite of your candy stick."

"I think it would be kind to share."

Molly was pleased to see the little girl break off three small pieces and share them with the others.

"Thank you, Flora. Now I think we'll take time for some lessons." Molly turned to her oldest niece. "Sarah, why don't you go over your sums with the others?"

"Yes'm." Sarah's smile faded. She resented having to play the part of teacher and second mother. Reluctantly she began calling out a series of numbers and realized at once her aunt's wisdom. The younger ones were forced to forget their differences while stretching their minds to add or subtract, multiply or divide.

Miles later Molly turned to call over her shoulder, "That's enough sums for today. How about a song?"

The girls needed no coaxing to follow her lead. As they topped a rise, they were singing at the top of their lungs one of Molly's favorite hymns from Sunday services.

". . . Bless the beasts of burrrrrr . . . dennnnnn . . ."

At the sight before them, their words died abruptly.

Two bodies lay on the ground, one faceup, the other on its side, arm extended over the head. The grass around them was trampled; the earth stained with their blood.

"Are they dead, Aunt Molly?" Sarah's voice was hushed with horror.

"I don't know." Molly drew the horse and wagon to a halt and climbed down, cradling her rifle in the crook of her arm. "Stay here."

The suddenly silent girls needed no coaxing as they watched her bend to the first, gingerly touching a finger to the throat. The man's face was too bloodied and battered to distinguish age or features.

"This one's alive, though barely."

Sickened by all the blood, Molly moved to the second and felt for a pulse. Like the other, this man's face was bloody and swollen beyond recognition. A gun lay on the ground nearby, just out of reach.

"I think this one's alive, too. Pretty feeble, and too thready to be certain, but I think his heart's still beating."

The signs of a ferocious battle were everywhere. There was no doubt that these two had fought desperately, first with guns, and then with their fists, until they could no longer stand.

Molly had no idea how long they'd been here, but this much she knew: Though they may not survive the ordeal of a long ride in a bumpy wagon, there was no choice but to transport them to her farmhouse as quickly as possible.

"Fetch our blankets," she shouted.

The four girls scrambled around the back of the wagon, moving heavy sacks until they'd located their quilts and blankets, folded underneath.

"Here, Aunt Molly." Sarah paused beside her aunt, then went sickly pale at the sight of the man's face.

"Look away." Molly rolled each man onto a blanket, while ordering the girls to unhitch the horse.

After tying one end of the horse's harness around the blanket, she moved along beside the animal as it slowly dragged each man to the wagon. With the girls pushing and Molly pulling, the two men were secured in the back, made snug by the heavy sacks positioned around them to keep them from being jolted any more than necessary. When the horse was once more hitched to the wagon, Molly and the girls scrambled aboard. Because she didn't want the children looking at those battered faces, she herded them onto the front bench alongside her and cautioned them to keep staring forward.

With a flick of the reins, they headed toward the farmhouse in the distance.

"If they die, do we have to bury them?"

Leave it to Flora to think of the worst, Molly thought. "No, luv. If they die, I guess we'll have to haul them to Delight, so their next of kin can be notified after they're buried in the cemetery there."

"You mean we'll get another trip to Delight?" Flora turned to the others. "I hope they die quick."

"Oh. That's disgusting." Sarah huffed and looked indignant, while the other two girls clapped their hands in excitement.

"They don't mean these strangers any harm." Now that the horse sensed an end to the journey, Molly had to fight to keep it moving slowly. Her arms ached from the effort. "But, Flora, luv, you can't hope for a man's death, even if it results in giving you something you'd like."

"I can't?"

"You can't. No. Life is precious."

The little girl gave that some thought before her face was alight with a bright smile. "All right, Mama Molly. I hope they don't die quick then. But I hope they die sooner or later, so we can go back to town. That was the bestest time."

"Best," Sarah corrected.

"For you, too?" Flora turned to the others. "You see? Even Sarah liked it."

The older girl rolled her eyes and crossed her arms over her chest in despair. Seeing it, Molly had to bite down hard on the laughter that threatened.

And wasn't it grand, she thought, that on a day such as this, in the midst of life and death, these little imps could give her a reason to laugh?

"WHERE ARE WE going to put those two?" When the wagon rolled to a stop in front of the farmhouse, Sarah eyed the two men who resembled mummies, wrapped in blankets up to their chins.

"The summer porch, I'm thinking." Molly hopped down and took a deep breath, to prepare for the task ahead. It would take a great deal of hard work to haul these two heavy bodies.

"You could use my bed." Flora jumped down to stand beside Molly. "I'll sleep with Charity."

"I'm not putting a stranger in your room. Besides, by having them together on the summer porch, you four can keep an eye on them during the day while I'm tending the chores." Molly led the way inside. "Come with me, girls. We'll have to prepare two beds." She turned to Flora. "Bring Addison up from the barn, and ask if he'll lend a hand."

They carried as many down quilts and blankets as they could spare to form two bedrolls, carefully folding them to cushion the weight of the two men. Between the two bedrolls Molly positioned a rough wooden bench, and instructed the girls to fetch basins of water, some sharp kitchen knives, and her father's supply of Irish whiskey.

At Sarah's arched brow, Molly smiled. "My da always used it to clean wounds. He said that even if it didn't always work, at least a wee sip or two would make the pain easier to take."

She stood and looked around with satisfaction. Her brother had built the enclosed summer porch on the north side of the farmhouse. With windows on all three sides, it offered a cool haven on summer evenings. In winter, no one ever wandered out here, because the warmth of the fireplace in the parlor couldn't reach this far. But for now, despite the hazy heat of August, the room was shaded and cool.

This would make a fine infirmary. Not that she thought they'd be using it very long. Judging by the looks of those two in the wagon, they had little time left on this earth. But at least their last moments would be spent in comfort. Or as much comfort as she could offer, given their condition.

She turned away. "All right. Let's figure out how to get those two inside."

She found the old man standing beside the wagon, studying the two bodies. He'd been mucking the stalls, and bits of straw and manure were stuck to his bare feet. His face, dark as mahogany, glistened with sweat. A faded shirt, unbuttoned, had been hastily pulled over his torn britches and tucked into his waistband.

He touched a hand in greeting to the brim of a felt hat. "Miss Molly, Flora says they're alive."

"Barely. I'd like to take them to the summer porch."

With Molly and the four girls grasping one end of each blanket and Addison holding tightly to the other, they managed to lower the two men from the back of the wagon. With much huffing and puffing, they inched first one deadweight, then the other, into the house and across the parlor to the summer porch.

Through it all, neither man moved.

Exhausted from the effort, Molly walked with Addison to the wagon and was grateful when he helped her carry her supplies to the house.

When the wagon had been emptied, she extended her handshake. "It's grateful I am, Addison. As always, it was a relief to be able to go to town knowing you'd see to my stock."

"I was happy to help, Miss Molly."

She nodded toward his supplies, which she'd stored in a huge sack. "I had Mr. Chalmers at the mercantile add some cornmeal."

"I'm much obliged." He touched a hand to the brim of his hat before shouldering his supplies and walking off across the field.

Molly came to a decision. "Before I have a look at their wounds, I'd better see about our supper, so that you four don't fall asleep at the table."

In the kitchen she tossed a hunk of beef and some garden vegetables into a kettle over the fire. While supper simmered, she drove the team to the barn, where she unhitched the horse and turned it into a stall.

Returning to the house, she rolled her sleeves, thrust her hands into a bucket of water, and thoroughly scrubbed before heading toward the summer porch.

"Will you need my help, Aunt Molly?"

Hearing the thread of nerves in Sarah's voice, Molly turned. "That won't be necessary, luv. It's stuffy in here, since the house has been closed up. Why don't you take the girls outside and set the table under that big oak."

"Yes'm." Greatly relieved, Sarah herded the others out the door.

Molly squared her shoulders and stepped through the doorway, preparing herself for the unpleasant task ahead.

TWO

Molly filled the basin with hot water from the kettle she'd heated over the fire. Dropping to her knees beside the first bedroll, she eased off the man's boots that were dusty and worn, attesting to a long, hard ride.

As soon as his left boot was removed, she could see the flesh around his ankle begin to swell and discolor. Probing his leg, she determined that it was broken. She hurried to the barn for several lengths of wood.

Returning to the summer porch, she washed the leg and cleansed it with whiskey before tying the splints as firmly as she could.

Picking up a knife, she cut away the rest of the stranger's bloody clothes. As she stripped them aside, fresh blood began oozing from half a dozen wounds.

She had to bite down hard against the shock of all that blood. She'd tended her father through his long illness, and then her brother, Daniel, after the runaway team had overturned his wagon, killing his beloved Kathleen and leaving him with a broken back. He'd lingered another week, without ever leaving his bed.

Tending these two strangers wasn't nearly the challenge her loved ones had been, she reminded herself. After all, though she hoped to ease their pain, she wasn't actually suffering with them, as she'd done with family. Then, each wince, each sigh or moan, had been like a dagger through her heart.

This first man appeared to be no older than she. Tall and strongly built. Dark hair fell in matted clumps to his shoulders. She washed the blood and dirt from his face, revealing a swollen upper lip and a black eye.

Stealing herself, she began probing the worst of the wounds in the shoulder and chest area, and determined that it was from a bullet that had entered through the chest area and had exited at his side. Since he hadn't died before this, she could only assume that the bullet hadn't torn through any vital organs. But the wound was filthy and most probably infected.

She worked quickly and efficiently, washing him thoroughly with lye soap and sponging water gently over his body. She followed this with a splash of whiskey to each wound, before binding the ones that were bleeding with clean linen strips.

Drawing the blanket over him, she moved to the man in the next bedroll and removed his boots before cutting away his clothes. This man appeared slightly older than the other, his lean body corded with muscles.

She was shocked by the ugly wound in his shoulder. When she rolled him slightly, she could see that the bullet hadn't exited, which meant that it was still lodged in his flesh, causing it to fester.

Working quickly she probed with the edge of her brother's hunting knife, until she found the bullet. As she plunged the blade deep into his flesh, hoping to dislodge the bullet, the man let loose with a string of curses. His left hand closed around her wrist in a grasp that threatened to snap every one of her bones.

"Bloody fool!" Her voice was thick with brogue. "It's your miserable life I'm trying to save."

She reared up, prepared to bash him in the head with the basin. In that instant all the fight seemed to drain out of him, and his fingers went slack, his hand dropping like a stone to his side.

Molly had to take a moment to catch her breath before returning her attention to the task at hand. Once more she probed, found the edge of the bullet, and dug the knife blade deep until the offending metal was dislodged. The man moaned as a fountain of blood spurted. She poured a liberal amount of whiskey on the open wound before binding it firmly with clean linen.

That done, she moved to his other wounds, which were minor in comparison, needing only a splash of whiskey to cleanse them. While she examined him, she noted several old scars, as well. This man had been in his share of battles.

Finally she washed the blood and grime from his face, noting the deep gash over his brow, and the purplish bruise from his closed eyelid to his cheek. This would have been caused by more than a fist. Perhaps a gun barrel, she thought while she gently sponged. He seemed to have all his teeth, despite the fact that his jaw was discolored from the punishing blow. She hoped it wasn't broken, but in the event that it was, she tore strips of clean linen and wrapped him from jaw to head, until he resembled a mummy. There was no help for it, she thought with a sigh. If the jaw was indeed broken, this would not only help it mend, it would ease his pain.

As she drew the blanket over him, she leaned back, drained from the exertion. These two men had been evenly matched. Both tall, muscled, and apparently healthy. At least healthy enough to have survived a great deal of time in the heat of the sun and the dirt of a Wisconsin field. But what had driven them to fight with such desperation?

Perhaps one of them would recover enough to tell her the reason. For now, she had a family to feed.

Content that she had done all she could, she got to her feet, gathered their bloody clothes and the basin and tools, now tainted with their blood as well, and made her way to the kitchen to serve up supper, and then, hopefully, to bed.

THE FOLLOWING DAY Molly glanced at the four girls, fresh from their chores, spilling out the door of the barn and into the yard. She envied them the ability to feel completely rested and leap into a new day after their grueling journey.

"I just checked the two strangers. They haven't stirred." She lifted a heavy jug and filled four cups with frothy milk, as the girls took their places around the wooden table set in the farmyard under a giant oak. "I should be back by the time you've finished your noon meal."

"Back?" Sarah's head came up sharply. "Where are you going, Aunt Molly?"

"To fetch their horses, and whatever belongings I can salvage." With the milking and the morning chores behind her, Molly climbed into the saddle of her old mare and turned toward the distant field. "I'll be back before supper."

Sarah's eyes widened with nerves. "What if one of those men should call out for help?"

"You can see to their basic needs. A dipper of water. A cool cloth."

"Can we go with Sarah, to see what they look like?" Flora glanced over at the others, hoping they would back her up. Instead, little Charity looked terrified.

"I don't think you want to see them yet. They're still too bruised and swollen. But if you promise to stay by the door, you may peek in."

Charity shuddered. "I don't want to see them."

"I do." Delia gave a quick nod of her head, sending red curls dancing. "Just 'cause she's oldest, Sarah shouldn't be the only one allowed to see the strangers."

Molly decided to nip this in the bud, or the girls would spend the rest of the afternoon tiptoeing in to stare at the men. "Unless Sarah needs your help, I'd like you to stay out here until I get back."

Flora piped up, "Even if they're dying?"

Molly gave a sigh. It would seem this child was determined to get back to Delight as quickly as possible, by whatever means available. And the death of one or both of these strangers seemed her best chance. "I want you girls to stay together out here until I get home. If they need help, let Sarah go to them alone."

"Yes'm. But what if—"

Sarah clapped a hand over Flora's mouth when the little girl opened it to ask yet another annoying question.

With a nod of satisfaction, Molly set out across the field. She studied the rich, black earth, alive with green growing crops. While her neighbors raised wheat, acres of it, she grew corn, beans, and best of all, hay. Hay to feed her herd. Enough hay to cut and store to get them through the long Wisconsin winter.

It never ceased to amaze her that her big brother had settled in this spot, so far from the place where he'd been born.

Molly had been in this country since she'd been Sarah's age, and yet she still felt a tug on her heart whenever she thought of that lovely green land across the sea. Their little farm in Cork would fit in one corner of this vast farm. There'd been no more than a dozen or so cows. A snug little cottage. A bit of land for growing things. And yet, with the help of her grandmother, her mother's mother who'd come from Scotland, they had turned their little dairy farm into a profitable business. And all because of her grandmother's recipe for making cheese.

It had been her brother's dream to bring the recipe to America and have a dairy farm that would be the envy of all.

With the death of her family, Molly had been forced to scale back that dream. Now, it was enough if she could feed her family of growing girls, with enough left over to barter for their necessities. But it was satisfying to know that her neighbors were eager for her milk and cheese.

Each time the people of Delight tasted it, they went into raptures over the smooth texture, the sharp tang of it.

Her grandmother would be proud.

Up ahead she saw two saddled horses grazing, their reins trailing. Dismounting, she picked up a man's blood-stained jacket lying in the grass. Checking a bulge in one of the pockets she discovered an enormous wad of bills. Though she didn't take the time to count it, Molly knew that it was more money than she'd ever seen in her life-time.

Was he a banker then? A wealthy farmer?

Had the other man been trying to steal this man's money?

It made sense. A wealthy man, and a thief determined to steal his money, by whatever means possible. The thought sent a ripple of unease along her spine.

A little farther on she found a second coat, though she nearly stepped over it since it was half buried in sand. She stooped to pick it up. As she did, she felt the stab of something sharp prick her finger. Turning over the jacket, she saw the grimy badge of a U.S. marshal pinned to the lapel.

Going through the pockets, she found several documents addressed to Marshal Hodge Egan. There was a remnant of a train ticket from Chicago, ragged and torn no doubt by the conductor's hand. One of the papers, carefully folded, was a poster, listing the name of Eli Otto, wanted for murder and bank robbery. Though there was no picture of the thief, he was described as tall, with dark hair and eyes. The poster carried a warning that he was armed and extremely dangerous, having already killed three people, one of them a lawman. There was a reward of one thousand dollars for the return of the outlaw, dead or alive.

A thief. A murderer, who was extremely dangerous.

Molly thought back to the two men who were now lying in beds in her farmhouse. Both could fit that description. She'd had to struggle to lift all that bone and muscle into and out of her wagon. Both men were tall, strong, with dark hair, though she couldn't describe their eyes.

Walking in methodical circles around the area, she retrieved a rifle, two handguns, and a very sharp, very deadly knife that had a flat piece of metal that folded over the blade, no doubt to conceal it in a pocket or boot.

It was clear to her that each man had used everything available to fight off an opponent.

As she tied the coats behind her saddle, her mind was racing.

No wonder they had fought with such desperation. It truly had been a life-or-death situation.

Under her roof at this very moment she was harboring both a man of the law and a dangerous criminal, with no way of telling which was which.

Even worse, she had left her four girls alone with them. And though one of those strangers might be willing to give his life to save them, the other would do whatever necessary to escape, even if it meant harming helpless children.

Catching up the dangling reins of their two horses, Molly pulled herself into the saddle of her mount and urged the old mare into a heart-stopping, pulse-pounding gallop.

With each mile, the accusation rang through her mind. What had she just done? Oh, sweet heaven, she was giving aid and succor to a dangerous gunman who had killed before, and would no doubt do so again, given the opportunity. But she could see no way out of this dilemma. Without knowing their identities, in order to save an honest man, she would have to fight to save the life of a man with no conscience, as well. And she would have to do all this while finding a way to keep her little family safe from harm.

"How are we supposed to figure out which is the marshal and which is the thief?" Sarah stood in the barn, hands on hips, and watched as Molly wrapped the weapons in a length of faded linen before climbing to the loft to hide them under a pile of hay.

"For now, we'll have to assume that both men are dangerous."

"The chief of police in Delight would be able to figure it out. Couldn't he contact someone for a better description of the thief?"

"I'm sure he could. If we could take the time to go back to Delight. I'm not about to leave two men out here to die while I go gallivanting off to town."

"But, Aunt Molly . . ."

"Give me time to think on this, Sarah. I'm sure there's a way to figure out which is which. For now, I want you to see that the girls are never alone with those men."

"You said yourself they haven't moved since you first got them put to bed. They're probably not going to make it through another night."

"That may be so. But I don't want to take any chances. I intend to have a talk with the girls right now." Molly descended the ladder before unsaddling the three horses and leading them into separate stalls. "Whether or not they survive, I have to get on with my farm chores. Whenever I'm otherwise occupied, it'll be up to you to see that the younger ones don't take any foolish chances. They're just little girls. They may not understand the seriousness of all this."

"Yes'm."

Sarah followed her aunt outside, where the three younger girls were climbing trees. Flora had climbed to the highest branch and was now hanging upside down, her chubby little knees the only thing keeping her from a dangerous, if not deadly, fall.

There was a time when Molly's heart would have stopped at the sight of that fearless little imp and her latest fate-tempting prank. For the moment, she had far more serious concerns on her mind.

She cupped her hands around her mouth to be heard over the shrill sounds of childish laughter. "Girls, I need to talk to you."

One by one the three shimmied down the tree and gathered around Molly.

Minutes later, after she'd explained that one of the wounded men was a U.S. marshal and the other a bank robber, they looked suitably impressed.

"A real live bank robber." This from Flora.

"Is there a reward for the robber?" The instant that Delia asked the question, the others perked up with new interest.

"There is. One thousand dollars." Molly saw the sudden interest in all their faces. "I would suppose it should be claimed by the marshal."

"But we found him." Flora's little hands went to her hips and she tapped her foot in frustration. "It ought to be ours."

Molly bit back a smile. "That's not really our concern right now. What is important is the fact that we don't know which man is the thief and which is the lawman. Until we do, I expect you girls to stay away from both those men."

The girls were glancing at one another with equal parts of revulsion and unconcealed excitement.

Though Molly worried that they weren't showing the proper respect for the danger they were facing, she had to concede that living in the middle of a wilderness as they did, this was probably the most exciting thing that had ever happened in their young lives.

Oh, to be so young and innocent. And foolish.

Watching and listening, Sarah couldn't help asking, "Even if we stay away, what about you, Aunt Molly? Someone has to tend their wounds."

"I do. Yes." Her brogue thickened, as it always did in times of crisis. "But from now on, I'll keep my rifle handy while I tend them. They're weakened enough from their injuries that they'll not likely overpower me."

While the others nodded gravely, Flora had the last word. "So it doesn't matter if they die from their wounds, or if you shoot them, Mama Molly. Either way, once we take their bodies to town, we'll find out which one was the marshal and which was the bank robber, and collect the reward. Do you think it would be enough to buy a whole jar of Mr. Chalmers's candy sticks?"

This time Molly did laugh out loud, before tousling the girl's dark tangle of curls. "Come on. We've had a long day. It's time we thought about supper."

MOLLY LAY IN her bed, wishing that the silence of the night would soothe her feverish mind.

In the slant of moonlight she looked around her familiar surroundings. Her meager wardrobe, such as it was, hung on pegs along one wall. A couple of faded gowns. A few of her brother's shirts and britches, which she found more comfortable for farm chores than her own gowns. She'd had to roll the sleeves and cut off the pant legs to fit her smaller frame. A battered straw hat, to shade her fair skin from the ravages of the summer sun. A pair of dung-caked boots she wore for mucking the stalls. Her mother's old nightshift, which billowed about her slender body like a ghostly tent. Though she rarely wore it, she liked having it here. It still carried the scent of her mother, who had always smelled of lilacs. The old woman had loved those lovely spring blooms. As soon as they burst into flower each spring she would cut enough to scent every room of the farmhouse. Long after they'd faded, the house, and her mother's clothes, would remain perfumed by them.

Her mother's chipped wash basin and pitcher were here, as well as the pretty linen towel her sister-in-law had embroidered for her the first year she'd arrived from Ireland. It pleased Molly to use it, and remember the love and pride she'd seen in her brother and his sweet wife, who had died much too young.

She rolled to one side, then the other, too agitated to sleep. It wasn't wise to dwell on those who had died. She needed to think, instead, about how to protect the living. Those young innocents, asleep in the next room, were depending on her.

Neither man asleep on the summer porch had moved enough to convince her that they would survive. Though their hearts continued beating, and they were still breathing, there was no other sign of life. Except for that one terrible moment when the stranger had bruised and nearly broken her wrist, neither man had made a sign of protest as she'd poked and probed their wounds. They hadn't so much as flinched when she'd poured liberal amounts of whiskey onto raw flesh to cleanse the wounds.

She doubted either would live to see many more mornings, but just in case, she'd hidden their freshly washed and dried clothes and boots in the barn, along with their weapons and the wad of money. If either man should wake during the night, he wouldn't get very far naked and barefoot, without the money they'd both obviously risked their lives over.

But if one or the other should survive, how would she determine his identity? If a man had a lick of sense, he'd claim to be a man of the law. Only a fool would admit to being a bank robber on the run from the law.

So, how to trick them into admitting the truth?

The thief had been identified as Eli Otto. She could begin by calling each man by that name. If one or the other reacted, she might have what she wanted.

There was also the matter of that U.S. marshal's badge. A lawman would take pride in that. But how would an outlaw react to it?

So many things to consider. Her head actually ached from the thought of all the ways a thief might try to get away with his evil deeds.

Despite the way her mind darted from one problem to another, her body was forced to give in to the exhaustion this day had wrought. Before she could complete another thought, she was asleep.

THREE

———◆◈◆———

BEFORE DAWN MOLLY was up and dressed and making her way to the summer porch. Both men lay as still as death. Their wounds had once again bled through the blankets.

Molly paused beside the first cot and touched a hand to the man's brow. It was cold and clammy, though the blanket around him was drenched in his sweat as well as his blood. His breathing remained shallow, his chest barely rising and falling in an uneven rhythm.

She pressed a finger to his throat and felt his pulse jerk.

She bent close, hoping to gauge his reaction. "Eli? Eli Otto?"

Though his eyes remained closed, she thought she detected a slight movement behind the lids.

She would need much more than this to determine his identity.

She lay a hand on his shoulder and gave it a shake. "Are you awake, then? Can you hear me?"

He made not a sound.

Deflated at his lack of response, she worked quickly to change his dressings and disinfect his wounds.

When she bent to the second man and touched his brow, she quickly withdrew her hand. His skin was as hot as a stove at suppertime. Like the other man, a fever was obviously raging through him.

She'd been so careful to cleanse their wounds. But somehow, despite her best efforts, both men were fighting infection. Not surprising, considering the length of time spent sprawled in the dirt, with festering wounds from bullets and fists. Both had lost far too much blood.

Working quickly she removed the bloody dressings and began washing the area carefully before pouring a liberal amount of whiskey on the wound. As before, the man's hand instinctively reached up, though his eyes remained closed. This time Molly was ready for him, and she snatched her hand away before his strong fingers could close around her wrist, leaving him clawing at air.

Just as quickly as it had come, his momentary burst of energy deserted him. His hand dropped limply to his side and Molly went on with her chore, carefully binding his wounds, checking his pulse.

When she was finished she bent close to whisper in his ear, "Are you Eli? Eli Otto?"

His lids flickered, the only indication that he was struggling to surface.

Her heart skipped a beat. Had he recognized his name?

Or was it merely the sound of her voice that had him reacting?

"Can you hear me?"

Though she spoke to him again, the initial effort seemed to have drained him. He showed no sign of hearing her, or of being aware of what was happening around him.

His face, still swollen and puffy, attested to the savage beating he'd endured. The swelling was more pronounced this morning. The entire face had turned hues of purple and green and brown. It pained her to look at it.

Having done all she could, she smoothed the blanket over his chest and placed a damp cloth on his forehead before walking from the room.

As she made her way to the barn to begin the morning chores, she wondered if either man would still be with them by afternoon. They'd survived this far, even though she'd given them no chance at all. But it was too soon to get her hopes up. She'd seen enough death to know that it could come at any time.

Another thought worried the edges of her mind. Though she'd forced a few drops of water between their parched lips, it wasn't enough nourishment to sustain them for long. If they didn't soon wake and begin to eat, whatever strength they had would be lost, and life would slowly ebb.

Perhaps that would simplify her task of determining which man was evil and which one good. If neither survived, she would leave it up to the chief of police, Dan Marlow, to determine their identities before consigning them to the grave. And if only one survived, she would deliver him to town, naked and without a weapon, if need be, to let the authorities in Delight decide his fate.

Pushing aside all thoughts of the strangers on her summer porch, Molly began milking the cows, pouring the buckets of milk into big jugs, which she arranged on a flat wooden cart hitched to her plow horse. She led the horse-drawn cart to the cool, dark cellar dug beneath one end of the farmhouse, entering from the outside through heavy doors that lifted up to reveal a sloping ramp made of earth wide enough to allow a horse and cart to enter with ease. The cellar could also be entered from inside the house, by lifting a trap door in the kitchen floor and climbing down a rough wooden ladder.

Her brother had given a great deal of thought to the design of his cellar, for it was essential to the success of his family legacy. It was here, in the cool, damp underground, that milk was transformed into so much more. Butter. Buttermilk. Cheese. Especially the cheese. Some pale yellow. Some smooth and white, or pocked with holes, as delicate as lace.

By the light of a lantern Molly set the jugs on shelves, arranging them so that the freshest was in the front of the shelf for their meals, while others, in various stages of fermentation, were placed behind. The air was ripe with the sharp tang of sour milk that would have been offensive to most who encountered it. To Molly it smelled of home and never failed to bring a smile of satisfaction to her lips.

She blew out the lantern and hung it on a peg, then carefully closed the doors before returning horse and cart to the barn.

As she started toward the house she waved to the girls, who were busy hanging the wash on a line hung between two big trees. Bless Sarah, she thought, for finding chores to occupy those busy little minds. It would keep the younger ones from asking a hundred questions, or worse, tiptoeing onto the porch to chance a look at the strangers sleeping there. She'd caught them herself, half a dozen times or more, peering down in horrified fascination at the grotesquely disfigured faces. Flora had actually been caught daring the others to look when they'd preferred to look away.

Despite the children's curiosity, she hoped she could impress upon them the danger of getting too close. Though the two men seemed helpless, there was no way of knowing their reaction if they should recover their strength.

One of them was a ruthless killer. But how to convince her girls of that fact? She didn't want them so frightened they couldn't sleep. She just didn't want them taking any unnecessary risks until she could determine how to go about getting these two men to town. She would be more than happy to turn this nagging problem over to others. The sooner the better.

"Mama Molly?"

"Yes, Flora?" She paused to glance at the little girl tugging on her skirts.

"We hung the wash and collected the eggs." Flora wrinkled her nose. "Now Sarah wants us to clean the chicken coop."

Molly knew that look. Of all their chores, the one the girls most disliked was cleaning the henhouse. It meant using the long-handled scrapers her brother had fashioned from scraps of lumber to remove an inch or more of droppings from the roosts and floor. The debris was then shoveled into one of the small wagons, and hauled to the field, to be spread on the ground and mixed in with the earth as fertilizer. Though the chore wasn't as physically demanding as mucking the stalls, a chore Molly reserved for herself, it was equally unpleasant.

"I've an offer for you." Molly knelt down, so that her eyes were level with the little girl's. "By the time you finish cleaning the coop, I'll have bread hot from the oven."

Two brown eyes went wide with joy. "With apple butter?"

Molly nodded.

"Can I have two slices?"

"If you'd like."

She grinned as Flora danced away, calling out to the others, "Hurry up. Let's get to the henhouse. Soon as we're done we can have warm bread with apple butter."

Molly was chuckling as she walked into the kitchen, perfumed with the fragrance of bread baking. Bless that child. It took so little to make her happy.

She removed several loaves of bread from the oven and set them on the scarred wooden table to cool. Then she picked up a bucket of water and headed toward the summer porch, to tend the strangers.

HODGE'S FIRST THOUGHT was that he'd died. The fire burning around him, through him, inside him, had to mean that he was now suffering the fate he'd always assumed would be his. Now he'd have an eternity to pay for every mean, rotten thing he'd ever done in his lifetime. And there'd been enough of them to fill a couple of eternities.

At a slight sound he moved his head. No more than a fraction, but enough to have pain spearing through his brain.

Not dead, he thought. Not if he could still move and feel. But the degree of pain told him that he wasn't far from death. That must mean that Eli's bullet had found its mark.

But hadn't Eli been out of bullets? Wasn't that why the gunman had come at him swinging instead of shooting? He could vaguely recall a blow from the thief's gun barrel that had knocked him flat and left him dazed. Too late, he'd realized that Eli had tossed aside his own rifle and had gone for the one Hodge always carried in a boot beside his saddle. He struggled to recall what had happened next. He'd managed to get to his feet, but that blow had left him dazed and disoriented, and he'd heard the terrible sound of a gunshot echoing through his head.

Had he been shot by his own gun? He couldn't swear to it. His brain was so addled by pain, he couldn't seem to hold a coherent thought for more than the blink of an eye. But it would seem that he'd let down his guard for a moment and was now paying the consequences.

He recoiled at the touch of something cool on his fevered flesh. He knew what was happening. Eli Otto had come back to finish what he'd started. In his mind he reared up and took aim with his trusty Sharps, sending the bank robber to hell.

Then, exhausted from the effort, and satisfied that he'd done his best to repel the attack, he slumped back against the bed linens.

He could hear the whisper of a voice, as if from a great distance. "If you persist in fighting me, I'll just have to tie your hands. Like it or not, I'm going to save your bloody hide, even if I learn later that it wasn't worth the effort."

A smile touched his swollen lips. He knew that voice.

He was twelve, and back in his childhood cabin. His tough, older sister Hildy was patching him after a knock-down, drag-out fight with the Simpson brothers, who had decided to claim Eagle Creek for the exclusive use of their herd. When they'd chased off his cattle, he'd known that he had no choice but to stand and fight the three bullies. Without a ma or pa to turn to, it had been just him and Hildy against the raw, untamed Wyoming winter fast approaching. And so he'd stood, unwilling to give an inch, while their fists beat his body senseless and their laughter tore at his soul. They'd told him if he came back, he'd better come with a gun. Because Eagle Creek was theirs.

He'd dragged himself, bloody and beaten, to the little shack he and his sister called home. And though it had been weeks before he'd healed enough to sit a horse, he drove his cattle back yet again, this time with his pa's old Sharps breech-loading rifle in the boot of the saddle.

After the ensuing battle, the word quickly spread that the Egan kid had become a man. A fearless man. And one to be reckoned with.

That was the day he'd left his boyhood behind. The day he'd learned the power of a gun.

The day that had forever changed the direction of his life.

Now, all these years later, Hodge tried to tell Hildy he was sorry for fighting her. But try as he might, he couldn't seem to make his mouth work.

Damn the Simpsons and their fists. Had they broken his jaw?

"That's better." He could hear the voice, though it now sounded strange to his ears. "As long as you don't fight me, we'll both be better off."

Not Hildy's voice. This was a strange female, with an Irish lilt to her voice.

Molly pulled away the bloody dressings and poured a liberal amount of whiskey on the wound.

Hodge tried to swear, but the words couldn't come out. The female was trying to finish him off. He knew he ought to fight her, but there was no fight left in him.

He gritted his teeth against the pain. As his flesh burned to ash, he could feel the darkness descending, and this time, he surrendered to it.

Maybe death would be easier than living with this searing pain.

With a sigh he slipped into blessed unconsciousness.

"The henhouse is clean, Aunt Molly." Sarah led the others into the kitchen, where the big wooden table was already set for a midday meal.

"Thank you. That's a big chore to have behind you." Molly watched as the girls paused beside the basin of water and washed up to their elbows as they'd been taught before taking their places around the table.

"Hot out there today." Sarah splashed water on her face and dried it with the linen cloth.

"It is, yes. A good time to think about working in the cellar until the worst of the heat has faded."

"We're going to help make the cheese?" Charity's eyes sparkled. "Not just Sarah, but all of us?"

"It's time all of you learned." Molly circled the table, topping off their glasses. "After all, the making of cheese is to be your legacy."

"What's wrong with our legs?" Flora lifted one sturdy brown leg to study it, and then the other.

"Not legs. Legacy." Molly slathered apple butter on a slice of warm bread and handed it to the little girl. "It's what I can leave you, just as my gram left it to my mum, and my mum to me. One day when you're grown, you'll be glad to know how to make the finest cheese in the land. It will mean that you'll never have to go hungry. And if you're wise, and willing to work hard, you'll be able to make a fine living off your cheese."

Flora took her time licking her fingers, unwilling to miss a single drop of her favorite apple butter. She indulged her love of this sweet treat the way she indulged everything in her young life—with unrestrained pleasure. "I'm going to marry a rich farmer, and then I'll never have to work."

Molly turned from the stove to stare at the little girl. The words coming out of her mouth had sounded just like the child's wild, gypsy mother. But how could that be? Flora had been an infant when her mother had last seen her.

Were some things just implanted in a baby's brain before birth?

"I would hope," she said carefully, "that all of you would choose to be masters of your own fate."

"You mean we should be like you, Mama Molly, and never marry?"

She felt an odd little ache around her heart. Did her own children see her as a dried-up old spinster? A misfit? "That's not what I mean at all, Flora. I just want all of you to be strong enough to live your own lives. And if you find someone who loves you just for yourself, and you feel the same about him, then marriage would be grand."

"That's good."

"Why?" With a cup of tea in hand, Molly took her place at the head of the table.

Flora glanced across at the oldest, busy spreading apple butter on a slice of bread. "Because Sarah's going to marry Samuel Schroeder."

"Oh!" Sarah dropped her bread and glared at the little girl across the table. "Flora, you're disgusting."

"'Cause I told the truth? You said yourself that you thought Samuel Schroeder was just about the best-looking—"

"That's enough." Biting her lip to keep from laughing, Molly held up a hand to put an end to this before it went any further. She could see the others turning from Sarah to Flora, trying to keep up with the flow of conversation. It was clear that neither Delia nor Charity had an interest in Sarah's love life, or lack of it. Flora, however, was another matter altogether. This child seemed destined to see and hear everything. And repeat it to as many people as would listen.

"Why don't we take the rest of our meal with us to the cellar? That way we can nibble our bread while we test the cheese."

As she held the trap door and waited for the others to climb down the ladder, Molly was still grinning.

Poor Sarah. It must be impossibly difficult trying to keep a secret from this curious bunch. Especially when one of them was as sly a pixie as had ever been born.

FOUR

"WHEN WILL WE be going to town, Mama Molly?"
Flora sat on a three-legged stool and watched as Molly
began to unwrap a length of fine muslin, revealing a hunk
of pale yellow cheese.

She looked up. "We just got back."

"But you said we'd have to take the dead men to town."

Molly cut a tiny slice from the cheese and tasted it before passing tiny slices around to the others. Satisfied that
it was aging to perfection, she wrapped it and returned it
to its place on the shelf before opening a second bundle.
"They aren't dead, Flora. They're very much alive."

The little girl gave a long, drawn-out sigh. "But when
are they going to die?"

"That's not for us to know." Molly handed the wrapped
cheese to Sarah before crossing the cellar to kneel in
front of the sad little girl. "Luv, I have to do everything
possible to help them live."

"But why?"

"Because it's the right thing to do. And if they should die, then we'll take them to town. If they should live, my job is to help them get better."

"Even the bad man?"

Molly nodded. "Even the bad man."

"But they're just going to hang him."

"Maybe. That's for the law to decide. But while I'm tending their wounds, you have a job to do, too."

"I do?" Dark eyes went wide with wonder.

"You have to help Sarah with the chores that I don't have time for. And when you say your prayers each night, you have to remember to pray for those two strangers, as well."

Little Charity was clearly shocked. She hurried over to stand beside Flora. "I don't think we should pray for a bad man, Mama Molly."

"Don't you think he needs prayers, too?"

The two little girls looked at each other, before Flora answered for both of them. "Is it all right if we pray that he dies?" In an aside she added, "That way, we did what we ought to, and we still get to go to town."

Turning away to hide the grin that split her lips, Molly decided it was time to change the subject. For now, she would immerse her girls in the joy of making her grandmother's cheese.

"We take the rennet, which we obtain from the lining of a calf's stomach, and add it to the milk. This is what causes particles of the milk to clump together into this solid gel." She opened a length of cloth to show the girls what happened when she cut into the gel. Liquid containing protein and milk sugar drained out.

Molly held it up. "This is whey. It makes grand feed for the animals. The solid part left behind is called curd, and this is what we'll use to make our cheese."

She pressed several pieces of curd together and wrapped them, then shoved them far back on the shelf. "Over time, this will darken and thicken and begin to taste distinctly like cheese."

"How did your grandma learn this?" Delia tasted the whey and made a face.

"From her grandma. I'm sure someone learned this by accident, probably when they were using a calf skin to haul milk, and the rennet in the calf skin turned the milk to cheese. But now that I understand the process, I can expand on it. I hope, by the time you girls are all grown up, our farm will become famous for its variety of cheeses."

For the next hour, hidden away in the cool, dark cave of the cellar, Molly cut them tiny slices from each wrapped bundle of cheese, nodding in agreement when it was firm and sharp, shaking her head when it was mushy or tart. And all the while, they washed each bite down with glasses of cold milk.

By the time they climbed the ladder, the worst of the afternoon's heat had fled, leaving the day fresh for the remainder of their chores. As always, Molly blessed her brother for having created such a cool haven from the heat of Wisconsin's summer. In the dead of winter, when the world lay frozen, the temperature in the cellar would remain equally comfortable, keeping their milk and cheese and cache of garden vegetables safe from spoiling.

ELI OTTO STRUGGLED up from the nightmare that held him in its grip. He was once again standing toe to toe with a man who refused to give up. A bullet in the chest, at least he thought he'd hit the marshal's chest, and still the bastard kept on coming. When he found his gun empty of bullets, he'd swung it with all his strength, landing a solid blow on the marshal's face, knocking him clean off his feet. Then he'd flung it aside and made a last, desperate scramble for the marshal's rifle. In his mind he heard the thunderous report of a gunshot. But which of them had fired first? Was he dead? Was the marshal?

He could recall falling backward from the report of the rifle, and then slipping away into a deep, dark tunnel. At least that's what he'd thought at the time. As though he'd been swallowed up by the earth while his life slowly ebbed.

Shallow, painful breaths had his chest rising and falling as he struggled to wake. Sweat beaded his forehead as he surfaced.

Not dead.

He tried to open his eyes, but it was too much effort. And so he lay, listening for anything that might tell him where he was. At first all he heard was silence. But as he became more alert, he realized that there were farm sounds. In the distance, cattle lowing. Birds chirping nearby. And something else. At first he was puzzled by the soft, steady hiss of air. And then his blood went cold as he recognized the sound of someone breathing nearby.

Where the hell was he? Certainly not in the field where he'd fallen. It was somewhere cool and soft, instead of the killing heat of the sun and hard-packed earth. So where was he? And who was sleeping beside him?

He tried to move, but his entire body was on fire.

The marshal had said he'd make him burn for killing a lawman.

Had the lawman set him on fire? Was the marshal sitting there watching? He wouldn't put it past the miserable bastard. In his whole life, Eli had never encountered a tougher, more determined foe.

Something was wrapped tightly around him, pinning his arms at his sides. Had Hodge Egan bound him before setting him afire? Try as he might, he couldn't summon the strength to free himself.

Something was very wrong here. The fire in his body. The lifelessness of his limbs. And worst of all, that sound of breathing nearby.

The fear that he may not have eliminated his adversary after all cast Eli into the depths of a new and more horrifying nightmare as he drifted into a deep, dark, troubled sleep.

"WELL." MOLLY TOUCHED a hand to the first man's forehead. Though he was still feverish, he jerked back the moment she touched him. "Looks like you're beginning to wake." She leaned close. "Are you Eli? Can you hear me?"

His eyes remained closed, though she could detect movement behind the lids.

"I know you hear me. Can you look at me?"

There was more furious movement, as though the man was struggling to wake, but the lids remained closed.

She moved to the other bed and touched a hand to the stranger's forehead. His fever seemed to have faded a bit. His skin was no longer clammy to the touch.

She bent over him. "Are you Eli? Can you open your eyes?"

She saw the lids flicker, before his eyes slowly opened. At least one eye opened. The other, swollen and puffy, could barely focus.

"Ah." She breathed the word slowly. "You've come back to the land of the living, it would seem, Eli. That is your name? Eli Otto?"

She saw the confusion in the man's eyes. "You'd be wanting to know where you are and what's happened to you. My name is Molly O'Brien. You're on my farm. I found you wounded out in my field and brought you to my house."

Hodge couldn't tear his gaze from the vision that swam before him. Eyes green as a sea of prairie grass, in a face that reminded him of an angel. Except that this angel had a sprinkle of freckles across her tiny, turned-up nose. Hair the color of fire spilled in wild curls around her face and down her back.

He tried to speak, but discovered that he couldn't open his mouth. His puzzled gaze flew to hers.

"I've tied your jaw shut. There's so much swelling, I can't tell if it's broken. I thought it best to err on the side of caution." She straightened. "I'll bring you something to drink."

She was gone with a rustle of skirts.

Whiskey, he thought with fierce desperation. *Please, God, let it be whiskey. Gallons of it.*

"Here, now." Hands lifted his throbbing head none too gently, until several pillows were placed behind him.

The sash that had been wrapped around him from head to jaw was removed. A spoon was pried between his parched lips and he felt cool water slide down his throat.

Not whiskey, was his first thought, and his hopes plummeted. But after several swallows, he realized he'd needed this more than alcohol. His body felt as dry as the cracked, sunbaked earth he'd seen one summer in Arizona when he'd tracked a gunman across the West.

He drank, sip by sip, until with a firm shake of his head, he indicated that he wanted no more.

"Good. I'll see what else I can find to make you comfortable."

She hurried away and he closed his eyes, thinking about downing enough whiskey to knock him senseless. Would a glass do it? Half a bottle? In his current condition, it would probably take no more than a thimbleful.

She was back, kneeling beside him. "You need sustenance, but since you're in no condition to chew, I thought you could begin with this." Molly held up a tall glass of something that looked like curdled milk.

When it got close to his nose, he sniffed and tried to evade. But she was having none of it. He was faced with two choices. Swallow or choke. He wisely allowed it to slide down his throat.

"Good." When the glass was empty, she tied his jaw shut and got to her feet. "We'll just let that settle a bit."

Settle? He watched her leave the room and wondered

how this crazed little female could possibly expect curdled milk to settle anything, especially his poor stomach.

Not curdled milk, he realized after a moment. Buttermilk. Though he'd had no time to actually taste it as it was forced down his throat, it had been fresh, and cold, and had gone down as smoothly as fine wine.

He hadn't tasted buttermilk since he'd been a boy in Wyoming. Then it had been considered a special treat. He and his sister, Hildy, used to fight over every last drop. There were times when it was all that kept them from starvation.

He closed his eyes and began to drift. He had to admit, despite the pain that burned through him, he was feeling somewhat better than he had a few minutes ago, thanks to that angel of mercy.

"ONE OF THE strangers woke up." Molly circled the table, ladling chicken stew into the children's bowls.

"Which one?" Sarah was busy cutting Flora's meat into small bites before tending to her own meal.

"The one with the broken leg?" Charity had begun hiding behind Sarah's skirts whenever she entered the summer porch, watching the strangers from a safe vantage point. Until now, she'd refused to even go near them. But the fact that the other girls had already stood beside their pallets and studied them closely while they slept had shamed her into stepping closer. Still, she ran like a rabbit if either of the men so much as sighed in his sleep.

"I'll bet it's the one with his head wrapped." Flora, be-

ing Flora, had spent endless hours boldly studying both
men and had already decided that the mummy was the
bank robber. It was, she insisted, because there was a
boldness about him that reminded her of a thief in the
night.

"That's the one." Molly took her place at the head of
the table and held out her hands. The others joined theirs
to hers and bowed their heads as she led them in a simple
prayer. "Bless this food, and those of us gathered here."

Before the amens were out of their mouths, they were
busy eating.

Sarah glanced over. "Did the man say anything?"

Molly shook her head. "I'm afraid he won't be able to
speak for some time. His jaw is so swollen, even if it isn't
broken, 'twill be too painful to open it more than an inch."

Ten-year-old Delia looked up. "How will he eat, Aunt
Molly?"

"I'll have to think of some easy foods that don't re-
quire chewing. He managed to swallow a glass of buttermilk, so that's a fine start." She buttered a slice of bread,
warm from the oven. "I believe a pot of chicken broth
would be just the thing."

Flora wrinkled her nose. "I don't think you should
waste good broth on him."

Molly paused in the act of sipping her tea. "Now why
do you say that?"

"If he's the bad man, we shouldn't help him get back
his strength. As long as he's too weak to move, he can't
hurt anybody."

Molly couldn't fault the little girl's reasoning. "True

enough. If he turns out to be the bad man. But what if he's the lawman?"

Flora thought about it a moment, before a sly smile crossed her face. "I guess we'll just have to starve both men."

Sarah rolled her eyes while the others looked from Flora to Molly, who was chuckling. "That's one way to insure our safety. But that would defeat the whole purpose of saving their lives in the first place. I believe I'll just follow my original plan, and do my best to keep them alive. Once they're strong enough to travel, we'll let Police Chief Marlow handle the problem."

"Yes'm." Flora bent to her supper, but from the look in her eyes, Molly knew the little girl wasn't at all pleased with the plan and was no doubt plotting a way to foil the bad guy, if and when he revealed himself to them.

"We'll want to go to sleep early tonight." Molly mopped the gravy with her bread. "The vegetables are ripening so quickly, I'll need all of you to help me in the garden tomorrow."

Flora's smile was radiant. "Does that mean we can skip cleaning the chicken coop?"

"It means," Molly said with a quick grin, "that you'll need to start your regular chores even earlier than usual, before we begin the harvest." When she saw the girl's grin fade, she added quickly, "But it also means that you can eat all you want while you pick."

Tomatoes, cucumbers, corn, and beans, all warm from the summer sun. What child could resist eating her fill? For that matter, Molly knew she would join them. She loved nothing so much as freshly picked garden vegetables.

Tomorrow night, she silently vowed, while the strangers sipped broth, she and the girls would feast on a garden of delights.

FIVE

———

MOLLY WAS SO deep into sleep that at first, she thought she was dreaming the man's voice that penetrated her consciousness. Moments later she realized that one of the strangers was crying out. Rubbing her eyes, she sat up before reaching for a lantern. Minutes later she was kneeling beside the man in the first bed, holding a dipper of water to his lips.

He shrank back from her, and she realized that the light of the lantern was blinding him. She blew it out and decided that she could work by the faint dawn light just beginning to streak through the windows.

"Where . . . ?" The word was little more than a croak.

"You're safe. You're in my house. Drink this."

The man drained the dipper and she filled it again, holding it to his lips as he drained it a second time.

"What about the . . . ?"

Though his voice was as rusty as an old gate latch, she

could make out his words, even though she didn't understand the question. "What about the . . . what?"

He gave a quick shake of his head, then moaned because the sudden movement caused his head to swim. He closed his eyes and waited for the dizziness to pass.

She bent close. "I made some broth, Eli. Should I call you Eli?"

He was too far gone to respond, or even to hear her.

Molly watched him for a few moments longer. Then, because he seemed to have lapsed into sleep, and because it was time to begin another round of chores, she picked up the darkened lantern and made her way to her room.

A short time later she was in the barn, tending to the milking. By the time the children were up and fed, she intended to have the morning chores behind her so that they could concentrate on the garden.

HODGE EGAN WAS drifting, neither awake nor asleep, but somewhere in between, wishing he could escape into deep, mindless sleep. Every part of his body ached. His head, his face, his shoulder felt like one giant toothache.

Something had caused him to wake suddenly. A bird? A child's cry?

He heard a sound beside him and waited for the woman to offer him comfort. A cool cloth, perhaps. A sip of water.

Whiskey.

Too much to ask for, he knew. But right now he'd take anything she offered that would ease his misery.

The sound increased. A sigh? A moan? And then slow,

easy breathing. Was the female sleeping nearby? It seemed too much effort to open his eyes and look around.

He touched a finger to his swollen eye and winced, before mentally cursing the miserable little thief who'd lambasted him with the rifle. When he got his hands on Eli Otto . . .

Had he managed to kill the bank robber? Or had Otto gotten clean away?

Next time the woman came to him, he'd have to remember to ask if she'd seen any sign of the bastard.

He heard the sound again. A moan. He opened his good eye, turning this way and that, trying to see with his limited vision. It was impossible in this faded light.

Where the hell had the woman put his pistol and rifle? Next time he saw her he'd demand they be brought to him, so that he could at least see to his own safety.

For now, he'd be content to just pass the time without too much movement, because the slightest effort caused untold agony. With that in mind, he lay perfectly still and eventually drifted into sleep. But even his sleep was troubled. His dreams were tormented with images of a menacing shadow hanging over him. There was danger lurking. He could feel it. Hear it. Smell it. He faced it in his dreams as he'd always faced it in life. Stumbling blindly into its clutches.

"REMEMBER, ONLY PICK the vegetables that are perfectly ripe. The rest can wait for another day." Letting go of the handcart, Molly assigned each of the children a row. "Sarah and I will dig the carrots and potatoes. Delia, you pick tomatoes. Charity, would you do the beans? And Flora, you can fill this basket with raspberries for our dessert tonight."

"That's not fair, Aunt Molly." Delia planted her hands on her hips. "You know Flora will eat while she's picking."

"You're all welcome to eat while you pick." Molly reached for a shovel.

"But we're stuck eating beans and tomatoes . . ." Delia looked to Charity for support. ". . . While Flora gets to eat raspberries."

"That's right, Mama Molly. I—"

Before Charity could jump in, turning this into a full-blown rebellion, Molly was quick to add, "Next time it'll be your turn to pick the raspberries, and Flora will pick tomatoes. Will that satisfy you?"

In reply, Delia stomped off, followed by Charity. Wearing a smug smile, Flora turned toward the tall, prickly raspberry bushes that Molly had transplanted from one of the nearby fields several years earlier. Over the past few years they had begun to produce a fine yield of fat, sweet berries.

As Sarah began digging beside Molly, the girl gave a huff of annoyance. "Delia's right, Aunt Molly. By the time Flora's done, we'll be lucky to get half a basket of raspberries for supper tonight."

"I know, luv. But sometimes we forget that she's only four. If I can encourage her to enjoy herself while she's doing chores, in time she'll do them for the sheer love of the work." Molly gave a long, deep sigh. "At least that's my hope."

She glanced around at her little family. What a sweet

picture they made. The girls wore bonnets and long, white muslin pinafores to protect their dresses. All summer they went barefoot, saving their boots for those occasional trips into Delight. Because she and Sarah had planned on digging, they'd worn their boots. Molly's were caked with dung from mucking the stalls earlier that morning.

Within the first hour of garden work the hems of their gowns were soiled. By the second hour their hands and faces, as well as the front of their pinafores, were filthy. And little Flora's mouth and cheeks and hands were stained deep red from the juicy berries. True to form, she managed to eat as many as she'd picked.

HODGE WOKE FROM a nasty dream, heart pounding, his body and the bed linens around him soaked with sweat. For long minutes he lay, breathing deeply, feeling completely disoriented. It took a few moments to realize that he hadn't been in a second battle. He'd merely been dreaming about the first one. A dream so real, he felt utterly exhausted from it, as though he'd actually been rolling around in the dirt, fighting for his life.

As his breathing slowly returned to normal, he became aware of something else. Or rather, someone else. Someone was nearby. He could hear the sound of soft, steady breathing.

The woman?

He opened his good eye. Light spilling in from the windows caused a stab of pain that had him quickly blinking it closed. Taking more care, he allowed his eye to open slowly, until the light no longer blinded him.

In order to see, he was forced to roll slightly to his side. Even that small movement had him gritting his teeth and muttering a series of rich, ripe curses.

He could see nothing, except a long wall and a closed door. He had no idea what lay beyond the door. Though it caused him excruciating pain, he rolled to his other side. And froze.

There was indeed a bed beside his. And someone was asleep in it. But it wasn't the woman. It was the coward who'd killed those innocent bank employees and a fellow lawman. The bastard who'd left him to die in a sunbaked field.

With a snarl of rage he tossed aside the bed linens, even though the pain that shot through him was almost more than he could bear.

At that very moment Eli Otto opened his eyes and caught sight of the man he'd hoped never to face again in this lifetime.

The two men, both crippled with pain, rose up out of their beds and came together in slow motion, like two ancient warriors hobbling into a battle to the death.

Eli's hand closed into a fist, but when he drew his arm back to deliver a blow, his wounded limb refused to obey, dropping weakly at his side.

Fueled by a black, blinding rage, Hodge took that moment to hurl himself across the distance that separated him from his enemy, slamming into him with such force, both men fell to the floor between the beds.

In a blur of pain Hodge willed his body, which seemed

completely disconnected from his control, not to fail him.

It was his last coherent thought before the darkness took him.

"WE HAVE MORE than enough here." Wiping an arm across her forehead, Molly glanced at the cart, filled with the rich harvest from their garden. "We'll eat what we can and store the rest in the cellar. That way, we won't have to pick again for a few days."

"Mama Molly, look." Charity pointed to Flora's basket, which was, as the children had predicted, only half full.

From the way the little girl was walking toward them, it was obvious that she was paying a dear price for her gluttony.

She went very still and let out a moan. "I don't feel good, Mama Molly."

Delia muttered, "Serves you right."

"Could I ride in the cart, Mama Molly?"

Prissy little Charity was horrified. "You'd squash the tomatoes."

"But I can't walk any more." Flora plopped herself down in the dirt between a row of cucumbers. "My tummy hurts something awful."

Molly paused, torn between a desire to get out of the hot sun and the realization that the little girl rarely complained. "Too many raspberries, luv?"

"Uh-huh."

"Can you make it to the house?"

Flora shook her head.

With a sigh, Molly turned to Sarah. "Think you can handle the cart?"

Sarah took up the handles, while Molly dropped to her knees and said to Flora, "Climb on my back."

The little girl did as she was told, and wrapped her chubby arms around Molly's neck. Tucking her arms around Flora's dangling legs, Molly started off at a brisk pace, bringing up the rear of their little party.

By the time they reached the doors of the cellar, Molly was dripping with sweat. She deposited Flora on the ground before lifting the cellar doors and helping Sarah roll the cart inside.

"Oh." Once inside Sarah dropped to the cool earth and nearly wept with relief. "This feels so good."

"It does. Yes." Molly tilted a heavy jug and poured each of them a glass of cold milk. While they leaned back enjoying the break from the broiling sun, she began setting the extra vegetables on shelves, and putting those they would eat for supper in a separate basket.

"I'll just return the cart to the barn and start our supper. I'll have a bucket of water on the porch. See that you wash before you come inside."

She braced herself for the blast of hot air as she stepped outside. A short time later she sat on the porch and slipped out of her boots. She leaned back, wiggling her toes, grateful that the worst of the day's chores were behind her. She plunged her arms into the cool water and soaped herself before rinsing. Then, unable to resist, she ducked her head into the water. Oh, it was grand to feel the shock of cold water running in rivers down her neck, her back. For good measure she stepped into the bucket and used a cloth to wash the dirt from her legs and feet, as well.

Once dry, she tossed the water on the wild honeysuckle that grew around the base of the porch and went to the pump to fill the bucket with fresh water for the children. That done, she hurried inside to peel the vegetables and prepare the dough she'd started earlier that morning for biscuits.

She could hear the giggles from the girls as they paused on the porch to wash. To Molly, it was the grandest sound in all the world. She loved the sound of her children's laughter.

She decided to use this time before supper to check on the strangers.

She crossed the parlor and opened the door to the summer porch. At once she realized that something was very wrong. Neither of the beds was occupied.

As she stepped around the first bed she caught sight of the heap of tangled bodies on the floor, lying in a pool of blood.

"Sarah! Girls!" With a cry for help, Molly knelt and touched a hand to each of the men's throats.

"Oh. Sweet heaven." Stunned, Molly sat back on her heels and let out a sigh of relief. Both men looked as they had when she'd first come upon them in that field. Despite the absence of dirt, there was so much blood. Far too much of it, streaming from their opened wounds.

"What's wrong, Aunt Molly?" Sarah stood in the doorway, while the others gathered around her, peering from the safety of her skirts.

Molly grabbed some blankets to cover their nakedness. "I'll need a hand with these two. And water. Plenty of water and fresh linens," she added.

At Sarah's directions the girls scattered and returned with a basin of hot water and a supply of lye soap and linens. Then they stood back and watched as Molly cleansed the freshly opened wounds and bound them.

Neither man offered much resistance. Except for an occasional moan or sigh, they seemed to have spent their energy on their earlier battle.

"What do you think happened, Aunt Molly?" Sarah smoothed the blankets over the man in the first bed while Molly tended to the second, who still lay on the floor.

"I suspect they woke up and realized their feud hadn't ended in death."

"What'll we do now?"

Molly looked grim. "It's obvious we can't leave them together in the same room. They'll use every opportunity to try to finish what they started in the field."

"Are we going to town then?" Flora danced closer, her upset stomach forgotten.

"Not likely, as long as they're in this condition." Molly finished binding the second man's wounds and came to a decision. "One of them will have to move to another room."

"What room?" Sarah thought about the horsehair sofa in the parlor. It seemed a shame to have the blood of one of these two strangers staining it.

"My bedroom." Molly tossed a bloody linen into the basin and got to her feet. "We'll put him in my bed."

"Where will you sleep, Aunt Molly?"

Her aunt sighed. "In the parlor."

Sarah eyed the two strangers. "Which man will we move?"

"This one." Molly pointed to the man on the floor. "Since that one has a broken leg, we'd never get him up and moving."

"And this one?"

Molly sighed. "I'll need all of you to lend a hand." Firmly knotting the blanket draped around him for modesty, she tugged the barely conscious man to his feet and lifted one of his arms around her shoulder, motioning for Sarah to take up a position on his other side and do the same.

With Flora holding the door, and Delia and Charity pushing at his back, Hodge Egan was coaxed and cajoled to move along between the two slender figures. Several times he slumped, nearly dragging them to their knees. But each time, with Molly's voice low and commanding, he rallied enough to take a few more steps, and then a few more. Once in her bedroom they maneuvered him onto the bed. With the others looking on, Molly tucked him up under the blankets.

Satisfied that he was as comfortable as the situation allowed, she shooed the girls out ahead of her. With a last glance at the sleeping figure in her bed, she closed the door and led the way to the kitchen.

SIX

❖◆❖

Hodge lay very still, struggling to sort out what had happened. The last thing he remembered was hurtling through space and landing on top of the bastard, Eli Otto. It infuriated him to know that the thief had survived their original battle. But where had he gone? There was no miserable bastard beneath him now. Did that mean that Otto had managed to escape yet again? Not likely, considering that he hadn't been strong enough to throw a single punch.

So, where was Otto? For that matter, where was he now? This wasn't the cold, hard floor. In fact, if he didn't know better, he'd swear he was in a big old feather bed.

At a soft, rustling sound he opened his eyes, and was pleased to see that his swollen eye was beginning to work. The vision was murky, but he could see. And what he saw had him going very still.

It was the angel, standing across the room, slipping a

voluminous white nightshift over her head. She turned away, so that all he could see was her profile as she reached up to hang the gown on a peg. She turned slightly and he had a quick glimpse of softly rounded hips, a tiny waist, and high, firm breasts. He blinked rapidly, trying to make the bad eye work. The view was still clouded, but it was enough to have his throat going dry.

Instead of a gown, she plucked a man's britches and shirt from a peg on the wall and dressed quickly. That done, she tossed back her hair and tied it with a ribbon before pulling on a faded straw hat. Picking up a pair of dung-caked boots, she left as quietly as she'd entered, without a backward glance.

He watched as the door closed. Then he took the time to study his surroundings.

This had to be her room. The bed was big and wide and soft, set on a frame that appeared to have been hand-hewn of rough timbers. Across the room several home-spun gowns hung along the wall on pegs. There was a basin and pitcher atop a wooden chest. The air, he noted as he breathed deeply, appeared to be perfumed with the scent of lilacs. Despite the clutter of gowns the room seemed bare of feminine frills. And it appeared to be spotlessly clean.

Why had she moved him into her room? And what had happened to Eli Otto?

He rolled to his side, and was forced to endure a jolt of blinding pain. He'd bet a year's wages he had a couple of broken ribs. Just one more part of his body that would need to mend, and mend quickly, if he had any hope of apprehending that no-good, lazy, shiftless, murdering thief.

"AUNT MOLLY!" SARAH lifted the trap door in the kitchen floor and climbed down the ladder to the cellar.

Molly looked up from the jug into which she was carefully measuring the precious cultures that would turn milk into cheese. "Something wrong, luv?"

"The man on the summer porch is hollering."

"If he's well enough to holler, he must be mending." She deliberated the wisdom of leaving this process before it was complete. It could mean an entire day's milking was apt to go sour. "Would you mind seeing what he wants? Or would you rather I tend him?"

The girl bit her lip. She was old enough to appreciate how hard her aunt worked. Still . . . After a pause she gave a sigh. "I guess I can do it."

Seeing her hesitation, Molly decided to help the girl out of a difficult dilemma without having to reveal her fear. "Why not take the others with you?"

"I don't need anyone's help."

"Of course you don't. But this way, if something needs fetching, one of them can get it while the rest of you stay together. If the man needs anything more than a bit of water, tell him he'll have to wait until I come up. I should have this finished in just a little while."

Sarah nodded and turned away to climb the ladder, relieved that she wouldn't have to face the stranger alone. After rounding up the others, who were playing a game of hide-and-seek behind the barn, she led the way to the house. In the parlor she paused before opening the door to the summer porch. The thought of having to deal with this man had her as skittish as a colt.

The younger girls, sensing her anxiety, glanced nervously from one to the other.

"Maybe we should wait for Mama Molly." Charity reached over to grasp Delia's hand.

Delia nodded in agreement.

"Let's go inside now." Unlike the others, Flora was practically jumping up and down with excitement.

"Aren't you afraid?" Delia demanded.

"Uh-uh." Flora's dark, glossy curls danced as she gave a vigorous shake of her head. "He's too sick to do much. Besides, I want to see his face without all those bruises, so I can tell if he's the good man or the bad man."

"No, you can't." Delia rose to the challenge.

"Can, too." Flora turned the knob, sending the door swinging inward, forcing Sarah and the others to make a move.

For a moment it looked as though Sarah would flee. But after a moment's pause, she straightened her shoulders and stepped inside, with the younger girls trailing behind her.

Sarah paused beside the man's bed and stared hard at his face. The last time she'd been this close, he'd been a bloody mess. Now, though there was a great deal of green and blue and black bruising along that strong jaw, she could see that he had a rather handsome face, with a wide brow, bold nose, and best of all, he had all his teeth.

She swallowed hard. "Do you need something?"

"Wah . . ."

Flora was quick to interpret. "He wants water."

Sarah turned to Delia and Charity, gripping each other's hands tightly. "Fetch the bucket of water and a dipper from the kitchen."

The two girls nodded and dashed away without saying a word.

While they were gone, Flora stepped closer and stood on tiptoe, hoping to see more of the man's face. At first his eyes were closed, and she thought he'd fallen asleep. Just then his lids snapped open and she found herself staring into piercing dark eyes.

He regarded her in stony silence before turning his attention to the girl who stood beside her. Something dangerous flickered in his eyes before he blinked it away.

He managed a slight curve of lips. "Wasn't . . ." He coughed, swallowed, and tried again. ". . . Expecting such . . . pretty little milkmaid."

Sarah's cheeks turned bright pink. Never in her life had she been called pretty.

"Here's the water," Charity and Delia called in unison as they hurried across the room.

They carried a half-filled bucket between them. Some of it sloshed over the rim and spilled on the floor, but they took no notice as they handed Sarah the dipper.

She realized that without lifting his head, the man would be unable to drink.

She glanced around nervously. "He needs something to raise him up."

"How about this?" Flora picked up a spare blanket from the foot of the bed and handed it to Sarah, who folded it several times before gingerly placing it beneath his pillow. As she bent over him she could feel his eyes watching her.

Nervously she scooped water from the bucket and held it toward the man's mouth.

Despite the swelling he managed to open it, all the while keeping his gaze fixed on her face. She flushed at his scrutiny and nearly bobbled the dipper before regaining her composure and fitting it between his lips.

She'd never been this close to a man before. Except for old Dr. Whitney. But he didn't count, since he was old enough to be her grandfather. This man wasn't much older than she, and she found herself extremely shaken by the intimacy of giving him a drink.

He drank his fill and managed another smile as she lowered the dipper.

Before she could step back he reached out a hand to her wrist. ". . . A very kind and generous milkmaid."

Delia's eyes were as big as saucers as she stared at her big sister. Beside her, Charity gave a little gasp at the man's boldness.

At his touch Sarah pulled back as though burned, and then seemed to take a great deal of time placing the dipper in the bucket and lifting the bucket from the floor.

"Well, if there's nothing else . . ." She seemed torn between wanting to bolt and hoping the man would ask her to stay.

". . . Head too high."

"Oh." She snatched away the folded blanket, and he moaned as the pillow cushioning his head dropped with a snap.

"Sorry." Embarrassed by her clumsiness, Sarah started toward the door, with the others trailing behind.

All except Flora, who was still standing beside the man's bed, watching him with those dark, liquid eyes that seemed always too big for her face.

Obviously in pain from the rough treatment, he flicked a glance over her and lifted a hand in dismissal. "G'wan. Get."

She stayed where she was, staring at him until he closed his eyes, bent on ignoring her. Even then she continued watching him until finally, at Sarah's hissed command, she turned away and walked to where the others were waiting.

When they'd closed the door and made their way to the kitchen, Molly was just climbing the ladder from the cellar. In her hand was a hunk of cheese for their lunch.

She took note of the high color on Sarah's cheeks. "Is everything all right, luv?"

Sarah nodded and turned away to replace the bucket and dipper.

As Molly began slicing the cheese and arranging it on a plate with slices of bread, Delia's voice was high with excitement. "The man on the summer porch called Sarah a milkmaid. A kind and generous milkmaid."

Molly looked up as she set the plate on the table and began filling glasses with milk. "Did he now? It's good to learn that he's getting his voice back and that he seems to have some proper manners. Did he say anything else?"

Flora piped up. "While Delia and Charity were fetching the bucket of water, he said Sarah was pretty."

The older girl whirled on her. "How do you know he wasn't talking about you?"

Flora's smile was at once sly and wise. "I know."

"You think you're so smart." Delia turned to Molly. "Flora said she'd be able to tell if the stranger on the summer porch is the good man or the bad one just by looking at him."

"So." Sarah tried to act nonchalant as she turned toward the little girl. "Tell us what you've decided?"

"I haven't decided yet." Flora pulled out a chair and helped herself to some bread and cheese. She calmly chewed and swallowed, then took her time draining the entire glass of milk. Wiping her mouth on her sleeve she said in a matter-of-fact tone, "I still need to see the man in Mama Molly's bed. But soon enough, I'll know which is which."

"Oh! Why would anyone listen to you? As if one look or a hundred could tell you anything." Sarah turned away and stormed out the door, allowing it to slam shut behind her.

In the kitchen the others quickly forgot the object of their discussion as they gathered around the table and began to eat their snack.

Molly found herself wondering, as she had so often, how a four-year-old innocent could seem so self-assured. Did Flora sense things that others didn't? Had the child's mother really enjoyed powers that others didn't possess? Then again, Flora might be merely compensating for the fact that her mother had abandoned her and left her with strangers.

Not strangers, Molly corrected. They may not be blood

kin, but Flora was hers now. As much as any child born of her own flesh. And she would defy anyone who argued otherwise.

"When we finish our bread and cheese and milk we'll head out to the fields to bring in the cows. Before we leave I think I'll toss a couple of chickens in a pot and make chicken stew for supper. How does that sound?"

The little girls clapped their hands.

"Chicken stew." They all knew it was Delia's favorite. "Is it a special day, Aunt Molly?"

"I believe it is."

"Is it someone's birthday?" Charity polished off the last of her cheese.

"I'm sure it's someone's birthday, somewhere. But the day is special here only because our chores are almost completed for another day, the strangers are healing, and soon, I hope, we'll be returning to Delight to turn them over to the chief of police."

"We're going to town!" Three little girls were grinning like pixies.

Hearing their voices raised in excitement, Sarah stepped into the kitchen. "What's going on?"

"We're having chicken stew."

She turned to her aunt. "What's the occasion?"

"Nothing special."

"Why is everyone shouting?"

"Mama Molly said we'll soon be going to town." Delia grinned at her big sister.

Sarah's mood brightened. "When, Aunt Molly?"

"As soon as the strangers are able to travel." Molly led the way out the door. "Come on. Let's fetch the herd home."

It was a happy band that marched across the field, and returned a short time later leading the cows to the barn. Whatever troubles there had been were now forgotten with the promise of another trip to Delight.

Over their special meal that evening, Flora reminded them with a sense of drama that there was still a chance they might be able to collect the reward on the bank robber.

Later, as they settled into their beds for the night, that tempting thought fueled all their dreams.

SEVEN

———◆◆◆———

MOLLY AWOKE ON the sofa and lay perfectly still, wondering what had caused her to wake from a sound sleep. With the days she'd been putting in lately, it would take the force of a tornado to break through her sleep-fogged brain.

A glance at the windows assured her it wasn't yet dawn. And it certainly wasn't storming. A full moon as bright as any lantern illuminated the midnight sky.

Suddenly she heard it. Not a storm, but something equally sinister. A soft, shuffling sound, coming from the direction of her bedroom. In a flash she was up and reaching for her rifle.

She pushed open the door and looked toward the bed, alarmed to find it empty.

Before she could turn away a hand closed over her mouth, cutting off the scream that died in her throat.

As her fingers tightened on the trigger, a hand closed

over hers in a steel grip, and a mouth pressed to her ear, sending tremors along her spine.

The voice was rusty as an old gate. "Drop it."

When she made no move to obey, the hand tightened on hers with a pressure guaranteed to break every one of her bones. Her rifle clattered to the floor at her feet.

The voice was tight, angry. "I know you're hiding him. Are you his woman?"

"I don't . . ."

The hand tightened over her mouth. "No denials. No lies, or I'll break your scrawny neck."

She had no doubt that he meant it.

The hand was lifted a fraction. "Where is he?"

Her mind racing, she sucked in a deep breath. Now was not the time for idle questions. "On the summer porch."

"That's better. Now where are my clothes and weapons?"

"I'll not tell you." Before the hand could once more cover her mouth she pushed free and turned on him like a spitting cat, kicking aside the rifle so that it was out of his reach. "Neither your weapons, nor his. You'll get nothing until I determine which of you can be trusted."

"That's easy enough to figure out. I'm Marshal Hodge Egan. And I intend to haul that miserable son of a bitch Eli Otto back to Milwaukee to stand trial."

"Stop that cursing." Molly's hands fisted on her hips. "I'll not permit it in this house."

Hodge blinked, and would have laughed if the situation weren't so damnably serious. "Now you listen to me, woman . . ."

"No." She shook a finger in his face like a school-marm. "You listen to me. Unless you can prove beyond a doubt that you are who you claim to be, I shall continue to treat both you and the man on the summer porch with the same mistrust."

"If you'll fetch my clothes . . ."

"And how am I to know which clothes are yours? One coat contained enough money to feed my family for a life-time. The other contained a lawman's badge and wanted poster that explained where that fine bounty came from." As her anger deepened, so did her brogue. "But since nei-ther of you was wearing a coat when I came upon you, how am I to know which coat belongs to which man?"

"I'm telling you. I am Marshal Hodge Egan and . . ."

"So you say. I'm sure the other man will do the same. Nobody but a blathering idiot would admit to being a cold-blooded killer."

Hodge was too incensed to be persuaded by her logic. In a burst of frustration he reached out, catching her by the upper arms. "Damn you, woman . . ."

"I said you'll not curse in my—"

With a muttered oath he dragged her close and, with-out giving a thought to what he was doing, covered her mouth with his. In the same instant, he was shocked by what he'd done. It wasn't at all what he'd intended. He'd merely meant to shut her up. But now that he was kissing her, he couldn't seem to stop.

He'd expected this prickly little female who could is-sue commands like a battlefield general to taste as tart as a sour apple. But the taste of her was sweet. What's more, the wisps of hair that brushed his hands were as soft as cornsilk. He thought about plunging his hands into all those wild red tangles, and instead had to content himself with the merest touch.

When she sucked in a breath and tried to push free of his arms, his ornery nature kicked in. He'd be damned if he'd let her win this contest of wills. She'd already given him notice that she thought she was in charge. Not this time. No, by God, not this time. He wasn't going to let himself be ordered about by any scrawny little female.

His arms closed around her, dragging her even closer to him.

He'd expected her to be bony, all elbows and knees and knotty hips. Instead she was incredibly soft, and her body fit against his like the missing piece of a puzzle. For the moment, his pain was forgotten, as his body responded in a purely masculine way.

It was, he realized, nothing more than male vanity. But it gave him enormous pleasure to know that his body, though battered, could still react to a female this way.

Forgotten, as well, was their contest of wills. Now there was just the pleasure of the moment. And what a pleasure it was. It had been too long since he'd held a soft, warm woman in his arms.

Molly's head was spinning. She knew she ought to fight him. It simply wasn't in her nature to allow herself to be bullied. But the press of his mouth to hers had her brain going all fuzzy, and her bones were feeling all soft and pliant, like wax to a flame.

She'd been kissed before, but never like this. A kiss that was at once rough and bruising. There was nothing soft or sweet about it, but almost brutal in its intensity. It drained her even while it filled her. Instead of coaxing, it demanded. Instead of soothing, it inflamed.

Something sprang to life deep inside her, like a deep, gnawing hunger that she hadn't even known was there.

As the kiss spun on and on, she found herself clinging to him, afraid to let go, for fear of her legs failing her.

She heard a primal, almost feral sound and realized it came from deep in her throat, like a growl of pain or pleasure. Or both.

Hodge answered with a moan of his own as he felt her gradual surrender. He knew he ought to do the right thing and step back. But not yet. Not just yet. He craved one more moment before letting go. And so his mouth moved none too gently over hers, teeth and lips and tongue invading, tasting, until she responded in kind.

Like one in a daze, Molly opened to him, allowing him to take the kiss deeper.

He drew in the taste of her, the scent of her, letting her warm breath fill his lungs. He'd thought her nothing more than a tough, weathered farm woman, but now he realized that he'd been wrong. There was such sweetness here. Such goodness. Like a fair prairie wildflower opening to the sun and revealing its beauty.

She was stirring up feelings he'd thought buried forever. Feelings of tenderness. He'd put such things aside years ago, and had grown accustomed to the sly, painted women who worked the gentlemen's clubs. Women who knew how to dress to draw a man's attention. Women who knew just how to walk, to move, to stir a man's appetite. Women who knew how to pleasure a man, and then walk away without asking for more than he was comfortable giving.

In some small, dark corner of his mind he could hear alarm bells going off. He could tell, by her first tentative reaction, that she wasn't accustomed to being kissed. And why not? Any man with half a brain could see that this woman wasn't the kind a man could trifle with and then go on his merry way. She'd likely hog-tie him, force him into marriage and misery, and steal his future.

No matter how pleasurable the kiss, this little female was nothing but trouble.

Calling on all his willpower, Hodge lifted his head, though he continued holding her, afraid that if he let go, he might embarrass himself by stumbling like a drunk.

"Sorry."

Molly dragged air into her starving lungs. "And well you ought to be . . ."

"Not about the kiss." By the light of the moon she could see the dangerous curve of his lips, the gleam of his teeth. "But I'm sorry about the cursing."

Her eyes went wide. He could actually feel the heat from her temper spiraling upward, turning those green eyes to hot sparks. "And you think you can just kiss me without a by-your-leave?"

"Woman, the way you kissed me back was answer enough to that."

"Oh, you hateful . . ." Her words died in her throat when she saw the way the color fled from his face and he went sickly white. She managed to catch hold of him just before he slumped to the floor.

Moving quickly, she steered him toward the bed. He

toppled forward and lay, breathing shallow, skin pearled with sweat.

"Now you've done it." She studied the way blood oozed through the dressing at his shoulder.

Working quickly she stripped away the bloody linen and began disinfecting the wound before applying a clean dressing. While she worked he hissed out a breath and she could see him clenching his teeth against the pain.

"Serves you right." She would not allow herself to feel compassion for this bold, hateful man. "Next time, maybe you'll think before you try stumbling out of bed. If you hadn't fallen, I could have had the pleasure of dashing you to the floor myself."

"Not likely."

"Oh, you think too highly of yourself. Do you know what I think?"

When he made no response, she watched as his eyes rolled back in his head before his lids flickered, then closed. His breathing was strained, shallow.

She covered him with the blanket and stood a moment, watching while he fought sleep.

As she let herself out of the bedroom, she wondered at the way her hands were shaking. The mere touch of this stranger had made her as jumpy as old Bossy when wolves were howling in the nearby hills.

Dropping onto the sofa, she took in a deep breath. The taste of him, dark and mysterious and so purely male, lingered on her lips. The feel of those hands, so strong they could easily snap her bones like twigs, was still imprinted on her flesh. Flesh that was far too heated for comfort.

She'd been so certain that she could get through this

situation without danger to herself or her girls. Hadn't she faced plenty of trouble in her life? But that was before. Before she'd tasted this stranger's kiss.

She touched a hand to her heart. Now there was a new and more deadly danger she would have to face. Her own foolish heart, which was still pounding like a runaway wagon at the mere thought of him.

The feelings whirling around in her mind were so raw, so alien, she had no defense against them.

Feeling completely lost and confused, she closed her eyes, hoping for sleep to come and wipe her mind free. But it wasn't to be. For the next few hours, while the night fled and ribbons of dawn began to streak the sky, she replayed that scene with the stranger, feeling again the little thrill as he'd pulled her close and boldly kissed her the way no man had ever dared to kiss her before.

It wasn't his boldness that shamed her, but rather hers. In the quiet of the night she was forced to admit that she had not only allowed his kiss, but had actually encouraged it. Had enjoyed it. And if truth be told, she found herself wishing with all her heart that he could be here right now, to kiss her again.

With a moan of frustration she turned on her side and squeezed her eyes tightly shut, hoping to blot out the image of that shocking scene with the stranger in her bedroom.

Whether gunman or lawman, he was purely evil. And he'd awakened something in her that had her more frightened than she cared to admit.

EIGHT

"MAMA MOLLY." FLORA danced into the barn, where Molly was hauling the milking stool to yet another cow. "The man on the summer porch is awake and hollering for something to eat. Sarah wants to know what she should do."

Molly looked over with a sigh. "Tell her to bring him some buttermilk. That should hold him until I'm finished here."

"Yes'm."

As Flora started away Molly reached out a hand to stop her. "And Flora, I want you and the others to stay with Sarah. She's not to be left alone with that man."

"'Cause he could be the bad man?"

"That's right. Until we know, we're to take no chances. Do you understand?"

"Yes'm."

The little girl skipped out and Molly bent to her task, her mind as busy as her hands. If the man was asking for food, it meant he was healing. And that meant she could soon haul him and the other man to town, to let the police chief deal with this problem. And then, hopefully, her life could get back to normal.

Normal. Nothing had been normal since she'd come upon those two.

Every time she thought about that scene with the stranger in her bedroom, she could feel the heat rise to her cheeks. As much as she tried to erase it from her mind, it was impossible. She felt like such a fool. For all she knew, she'd been kissing a dangerous outlaw. In fact, she was more and more convinced of it. How could he be a man of the law when there was such a feeling of ruthlessness about him? He was rough and dangerous, and she would have to steel herself against any further feelings for him while she tended his wounds.

Even when these men were out of her life, would things ever feel normal again?

"THAT'S IT?" ELI drained the glass of buttermilk and handed the empty glass to Sarah.

She and the girls had propped his head up by stacking several mounded quilts behind him. He lay back, feeling weak as a newborn, while four pairs of eyes watched his every move.

It was creepy and unsettling. And yet, he found himself enjoying their attention. It was a lot like being back in that schoolhouse in Sheboygan, when he would mock the teacher behind her back, drawing laughter from the bigger boys. Of course, whenever he was caught, he'd had to taste Miss Seaberry's rod. She did enjoy using that cane on his backside. But it was worth the price, to have the older boys treat him like one of them. By the time he was ten, he was hiding in the woods until school was in session. Then he would take himself to town and sneak into the back room of old Uriah Perry's mercantile, where he'd help himself to the old man's stash of whiskey while Uriah was out front, dealing with customers.

Oh, those were grand days. By the time his Aunt Reba found out that he wasn't attending school with the others, he'd had a taste of freedom that he wouldn't easily forget. Even after his aunt started accompanying him to the schoolhouse, he'd found a way to slip out of the teacher's clutches. There was always a need to go to the outhouse, which was situated close enough to the woods to allow him to be gone before he was missed. And by the time he was eleven, he was taller than his aunt and his teacher, and both women had given up trying to force him to play by the proper rules of the good people of his town.

He'd walked away from his aunt's miserable little farmhouse and the town of Sheboygan without ever looking back.

Now he made the rules. And others danced to the tune of his rod, which he yielded with fierce glee.

"Aunt Molly said that buttermilk will have to hold you until she's finished the milking. Then she'll be back to fix you something more substantial."

He blinked, forcing himself back to the present. "Your aunt and uncle own this place, huh?"

He saw the way the younger girls covered their mouths to hide their laughter.

"I say something funny?"

"You said uncle." Delia laughed aloud. "Don't let Aunt Molly hear you say that."

He studied the red-haired girl, a mirror image of her older sister. He'd never had any use for red hair or freckles. They reminded him of Irma Stanton, a girl in his old schoolhouse who used to taunt him because he couldn't read. "Why's that?"

" 'Cause Aunt Molly doesn't have a husband."

"There's no man around?" Intrigued, he turned to the oldest. "I'm in a house full of women?"

Sarah flushed and studied the toe of her boot. Aunt Molly would be furious when she learned that they'd been telling this stranger their business. Thinking quickly, she said, "There's Addison."

Eli's eyes narrowed. "Who's that?"

"He lives alone in the woods. Every once in a while he comes by and lends a hand with the calving or the plowing. In return, my aunt buys him tobacco and coffee and things in town."

"Why doesn't he buy them for himself?"

"I guess he doesn't much care for people. Except Aunt Molly."

"You mean he's sweet on her?"

That had the girls laughing harder.

"What's so funny?"

Delia's face turned as red as her hair. "It's just that . . ." She turned to her big sister. "You tell him, Sarah."

Sarah flushed when she realized she had Eli's full attention. Each day, as the swelling in his face improved, he became more handsome. He was, she could see now, much younger than she'd first imagined, despite that stubble of dark hair on his chin. Why, he was probably no more than four or five years older than she. And so good-looking. There was something wild and dangerous in his eyes in those unguarded moments when he thought nobody was looking. Not at all like the boys she knew in Delight. Just looking at him made her feel older. And bolder.

"Addison told us he was a slave during the War Between the States."

"A negro?"

The girls arched a brow, and Eli realized they'd never heard the word before. Just how far from civilization was he? "That war was almost thirty years ago."

Sarah played with the sash at her waist. "After the war Addison made his way to Wisconsin, and he's been living alone in the woods ever since. He said he much prefers his own company to most of the folks he's met in his lifetime."

"That's crazy. You ever been to his place?"

Sarah shook her head. "Aunt Molly said we have to stay away, out of respect for his privacy."

"That's what she tells you. What she means is, there's no telling what a crazy old coot like that might do if he found a bunch of helpless females poking around his hidey-hole. He might want to wring your necks like chickens."

Little Flora felt the need to defend the old man who

had never been anything but kind to her and the others. "Addison would never do anything to hurt us."

"Yeah? And how would you know, kid?"

Her little chin lifted. "He saved my life once."

The others nodded.

Charity's eyes went wide, remembering. "Flora decided she was going to fly. She climbed the tallest tree she could find and when she reached the top, she started flapping her arms just before she jumped."

"Crazy kid."

At his remark, Flora's little hands fisted at her hips.

"As usual, Flora didn't think before she jumped." Delia rolled her eyes. "The tree was hanging over a creek bed, and by the time she hit the water, she landed with such a splash, we all started crying thinking she would drown."

"Just like a bunch of helpless females to stand around crying."

"Did not." Flora felt the need to defend the others. "Charity jumped in to save me. Only she couldn't swim either. We'd have both drowned for sure if it hadn't been for Addison."

Sarah nodded. "Before any of us could move, old Addison came running out of the woods and raced ahead to the shallows, where he hauled the two out by their petticoats. He wrapped them up in his shirt and carried them home." She put a hand to her heart. "Poor Aunt Molly. When she heard what happened, we figured she'd give them both a good thrashing, especially Flora."

"That's what she deserved," Eli said firmly.

Sarah interrupted. "Instead, Aunt Molly just got awfully

quiet and ordered us to go sit in the sun while she fixed us some buttermilk."

Eli gave a grunt. "If you'd been mine, brat, I'd've tanned your hide."

"Well I'm not yours." Flora was eyeing the stranger with a look of disgust. "How come you haven't told us your name?"

"Figured you already knew it."

Delia could see her aunt heading toward the house, hauling a cart filled with buckets of milk. Distracted, she blurted, "We know you're either a marshal or a bank robber."

As soon as the words were out of her mouth, she clapped a hand over it while her face flamed.

Well, now. Wasn't that a hoot? Eli saw the looks that passed from one girl to the other. Their faces reflected fear, horror, and in the oldest, annoyance.

Very deliberately he forced himself to smile. "Well, now you won't have to worry your pretty little heads about it another minute. The truth is, my name is Marshal Hodge Egan, and I'm on the trail of a bank robber named Eli Otto. Would've had him by now if I hadn't broken my leg."

"So you say." Flora backed away, and the others, mortified by all that had been revealed, did the same.

"If you'll bring me my badge and my gun, I'll prove it."

"Prove what?" Molly stood framed in the doorway, her face flushed from the heat of the day.

"That I'm the marshal."

She looked from the man in the bed to the faces of her girls, and could see Delia's lips trembling.

"I'm sorry, Aunt Molly. I didn't mean to say anything but . . ." The little girl dashed from the room, tears spilling down her cheeks.

Molly turned to Sarah for an explanation.

The older girl gave a toss of her head. "Delia told him we don't know if he's the marshal or the bank robber."

Molly hissed out a breath and struggled for composure. When she looked at the man in the bed, she wondered about the look in his eyes. Though he was neither laughing nor frowning, she thought she detected a look of smug satisfaction before he blinked it away.

"The girls told me you're hungry. I'll be back with some food in a bit."

"Thank you, ma'am." Eli tried for his best manners. "That would surely be appreciated."

As Molly turned away, she could see the door to her bedroom standing open. The man in the bed was wide awake. And from the intense look on his face, had heard every word of their conversation on the summer porch.

Just how much had the girls revealed?

She couldn't blame the children. The fault lay squarely on her shoulders. Hadn't she made the same admission last night to the stranger in her bed?

She'd been a fool to allow the girls to be left alone with these men for even a few minutes. Even though neither man was in any condition to be a physical threat to her girls, there were other dangers, equally daunting. Now that both men knew that she was unaware of their identities, they were bound to do everything they could to persuade her to trust them. What was worse, with their injuries beginning to heal, both men would begin to take careful note of their surroundings. And one of them would be making plans to escape.

It was time to think about hauling them to Delight, no matter how painful the journey might prove for them, or how difficult for Molly and her girls.

NINE

◆◆◆

HODGE LAY BACK, straining to hear as the woman and girls made their way to the kitchen. The woman's voice was too low to understand the words she was saying, but from the respectful silence that followed, he suspected that the children were getting an earful about having violated one of her rules.

The kid had played right into Eli's hands. Within the space of a couple of minutes that bastard had learned that there was no man around to protect them, and that these females didn't have a clue as to which of the strangers taking up space in this farmhouse was the marshal and which the bank robber.

If all Eli Otto had done was rob a bank, it would be bad enough. But this was no mere thief in need of enough money to keep body and soul together. While he'd trailed Otto through the wilderness, Hodge had read the reports that went back more than a dozen years, since the thief was no more than a boy. Eli Otto didn't just steal when he needed to. He enjoyed the life of crime he'd chosen. What was worse, like a ferocious storm that flattened entire towns, this criminal had left a string of innocent victims in his wake. From the testimony of those witnesses lucky to be left alive after his crimes, it was clear that he felt no remorse. He was a vicious, cold-blooded animal who had learned how to use his looks and charm to take whatever he wanted. What's worse, that feral animal had just learned that he was in the company of a woman and a handful of girls. And the only thing that stood between the fox and the hens was a man of the law so weak, he could barely stand.

Hodge knew that he had to find a way, and quickly, to persuade the woman to give him back his gun. Without it, the first chance Eli Otto had of getting to him in the night, he'd surely be dead. With the woman and kids following close behind.

Hodge struggled to sit up and felt the room spin. With a string of curses for this weakness that held him prisoner, he fought through the pain and managed to swing his feet to the floor.

Where the hell had that damnable woman hidden his clothes? How was he supposed to defend her and her kids when he was stark naked? Furious, he thrashed around until, defeated by his own weakness, he dropped to the floor like a stone.

ON THE SUMMER porch, Eli Otto's thoughts ran in the same vein. More than clothes, he needed a gun. And he needed it now. Thanks to the kid with the big mouth, he now knew that he hadn't been dreaming when he'd had that strange encounter with the marshal. It hadn't been a nightmare. It had actually happened. They were both here under the same roof. And from what the kid said, Hodge Egan hadn't been able to prove his identity either.

Good news for Eli. Right now, he had as much chance of claiming to be the marshal as Hodge Egan. What a hoot. Wouldn't it be a fine joke to play on all of them if he could persuade them to trust him instead of Egan?

He lay back, his mind working overtime, circling this way and that like a hawk tracking prey.

As he saw it, the oldest girl was the one to work on. The woman wasn't about to trust either of them. And the kids, especially now that one of them had spilled their secret, would be too cowed to cross the line again. But the oldest girl was the one who had to run and fetch whenever the woman was too busy. Since she was forced to spend the most time with him, he'd have to find a way to earn her trust.

His lips curved into a grin. When it came to worming his way into a woman's heart, he was an expert. Hadn't he known since he was a kid just how to work his aunt Reba? Until the day that she'd been given undeniable proof of his many youthful crimes, she'd been his staunchest defender.

Since leaving Sheboygan he'd had plenty of experience with women, from simple farmers' daughters, to the harlots who plied their trade in the cribs of every city from here to St. Louis. He'd mastered a hundred ways to turn on the charm. And though this one was younger than most of the women he'd conned in the past, he hadn't a doubt that he could handle her.

He lay back and closed his eyes while he mulled his next step. He couldn't afford any mistakes. He needed to make his escape in the next day or so. That meant that he had to work overtime to win the trust of the girl called Sarah.

"HEAVEN HELP US." Molly started into the bedroom, then came to an abrupt halt at the sight of the naked man crumpled on her floor.

Hearing the children coming down the hallway, she slammed the door shut to preserve modesty before hurrying to his side.

"Trying to escape, were you?"

"Es . . . ?" Hodge felt like a drunk. Though he knew the words, he couldn't seem to make his mouth work.

"Indeed. Slip away while I was busy elsewhere. Oh, you're a slick one." None too gently Molly pulled him to his knees before draping one of his arms around her neck and hauling him to his feet.

He moaned at the sudden shaft of pain, causing Molly to experience a quick jolt of guilt. Just as quickly she pushed aside her feelings as she inched him toward the bed. "I know you overheard everything said by the girls on the summer porch. And now you thought to escape before I could figure out what was what."

"Woman, you're too damned smart for your own good. You figure you can bully me into behaving, do you?" His gravel voice, so close to her ear, shot splinters along her spine.

She looked up. A mistake, she realized at once. He was staring down at her with a lopsided grin that did strange things to her heart. She looked away, her jaw clenched. "I'll do whatever it takes."

"Really?" He pulled back, nearly causing them both to take a tumble. "In that case, you'd be better off using honey instead of vinegar."

"Honey, is it? I've a good mind to let you fall. Then you'll taste my honey."

"If you do, I'll take you with me. Of course, in my present state of undress, that might be . . . interesting, especially if you should fall on top of me."

"Oh, you wicked man." She huffed out a breath. "Have you no shame?"

"None at all. In fact, there must be something wrong with me. I think I'm beginning to enjoy all this pain and humiliation at the hands of an ornery female."

"I'd be more than happy to show you pain and humiliation." Though she talked a good game, Molly was forced to wrap both arms around his waist to anchor him. He stood a good head over her and probably outweighed her by a hundred pounds of muscle. By the time she'd shoved and prodded him into bed, she was exhausted from the effort.

Though it cost him more pain, Hodge refused to show it. Instead he patted the edge of the bed. "Care to join me?"

Molly turned away in disgust. She'd been right about him. The man had absolutely no shame at all. There was no way he could wear the badge of a U.S. marshal. Only an outlaw would be so coarse.

With a huff of breath she yanked open the door and stormed out.

"YOU STAND RIGHT there, Sarah." Molly bustled into her bedroom carrying a tray and gave a nod toward the doorway, where the girl stood holding her aunt's rifle. Three little faces peered from behind Sarah's skirts.

Molly set the tray on a scarred wooden night table and picked up a wedge of cheese. "Eat this. 'Twill give you back some strength."

Hodge sniffed. "If it doesn't poison me. It smells foul. What is this?"

"Cheese. The girls and I make it in the cellar."

That would explain the sharp, pungent odor that drifted in and out from time to time. Hunger won out over sense, and he ignored the smell of it as he took a bite, chewed and swallowed. "I must be hungrier than I thought." He devoured the rest of the cheese. "That's mighty fine."

His compliment had Molly almost smiling. "That's what most of my neighbors say, too."

"You sell this?" He watched as Molly picked up a bowl of steaming soup and dipped in a spoon.

"I do, yes. Or rather, I barter it for goods I need." She held the spoon to his mouth and he practically inhaled the chicken broth. With each spoonful, he could feel his energy returning.

He watched the woman as she fed him. Up close her eyes seemed a deeper green. Her skin, despite the constant exposure to sunlight, was fair, and sprinkled with freckles. Her nose was small and upturned, and her mouth was slightly open, mirroring his movements.

He felt a sudden sharp longing to taste more than the food she offered.

The unexpected jolt of lust had him reaching a hand to her wrist. He felt her pulse leap before she shot him a frigid look.

"You'll not be touching me."

"Sorry." He grinned. "I didn't know there were rules."

"There are. If I'm to take you and the stranger in the other room to Delight to be identified, I must first get you strong enough to survive the journey. So I'll feed you, because I have no choice. And I'll dress your wounds for the same reason. But that rifle"—She nodded toward her niece in the doorway—"will insure that you will not abuse my kindness. Now lower your hand at once."

He uncurled his fingers and lowered his hand to the bed.

Satisfied, Molly slathered a hunk of bread with strawberry preserves and handed it to him.

Like everything else she'd fed him, it tasted like heaven. The bread was still warm from the oven, and the sweet preserves melted in his mouth, leaving him wanting more.

"There's tea here." She handed him a cup and nodded toward the steaming pot on the tray. "Can you manage that on your own?"

He nodded. "Yes." Almost as an afterthought he muttered, "Thanks."

"You're welcome." She stood and smoothed down her skirts before walking around the bed and motioning for Sarah to move aside.

When he was alone, Hodge closed his other hand around the warm cup and sipped before lying back against the pillows. What in hell was wrong with him? There was a killer in the next room, and the last thing he needed right now was the distraction of a female. Especially that one.

Not his type, he thought glumly. He much preferred a perfumed female in a satin gown, with smoky eyes and rouged cheeks. A woman willing to share a quick tumble in the sheets before making herself scarce.

This one had work-roughened hands that were none too gentle whenever they touched him.

And they didn't touch him nearly often enough.

He grinned. It had taken her an eternity to feed him, and through it all, he'd had the most unreasonable urge to curl his arm around her neck and draw her face down for a kiss. If he dared such a thing, he'd surely wear that soup. Still, it would have been worth it.

With a sigh he set aside his tea and closed his eyes. Now that he knew how the woman tasted, it was even worse. One kiss and he found himself wanting more.

She may not be as sweet as her strawberry preserves, but he'd bet a twenty-dollar gold piece that if he set his mind to it, he could sweeten her up considerably. Even though she'd make him pay for it afterward.

Another thing he'd bet on. Judging from the farm chores she did, despite that tiny body, he figured she'd pack a hell of a punch.

That thought ought to be enough to fuel his dreams for hours.

TEN

"Hot out there today?" Eli accepted the glass of buttermilk from Sarah's hands, careful to keep his gaze lowered. The girl had been as skittish as a colt since that tongue-lashing from her aunt, administered in the kitchen in a voice so low he hadn't been able to overhear the actual words. But he'd known, all the same, by the reaction of the younger ones, that they'd been chastized. He was determined to put this girl at ease so he could pry some answers with as little pressure as possible.

"Some." She stepped back and watched him drink.

He flicked a glance toward the three younger ones, who stood in the doorway, watching and listening. Apparently they'd all been warned to keep their distance. "I used to find it hard to do farm chores in the heat of the day."

Sarah's head came up. "You lived on a farm?"

He nodded. "With my aunt Reba."

"What happened to your folks?"

"They died when I was six."

Sarah felt an instant kinship. "Mine died when I was ten."

Eli allowed the silence to drag on for a moment longer before giving an exaggerated sigh. "Not at an outlaw's hand, I'll wager."

He could see that the girl was shocked. "Your parents were . . . killed?"

He stared off into the distance. "I suppose that's when I decided to become a man of the law. To avenge their deaths."

"That's a fine and noble reason."

"Not so noble, I guess." He shrugged. "I wasn't so much concerned about seeing justice done. I wanted to make certain that the outlaw that killed my parents wouldn't be around to make orphans of any more kids."

"I hate that word." Sarah shuddered. "Orphan." Her voice was barely a whisper. She thought of the people in town, whispering behind their hands in the months after her parents' death, and the looks of sympathy in their eyes whenever they engaged her and her sister, Delia, in conversation.

"Yeah. Me, too."

She dared a glance at the man in the bed from beneath lowered lashes. "Did you ever catch him? I mean, after you became a lawman?"

He took his time draining the glass, then held it out, forcing her to step closer. When she reached for it, he stared into her eyes. "I was this close to catching him."

"What stopped you?"

He rubbed his shoulder. "His bullet. But when I get out of this bed, he'll pay for his crimes."

Her eyes went wide. "You mean, the man in the other room is the one who . . . ?"

"Eli Otto." Eli's voice lowered for dramatic effect. "I'm going to take great pleasure in arresting him."

The three little girls in the doorway began whispering among themselves, and Eli could see that Sarah was getting ready to herd them away. "I wouldn't mind another glass of that fine buttermilk."

Sarah crossed to the doorway and handed the glass to Delia, who started toward the kitchen, with Charity and Flora trailing.

For the next minute or two, Eli knew that he would have Sarah's undivided attention. He kept his tone low, forcing her to walk closer to the bed in order to hear him. "I'll need to haul that outlaw to the nearest jail until I can wire the authorities for instructions on where to take him."

"That would be Delight."

"How far is Delight from here?"

"A day's ride."

"That far? Nothing closer?"

"There's nothing between us and Delight except wilderness."

"How often do you go there?"

Sarah shrugged. "A couple of times a year. Whenever Aunt Molly needs supplies."

"I suppose you have kin living nearby to keep an eye on the farm while you're gone."

"Aunt Molly is the only kin we have left. Our folks and hers are all buried out behind the barn."

"Well, at least you all have each other. The way I had my aunt Reba." He let that sink in before asking casually, "So who tends the herd and watches the farm whenever you leave?"

"Addison, usually."

"The old guy who lives in the woods. How does he know when you need him?"

"He and Aunt Molly worked out a signal. There's a big old wooden pole alongside the barn. She hangs a sheet from the pole. Whenever Addison sees it flapping, he knows to come over."

"That's real clever of your aunt. What if he gets busy and doesn't see the sheet?"

"So far, whenever we've needed him, he's always shown up."

"But you've never been to his place?"

Sarah shook her head. "Aunt Molly says a man deserves his privacy."

"Your aunt's a smart woman. I bet she's got lots of friends in the town of Delight." Eli saw the flush that stained the girl's cheeks and realized he'd hit a nerve. Apparently a spinster with four kids not her own wasn't too popular with the good folks of the town. "Do her friends in Delight ever pay a visit to your farm?"

"No. She . . ." Sarah looked up as the three girls returned.

She accepted the glass from Delia and carried it to the bedside. When the man emptied it, she held out her hand. "I'd better get back to my chores."

"Thank you for the buttermilk, Sarah." He allowed his fingers to brush hers. Just the slightest touch, while he gave her one of his most charming smiles. "I don't know what helps me feel better. Your aunt's fine hospitality, or the pleasure of your sweet company. Maybe, when your chores are done, you'll come back for a visit."

"I shouldn't."

"It's just nice to talk to someone who knows how I feel. The more I know you, the more I realize how much alike we are."

Sarah shrugged. "I suppose it wouldn't hurt to talk."

"There you go. I'll wait for you tonight. Maybe after the others fall asleep, we can talk about how it feels to lose our folks, and . . . things." He gave her his best smile as she backed toward the door.

"I don't know. I'll . . . see."

When he was alone, Eli sank back against the cushions and thought over all he'd managed to learn. These females weren't just alone, they were isolated. A day's ride from the nearest town. No kin or friends to pay a call. And the only help they could look for was an old coot living like a hermit in the forest.

This was too good to be true. Once he managed to get rid of the marshal, he was home free.

He had to persuade the girl to trust him. And there was no time to waste.

"HERE'S YOUR SUPPER." Molly set a tray on the wooden table beside the man's bed on the summer porch and began removing a plate, covered with a square of linen.

His eyes flicked open and he yawned and stretched before offering her a smile.

"Thank you kindly, ma'am." He caught sight of Sarah in the doorway, holding her aunt's rifle. The other three girls stood slightly behind her, peering at him from behind her skirts.

"I hope you don't mind if I wait awhile to sample your fine cooking."

Molly gave him a look. "Are you not feeling well?"

"As well as can be. But that fine buttermilk earlier filled me up. I'll just take some time and feed myself. And if I can't manage, I'll let you know. Maybe one of your girls could feed me."

Molly wasn't about to let that pass. Quickly tying his wrists and ankles, she gave him a long look. "If you need help, I'll be happy to come back and feed you."

"Thank you, ma'am." He waited until she'd picked up the tray and started away before adding, "If someone could put a pillow under my broken leg, I'd be obliged."

Molly hissed out a breath. She was weary from her farm chores and still had to feed the man in the other room before she and the girls could take their own supper.

"Sarah, would you see to it?"

"Yes'm." The girl set aside the rifle and obediently moved to his bed, with the other three watching from the safety of the doorway.

Leaving them to watch out for Sarah, Molly moved around them and walked to her bedroom. The stranger was awake, and scowling.

"Well, now, and it's happy I am to see you, too." She snapped down the tray with a clatter.

"Why should I be happy when I'm forced to lie here and watch the way that outlaw is playing with all of you?"

She turned to him, hands on her hips. "What are you talking about?"

"Have you ever watched a cat when it corners a mouse?"

At her blank look he gave a snarl of anger. "Eli Otto is as sly as any cat. And his claws are just as deadly. Right now, while you're in here with my meal, he's conning more and more information out of your innocent little niece."

"Sarah has been cautioned . . ."

"She's a girl of what? Thirteen?"

"Fourteen. She'll be fifteen next spring." Molly draped a clean linen towel across his chest and dipped a spoon into the bowl of steaming beef stew.

"If she lives that long. Right now that clever outlaw's coaxing all the information he needs to know. Bit by bit he's earning her trust while learning everything there is to know about you."

"Such as . . . ?" She dipped the spoon between his lips and he was forced to chew and swallow before he could speak.

"He now knows that you have no kin. Nobody from town ever visits your farm. The only man for miles around is named Addison, and he only comes to call when you hang out a sheet on a pole by the barn."

Molly sat back and regarded him with a look of stunned surprise. "How do you know all this?"

"I told you. The only thing you can trust about Eli Otto is the fact that he's the slickest con this side of St. Louis. To him this is all a game. He's manipulating all of you into trusting him. For your own safety, you need to give me back my weapons."

"I should have known." Molly got to her feet and shook down her apron.

"Known what?"

She gave him a chilling look. "You said all this just to get your hands on a gun."

"Are you saying none of this information is true? That I made it all up about you having no kin, and about an old man named Addison who lives in the woods and only comes running when you send a sheet up a pole?"

That had her stopping in her tracks. But only for an instant. With her spine stiff she started toward the door. "If you're strong enough to sit up all day and listen to every word being spoken in this house, you're certainly strong enough to feed yourself."

"You listen to me, woman . . ."

"No." Her voice was pure ice. "You listen to me. I'll not be told what to do in my own house. Especially not by you."

"Fine. Suit yourself. But I'm warning you, if there's a way to slip free of this place, that bastard on the porch will find it."

"You will not use such language in my home. And in case you aren't aware, that man has a broken leg. At your hands, I might add. I doubt he could get from the porch to the barn without fainting dead away."

"If there's a way to escape, Eli Otto will find it."

"And I'll be right behind him with my rifle at the ready."

"There are a lot of others who said that very thing. Now they're all dead."

"If you're trying to frighten me . . ."

116

"You'd have to have some sense to be afraid. And you . . ."

His words died as Molly's skirts fluttered and the door slammed shut with such force, the sound reverberated throughout the farmhouse.

From her position in the doorway of the summer porch, Flora watched Molly flounce away. Strange, how the man in Mama Molly's bed seemed to strike sparks every time those two got close.

Just the opposite of Sarah and the man on the porch. To the little girl's ears, his words were too smooth, too slick. Every time he looked at Sarah, young Flora felt something curdle in her stomach. She knew everyone thought she was just bragging, but she sensed things. And the thing she sensed every time she got near the man on the porch was evil.

She needed to see if she'd feel the same way about the man in Mama Molly's bed.

Leaving the others, she opened the door to the bedroom and stepped inside.

Hodge scowled, thinking Molly had returned for another round of battle. Seeing the little girl, he relaxed and waited for the cup of tea.

"Why do you fight with Mama Molly?"

"She's an irritating woman. Did you come to irritate me, too?"

Flora watched him sip his tea. When he was finished, her dark eyes peered directly into his. "Mama Molly saved your life."

He nodded. "I know that. And I'm grateful."

"You don't act like it."

"There's just something about that woman that rubs my fur wrong."

"She wanted you to live. I wanted you to die."

Her words had him gaping at her in surprise. "Why?"

"Because then we'd get to go back to town."

He let that sink in. "You like going to town?"

"It's fun. Mama Molly lets us visit with folks along the way while she barters cheese and milk and eggs. And once we're in town, we get to go to Sunday services and church socials and dances and such."

"I see. That must be quite a change from living way out here."

"I like being here." She gave an emphatic shake of her head, sending dark hair tumbling around her face. "But I like town, too."

"You didn't inherit your aunt's red hair, I see."

"She isn't my aunt. Not my real mama, either."

"Then how do you happen to live here?"

"My ma couldn't take care of me. So she left me here, knowing Mama Molly would take me in."

"How did she know that?"

"Everyone in Delight knows that Mama Molly can't turn away a stray." The little girl moved to the window. With her back to him she said, "She might not be my real mama, but she loves me, and this is my home." She turned back and met his stare without blinking. "You'd better never do anything to hurt Mama Molly."

She slipped out of the room without another word.

When she was gone, Hodge sipped his tea contemplatively. The kid had the oldest, wisest eyes he'd ever seen.

Someday, when she was all grown up, she'd make some poor sucker either the happiest man alive, or if he should cross her, the most miserable bastard in the world.

Despite his irritation at Molly, he found himself grinning at the thought of the woman that little girl would one day become. God help the man who fell for her.

And God help me, too, Hodge thought. *If I don't find a way to get that damnable woman to trust me, I can kiss my dreams of living the good life in San Francisco good-bye.*

ELEVEN

◆━━◆━◆━◆━━◆

HODGE LAY IN the big feather bed. Alone in the woman's room, with the door firmly closed, there was nothing he could do but watch as evening faded into night and the household grew silent, while he worked on the rope at his wrists and ankles.

He was grateful that the woman had let slip the fact that Eli's leg was broken. It was the only good news he'd gathered since landing in this godforsaken place. But he doubted a broken leg would stop that outlaw from figuring a way to take control of the situation. That's why it was critical that Hodge act quickly to foul Eli's plans.

He needed his gun, his badge, and his clothes. And he intended to fetch them tonight while the others slept. He figured if he took his time, moved slowly and carefully, he could remain upright long enough to complete his mission. Once he had his gun and badge, no matter how weak he felt, he'd bully the others into helping him haul the outlaw to town.

Judging from the look of this room, the woman kept a clean house. It stood to reason that she would have felt compelled to wash and dry his bloody clothes. If she was like most farm women, she would have them folded and stashed somewhere in the parlor. That was the only room that was rarely used except on Sundays or holidays. As for the weapons, he figured he'd find them in one of the parlor cabinets, along with a stash of whiskey kept for company, providing the female permitted drinking in her house. Seeing the way she'd bristled when he swore, he wouldn't be surprised if she considered whiskey to be an equally damning work of the devil.

That brought an image from his past that had him grinning. He'd been fifteen when he and his sister, Hildy, had gone to town for supplies. He'd left Hildy at the mercantile, while he'd gone in search of a man who'd offered to sell him a brood mare that would help increase their herd. The man allowed him to examine the horse, then agreed to seal the deal at the saloon, where the document could be witnessed by the local sheriff, who spent more time drinking than he did chasing outlaws. By the time Hildy found Hodge, he was polishing off his third glass of whiskey, and could barely remember his own name.

It had taken three ranchers to hold Hildy back, though she managed to verbally rip both the sheriff and the farmer to shreds, calling them every villainous name she could think of, before hauling her little brother out the door by his ear. There wasn't a man in the place who'd dared to laugh, though Hodge had seen a few sly grins from some of the older ranchers. That humiliation would have been bad enough. But on the daylong ride back to their shanty, he'd nursed a sick stomach and a pounding headache that had him thinking that death would be a welcome relief from the pain. Afterward he promised his sister that he wouldn't go near the saloon again until he was old enough to know the difference between a pint and a gallon. Even today, though he enjoyed an occasional taste of whiskey, the temptation to overindulge brought a flash of his sister's face to his mind's eye.

His grin turned into a frown. This woman, Molly, reminded him a lot of his sister. A tough, scrappy survivor. But the unforgiving life of a wilderness rancher had taken its toll, and Hildy had been dead before she'd ever known a man's love, or held a babe in her arms. All she'd had to show for her life was a stubborn kid brother from whom she'd bullied a deathbed vow to stay out of trouble and follow the law.

Well, he'd kept his promise, hadn't he? And look what it got him. Feeling more dead than alive in this sorry backwoods farm, trying to stay one step ahead of a cold-blooded killer bent on escape at any price.

The way Hodge saw it he had no choice but to save this foolish female and her kids from their own folly. He'd find his gun, his badge, and his clothes. And then he'd haul the bastard Eli Otto to the nearest town and see him locked up for good.

And then he was going to find himself a perfumed woman, a good cigar, some smooth whiskey, and a hot game of poker to celebrate.

* * *

"THEY'RE NOT EVER going to die, are they, Mama Molly?" Flora's tone revealed the depth of a four-year-old's disgust.

"Doesn't look that way, Flora." Molly smoothed the blanket and bent to brush a kiss over her cheek. "But we'll be going to town anyway."

"We will?" Excitement bloomed. "When?"

"As soon as those two are strong enough to make the trip."

The little girl's face fell. "Why can't we take them tomorrow?"

"If I thought I could get them into the wagon . . ." Molly let the words hang as she walked to Charity's bed to brush a kiss over her forehead.

"I'll help. We can all help." Flora wasn't about to let the issue die.

She glanced around at the others, but they remained silent as Molly went from bed to bed kissing each of her girls good night.

"Have you decided which one is the bad man?" Delia caught Molly's hand.

"Not yet, honey." Molly squeezed. "But sooner or later one of them will make a mistake and I'll figure it out."

"Promise?" Delia asked as her aunt bent to kiss her.

"Promise." Molly moved to the last bed to brush the hair from Sarah's cheek and press a kiss to the spot before picking up the lantern and making her way to the door.

"I know which is which." Flora's words had Molly glancing over. "The man on the summer porch is the out-law. And the man in Mama Molly's bed is the marshal."

Delia gave a snort of disgust. "And how would you know that?"

Flora shrugged. "I just do."

Molly couldn't help smiling at the child's somber words. She stood there a moment longer, savoring the sight of her girls all tucked in their beds. Despite their bickering and occasional grudges, they'd formed a bond. Family. They were all her family. She loved every one of them. And loved knowing that for another night they were all safe and sound in their home, where they belonged.

As she closed the door, she could hear their voices, hushed in the darkness.

Flora's, soft and impatient. "Sarah? Do you think the man on the porch could climb into the wagon with our help?"

Sarah's reply, weary and slightly annoyed. "How should I know?"

"Well, you take care of him the most."

"All I do is fetch him buttermilk."

"That's more than the rest of us can do. I don't like the way he looks at you."

"Go to sleep, Flora."

The little girl's voice was more tired then annoyed. "You're starting to sound just like Mama Molly."

Molly chuckled as she made her way to the kitchen. Now that the house was reasonably quiet, she wanted a cup of tea before going to sleep.

A scant hour later she made her way in the dark to the parlor, where she stripped off her clothes and pulled on her nightshift before settling down on the sofa.

Within minutes she was fast asleep.

HODGE CREPT FROM the bedroom and started along the hallway, pausing every few steps to lean against the wall and catch his breath. He couldn't decide if the floor was lopsided, or if the weakness in him was making him walk like a drunk. His vision kept blurring, and he had to stop and blink before stumbling on. By the time he'd made it to the parlor, a river of sweat was running down his back. His hair was damp with it; his palms clammy. His stomach was roiling, and he had to fight not to be sick.

Flush with success because he was still standing, he stepped into the room and stood a moment, to get his bearings. He cursed the clouds that scudded across the sky, completely obliterating the light of moon and stars. The room was as dark as a tomb.

With his hands outstretched like a blind man, he began moving ahead, until he felt the cool wood that could only be a parlor hutch. He enjoyed a moment of triumph. This was where a farm wife would store whiskey. And hopefully, the clothing and weapons she'd collected in the field.

He pried open the hinged door to the cabinet and fumbled around in the darkness, but the only things he encountered were crystal goblets. After running his finger around the rim of each, he gave a hiss of annoyance and moved to the next cabinet, where he found plates, cups, saucers. But no clothes. No weapons.

He moved to the last cabinet and eased it open. He felt something soft and found himself hoping, praying, it was clothing. But when he picked up the first object, he realized it was small and lacy. Some frilly table cover, no doubt, or perhaps one of those crocheted doilies women were so fond of.

He turned away in disgust and his fingers brushed something cold and hard and metallic.

His rifle!

The thought had him reaching out, but in that instant it was jerked aside before being shoved roughly against his naked chest.

Molly's voice was a hiss of anger. "One move and it'll be the last you ever make."

Though stunned, Hodge had enough sense to lift his hands in the air. "How did you hear me?"

"The old bull out in the pasture makes less noise than you. The way you lumbered around the room, I figured you were trying to raise the dead."

Now that his eyes had adjusted to the darkness, he could make out a vague figure all in white, from neck to ankles. Her hair fanned out around her like a fiery cloud.

"And since you've cost me my sleep, I'm not inclined toward patience. Sorry to foil your escape. I guess from now on, I'll have to use stronger rope before I blow out the lantern."

"If I'd planned on running, I wouldn't have stopped here."

"Maybe you just got lost in the darkness."

"Not likely. I could have followed the hall all the way to the kitchen, and then to freedom."

Her voice hardened. "Is that so? If you weren't planning on running, what were you planning on doing?"

"Finding my clothes, my badge, and my gun, and then forcing you to take the outlaw, Eli Otto, to town."

"You're still insisting that would be the man on the porch, and not you?"

He hissed out a breath and swore, low and deep. "You are the most damnably ornery woman I've ever met. Do you think, if I were that outlaw, I'd have given you a chance to stop me from making a break for freedom?"

"I don't know what to think. All I know is, you're here, buck naked"—Her tone lowered for emphasis—"And it's thankful I am for the darkness, since you obviously have no shame." She wasn't even aware that her brogue had thickened in anger. "And fumbling around in my parlor hutch, like a man hoping to find a gold piece in the sugar bowl. Now turn around and start back where you came from."

Hodge felt the thrust of the rifle in his gut, and his anger, always on a short tether, snapped. Without giving a thought to the risk he was taking, he caught hold of the butt of her rifle and tugged it viciously from her grasp.

Caught by surprise, Molly felt the rifle slip from her grasp, before it clattered to the floor.

"How dare you . . . ?" When she realized she'd lost control of the situation, she dropped to her knees in the dark and began feeling around for her weapon.

Hodge was on her in an instant, his legs pinning hers, one hand easily locking both of hers above her head.

Left with no other defense, she tried to bite him, but he used his other hand to cover her mouth. Though she twisted her head from side to side, and bucked like a mare with a burr under her saddle, she was unable to shake loose of him. Finally, realizing she was no match for his strength, she became subdued, her body rigid beneath his, her breath coming in shallow gasps.

"That's better." His words were whispered against her ear, sending a series of icy shivers along her spine. "I mean you no harm. You have to believe that."

Because his hand was still covering her mouth, she was unable to respond. But he saw the sparks in her eyes and could only imagine what she was thinking.

"If you promise not to fight me, I'll let you up." He gingerly lifted his hand a fraction.

There was a smattering of Gaelic, followed by, "May you burn in hell, you miserable—"

He clapped his hand over her mouth, cutting off the rest of her words. "I see you're not ready to cooperate. Then I guess we'll just have to stay here until you come to your senses."

Molly lay beneath him, her mind in turmoil. Now that she had a chance to think things through, the things he'd said earlier were beginning to make sense. If he'd planned on escaping, he wouldn't have bothered to stop in the parlor. Without this detour, he could have been safely away by now, and no one would have been the wiser.

Still, it wasn't in her nature to allow this man, or any man, to have the upper hand. Damn his brute strength! Without that, she'd have already forced him back to his bed, where she'd have surely bound his hands and feet so she wouldn't have had to deal with this until morning.

"Ready to call a truce?" He lifted his hand a fraction.

"Truce with a smug, bloody—?"

The hand that covered her mouth was rough. But when she looked up, she could see the way his eyes were crinkled with laughter.

Laughter? Was he daring to laugh at her?

The very thought had her temper boiling, while she squirmed and struggled to break free.

Hodge couldn't help himself. The angrier she got, the more ridiculous this became. As his sister had often said, he'd been cursed with a wicked sense of humor that often revealed itself at the most inappropriate times.

"Naughty, naughty, Molly O'Brien. Hasn't anyone ever told you what all that wiggling does to a naked man?"

Molly froze. Her eyes went wide. Her entire being seemed to vibrate as the reality of her situation sank in.

Her anger was forgotten. As was her need for revenge. Now her only thought was survival. There were other ways for a brute of a man to inflict pain and humiliation on a helpless woman, and she'd just given him the perfect opportunity.

Despite the darkness, she could see that he was looking at her with a dangerous, almost wolfish expression. As though the very thing that was sending terror though her had just occurred to him. And his enjoyment of the situation seemed to grow in direct proportion to her fear.

"You'll. Not. Touch. Me." She spoke each word like an outraged schoolmarm.

"Too late." He chuckled. "I already am." He lowered his face to hers.

When she turned her head to avoid him, his mouth grazed a tangle of hair at her temple, sending the most amazing curl of heat along her spine, as his next words whispered over her senses. "And God help me, now that I've started, I'm not sure I can stop."

TWELVE

———◆◆◆———

HODGE WAS ENJOYING Molly's misery. And why not? She'd gone from angry spitfire to meek virgin in the blink of an eye. Served her right. Annoying little female was all fierce bravado when she'd been holding that rifle. Now the worm had turned.

"That's better." His voice was a snarl. "I like my women warm and willing."

"Warm and willing, is it?" She managed to free her foot, which she mashed into his while struggling to roll aside.

"No sense fighting me." He pressed down hard on her foot, locking it beneath his, causing the rest of his body to press into hers, as well. At once he was aware of the way every hard angle of his body seemed to encounter softness. The flare of her hips beneath his. The rounded curves of her breasts under his chest. The tendrils of silken hair that tickled his arm as he continued pinning her wrists over her head in one big hand.

Hodge was sweating again, but this time it wasn't from the exertion of their struggle. He'd become too aware of this woman in a way he'd never intended.

She might not be warm and willing, but she was something even better. Flesh and blood, and soft as an angel. She might be small, but she was round in all the right places. And all woman.

She smelled of soap and water. There was a hint of cinnamon in her hair from the biscuits she'd baked earlier for their supper. Her eyes were watching him. Eyes the color of a field of grass. Hot and cool at the same time. Eyes that a man could easily drown in.

What in hell had he been thinking?

He'd meant this as a game. To pay her back for refusing to believe him. For sticking a rifle in his chest. For foiling his plans. But he'd stepped over a line. In his entire life, he'd never forced a woman. The very thought was repugnant to him. And this little game of revenge had somehow gone very wrong.

He looked down at her and felt a stab of remorse. "I'm sorry."

Molly blinked, wondering what new surprise he planned. She was having trouble following the twists and turns of his devious mind.

At her silence he felt a need to explain. "I'm sorry. Really. I let my temper get the best of me. But I never expected to go this far. As a man of the law, I've always held myself to a higher standard." He rolled aside, freeing her.

When she continued lying perfectly still, he scrambled to his feet and reached a hand to her, helping her to stand. Then he bent down and picked up the rifle.

Seeing her cringe, he held it out to her. "I hope you won't feel compelled to use it against me."

Molly took the rifle and continued staring at him in stunned silence. As his intentions sank in, she cleared her throat. "You really are a lawman."

He merely returned her look.

"Until this minute, I didn't quite believe it. Oh." She gave a shake of her head. "I thought it was you. Or I wanted to think so. But I was afraid that I'd never know for certain. Now I do."

"Because I didn't . . ." He let the words trail off.

"Because only a man of honor would do what you've done." She shivered, and turned away to keep from staring at him. "I'll fetch your clothes." With a smile she added, "They aren't here in the parlor."

"Where . . . ?"

"In the barn. I'll help you back to bed, and then get them."

She set aside the rifle and wrapped an arm around his waist. In turn he draped an arm over her shoulder, allowing her to lead the way.

All the way to the bedroom, she was achingly aware of the warm, naked flesh of the man beside her. Of the way her hand burned at the mere touch of him. Of the way his hips brushed hers as he moved ever so slowly down the hall. She could feel the heat of him through the barrier of her nightshift to her very core.

Once in her bedroom she helped him toward the bed.

He eased himself onto the edge of the mattress. But instead of lying back against the pillows, he took both her hands in his.

"Thank you."

"For what?" Her throat went dry. Did he know what his simple touch was doing to her? She looked down into his eyes and found him staring directly into hers.

"For believing me." He lifted her hand to his mouth and dropped a kiss over her knuckles, all the while staring into her eyes. "I don't know why it should matter so much to me, but it does."

And it was the truth, he realized. For some strange reason, this rigid, unyielding, damnably independent female had gotten under his skin in a way no other woman ever had. It was vitally important to him that she believe him. That she trust him. That she know, without reservation, that he would never do anything to harm her or her children.

"I do believe you, Marshal."

"Hodge." He brought her other hand to his mouth and pressed a kiss to her palm. "My name is Hodge. Hodge Egan."

"Hodge." A shudder passed through her. She could barely speak his name, because for some strange reason all the air in her lungs had fled.

"Molly." He wasn't smiling now. There was a new light in his eyes when he looked at her. A light that hadn't been there moments before. It wasn't the threatening, seductive look he'd given her in the parlor. That had been intended to strike fear in her heart. This was questioning. Probing. Hopeful.

This time she felt no threat of danger. Instead, there was a strange palpitation around her heart. It started with a flutter and spread through her body like ripples on a pond, leaving her feeling week as a newborn. She wondered that her legs could still hold her upright.

She struggled for her usual businesslike demeanor. "I should go now and fetch your things."

He continued holding her hands. His voice was low, pleading. "Don't go, Molly."

Oh, her poor heart. If she didn't flee this minute, it was about to burst clear out of her chest. "I'd better . . ."

"Stay with me awhile, Molly." He drew her down beside him on the edge of the bed and, when she offered no resistance, wrapped an arm around her waist.

What in the world was happening to her? Why had she become so . . . compliant? It had to be a momentary weakness.

Against her cheek he whispered, "I haven't the right to ask, but I'd like, more than anything, to hold you. To kiss you."

She turned to him. Their faces were inches apart. In some small part of her mind she wondered if he could hear the way her heart was pounding.

Without a word, she offered her lips.

And then there was no time to think as their mouths brushed, hesitated, then brushed again, as softly as the wings of a butterfly.

Now her heart was racing like a runaway train, and her throat had gone as dry as dust.

She pulled a little away and took a breath before turning to him again. This time, as she offered her lips, she felt his hands at her waist, rough, demanding, before he dragged her close and kissed her with a hunger that nearly devoured her.

Heat. There was so much heat, she wondered that she didn't simply burn to ash in his embrace. But instead of resisting, she returned his kiss with equal passion until he moaned, low in his throat, and drew her down, down, until they were lying together, so lost in the moment, the world seemed to have slipped completely away.

"God in heaven, Molly. I never wanted anything the way I want you."

"And I want . . ." She ran a tongue over her dry lips and tried again. "I want you, too, Hodge. I want this."

It was all he needed. He gathered her close and covered her mouth in a kiss so hot, so hungry, it spoke more eloquently than any words the raw emotions he was feeling.

And then his hands, those big, rough hands were moving over her, igniting little fires wherever they touched.

His mouth moved over hers, slowly, deliberately, drawing out the kiss until she sighed and her lips parted. His tongue tangled with hers as he tasted her sweetness.

She made a guttural sound, more animal than human, and he realized he was taking her too far, too fast.

He lifted his head to press kisses to her cheek, her forehead, the tip of her nose.

He stared down at this woman in his arms with a look of wonder. "Who are you, Molly O'Brien, that you can affect me like this?"

"I'm just a farmer."

"So you say. But you're so much more."

She blinked. "I am?"

He nibbled his way along her jaw. "You're just full of surprises. I think you act tough just to hide your sweet, sunny nature."

"I do?"

He nibbled his way lower, to the sensitive hollow of her throat. "You've never been with a man before, have you?" He felt her stiffen in his arms and ran a trail of kisses across her shoulder. "Not that I mind."

She pushed free of his arms and sat up, feeling the need to explain. "It's just that I've never wanted to, before. I mean there's never been a man that made me feel . . ." She stopped, mortified to be baring her soul to this man.

He gathered her close and muttered against her lips, "Molly, I'm flattered to know that I'm your first. But you need to think this through. What you're offering is something rare and precious. Any man would feel honored to be your first."

"You're not just saying that because you think I'm some dried-up old spinster?"

"You're neither dried up nor old. Spinster might apply to your grandmother, but it hardly suits the woman I'm holding in my arms." He brushed a kiss over her lips, then lifted his head to look down into her eyes. "But I want you to be sure. I don't want you to have any regrets later."

She met his look. "I'm sure. But if you're having any doubts . . ."

"I've made plenty of mistakes in my life, Molly O'Brien, but this isn't one of them. But be warned. I can't make you any promises. This night . . ." He kissed her again, drawing out the kiss until they were both breathless. ". . . This night is all we'll ever have."

Inside his mouth she whispered, "It's all I need. I'll ask for nothing more."

When they came up for air he reached a hand to the buttons at her throat. "I want to see you. All of you."

When his big fingers tangled in the buttonholes, Molly began to help him.

He waited a moment longer, then with a sigh of impatience he reached to the hem of her nightshift, tugging it over her head. He tossed it aside and it drifted to the floor. Neither of them noticed as his gaze moved slowly over her.

Molly had thought that at such a moment in her life, she would feel awkward or timid.

"God, Molly." His words were torn from a throat gone dry at the sight of her.

She flushed. "I guess I'm not very pretty."

"You're more than pretty, Molly. You're beautiful."

She might have doubted his words, but the look in his eyes had her heart swelling with emotion.

And then there was no need for words as they came together in a fierce embrace. His kisses were no longer gentle. She could feel the tension growing in him as he explored her body with teeth and tongue and fingertips, running hot, moist kisses down her throat to her breasts.

Here were feelings unlike anything she'd ever experienced. Dazed, she found herself clutching the bed linens while he feasted, devoured, pleasuring them both.

"Hodge. Wait."

He lifted his head. "You'd like me to stop?"

She heard the warmth of humor beneath the frustration. "Yes. No." She wrapped her arms around his neck and offered her lips. "Don't stop. Please don't stop."

"Yes, ma'am. I aim to please." He took her lips with a hunger that startled them both.

Molly was eager to touch him as he was touching her. Oh, she'd touched him plenty of times. As a doctor would tend a patient. But she'd never touched him like a woman yearns to touch a man. She longed to run her hands over those muscles that until now, she'd only been able to see. To touch the mat of hair on his chest. To trail her fingers across the flat plains of his stomach, and watch the way his eyes glazed with passion as she brought her hand lower.

With each touch, she could feel the excitement grow, the energy build, the need climb, until they were both half mad with it.

Hodge struggled to bank the fire that threatened to rage out of control. For Molly's sake he would hold back, move slowly, and give her time to savor each touch, each kiss. It was the only thing he could give her. This one special night would have to be enough for a lifetime.

His touch gentled. His kisses became almost reverent as he allowed her to set the pace.

Molly lay in his arms, steeped in pleasure. The demands of endless farm chores were forgotten. The worries that had plagued her no longer mattered. For now, for this night, they were alone in the universe. There was only this room, this bed, and a need so urgent it was all consuming.

With each touch of his hands on her flesh, with each kiss, her body grew more tense, her breathing more shallow.

Her excitement fueled his. He felt her tremble as he moved over her, damp flesh to damp flesh. He swallowed her sudden gasp as, with lips and fingertips, he brought her to the first peak.

He gave her no time to recover. All she could do was stare at him through a mist of passion as he took her to places she'd never been before.

His eyes remained steady on hers as he gathered her close and entered her. He paused, trying desperately not to hurt her.

Molly tensed, anticipating pain. Instead there was only a pleasure so intense she enfolded him in her arms, taking him in fully.

"Molly. Molly." He spoke her name like a litany as they began to move together, climb together.

Hodge filled himself with the scent of her. The fresh, clean taste of her. In the years to come, wherever life took him, he would remember her, remember this night, and be warmed by the memory.

And then all thought fled as they soared beyond the moon and shattered, like millions of tiny stars, in the midnight sky.

"YOU ALL RIGHT?" Hodge couldn't find the strength to move. He lay, still joined with Molly, his face buried in her neck.

She was quiet. Too quiet. His heart took a sudden, hard jolt. "You're supposed to breathe."

When he touched a hand to her cheek and felt the tears, he quickly levered himself above her. "Aw, God, Molly. I've hurt you."

"No." She closed a hand around his wrist and felt the wild throb of his pulse. "No. I'm just a silly old maid."

She gave a long, deep sigh. "I never dreamed it would be like this."

"Like this?" He had hurt her. He was staring down at her, cursing the darkness because he couldn't read the look in her eyes.

When she looked up at him, he could see, in the glitter of moonlight, the traces of tears that clung to her lashes. And then he saw the curve of her lips as she smiled.

Smiled.

It was the most glorious sight. He felt his heart contract before it started beating again.

She kept her hand on his wrist, as though needing to feel that connection with his pulse. "I . . . probably wasn't very good at that, was I?"

"Not good?" He pressed his forehead to hers and chuckled, low and deep in his throat. "Molly O'Brien, if you were any better at this, I'd have burned to a cinder."

"It was . . . ? You enjoyed it as much as I did?"

"Enjoyed is too mild a word. It was fantastic. You were fantastic."

She let that sink in a moment, feeling a glow of warmth all the way to her toes.

When she started to sit up, he caught her hand. "Where are you going?"

She looked down at the hand on hers. It felt warm. It felt so nice to be connected. "I thought I'd better go to the barn now and retrieve your things."

He heard the regret in her voice and kept his tone low and easy. "They can wait."

"I thought you'd want . . ."

"What I want, Molly O'Brien, is a little more time with you." He drew her down and into his arms. "Will you stay a while longer?"

She couldn't think of anything she wanted more. With a little laugh she nodded. "I suppose I could spare some time."

Against her lips he murmured, "If you agree to stay, I'll more than make it worth your while."

She grinned. "That's very generous of you, Marshal."

He nibbled his way to her throat, and felt her little purr of pleasure. "Folks who know me will tell you I'm a kind and generous man."

She sighed and gave herself up to the pleasure of his kisses. "There's so much I don't know about you."

"You see? I may have to keep you here for hours . . ." His tongue circled her breast and he heard her quick intake of breath. "Just so you can learn all there is to know about me."

She wrapped her arms around his waist and gave herself up to his ministrations. "And then you'll need to learn all about me."

"This could take all night."

And then there were no words as they took each other with all the frenzy of a summer storm.

THIRTEEN

———◆━◆◈◆━◆———

SARAH LAY LISTENING to the sounds of slow, even breathing all around her and wondered what had caused her to wake in the night. She could hear nothing out of the ordinary.

Had the man on the porch called out in pain? She sat up, trying to decide what to do. Aunt Molly had given strict orders that the strangers could never be tended alone. Still, it didn't seem right to wake the others on a whim. Besides, what harm could he do to her with his leg broken?

She felt such a kinship with him. With the boy whose parents, like hers, had died young. His loss had been even more painful than hers, because he'd lost his parents to an outlaw's bullet. And now he was dedicating his entire life to ridding the world of such outlaws.

What if he should be in need of water? She tried to imagine how she would feel, alone and hurt, with no one to help quench her thirst.

It simply wasn't in her nature to be cruel or thoughtless.

Tossing aside the covers, she slipped out of bed, crept across the room and let herself out, carefully closing the door behind her.

On the summer porch she tiptoed to the stranger's bed and looked down at him.

In the dim light he appeared to be sleeping, but before she could turn away he whispered, "Here's my pretty milkmaid."

"Oh." She brought her hand to her throat in a gesture of surprise. "You're awake."

"And have been for an hour or more. I was hoping you'd come to me. You're the answer to my prayers."

"You were praying?"

"In a manner of speaking." He nodded toward the edge of the bed. "Want to know what I was praying for?"

Hearing her aunt's voice inside her head, Sarah ignored his invitation and remained standing. "What?"

"For you to wake and fetch me a glass of that fine buttermilk."

"I'll have to climb down to the cellar. We keep it there in summertime so it won't spoil."

"Would you mind?"

She shrugged. "I guess not." She turned away. "This will take a few minutes."

He shot her his warmest smile. "I'm not going anywhere."

Sarah was grinning as she danced away and held a match to a lantern before climbing down the ladder to the cellar. He had a nice smile. And a playful sense of humor. She liked that about him.

She filled a tall glass with buttermilk and climbed to the kitchen. There she blew out the lantern to keep from waking the others, before making her way in the darkness to the porch.

After untying his hands, she helped him struggle to a sitting position, using several quilts as pillows to cushion his back.

She handed him the glass. "Looks like you're feeling stronger."

He nursed the buttermilk in short sips until it was gone. Instead of handing her the empty glass, he continued holding it. "If it weren't for this leg, I'd be good as new. And it's all thanks to you."

Sarah flushed. "I didn't do anything."

"Is that so? The way I see it, you did all the running and fetching and tending, whenever I needed it. Look at you now." He glanced at her bare feet, peeking from beneath the hem of the prim white nightshift. "While the rest of the household sleeps, you're here seeing to my comfort."

"It was just by accident."

"Do you believe that?"

At his question she shot him a curious look. "What do you mean?"

"Nothing ever happens by accident, Sarah. You woke up because you were supposed to be here with me."

"I was?"

He nodded. "You're my sweet milkmaid. My soul mate. I believe you're going to be the one who saves me and your entire family from that dangerous outlaw, Eli Otto."

"I am? How?"

He patted the edge of the bed and lowered his voice, so that she had to strain to hear every word. "The only way I can prove I'm who I claim to be is to go to the town of Delight."

"That's just what my aunt Molly said." Encouraged, Sarah settled herself on the edge of the mattress.

Eli leaned back and closed his eyes, knowing she would feel safer thinking him weak. He gave a long, low sigh that had her reaching out a hand to his forehead.

"Are you all right?"

"It'll pass." He closed a hand over hers. "You're an angel of mercy to care about me."

Sarah felt a little thrill at his touch.

He felt the way her pulse leapt and kept his hand on hers. "You're the kindest, most beautiful woman I've ever known, Sarah."

A woman! Again that little thrill at the knowledge that this brave, strong man thought of her as a woman, and not just a girl. For years now, she and Delia, Charity, and Flora were referred to as "the girls." But this man saw her as a unique individual. A woman. A pretty woman.

He allowed his eyes to open, and found her staring at him. She averted her gaze, but not quickly enough. He'd already caught the look of adoration that she couldn't hide. "I just had a grand idea."

She looked up. "What is it?"

"A way for me to prove my identity, and a way for you to be a hero to your family."

"How?"

"If you were to fetch me a horse and my clothes, we could be halfway to town before the sun comes up."

"I couldn't." She shrank back and was on her feet when he caught her hands in his. "Not without my aunt's permission."

"I would never ask my sweet milkmaid, my soul mate, to do anything wrong." He paused a bit before adding, "Of course, there's the matter of that reward."

"What about it?" She sank back down on the edge of the bed.

"Being a man of the law, I can't claim the reward for myself. But you can. I'm betting that much money would change your aunt's life forever." He watched Sarah's eyes as he added, "She could buy herself a fine big rig to take all of you to town. Even on the coldest, rainiest days, your family would be all warm and snug, and they'd have you to thank."

He saw Sarah smile at the thought.

"And she could hire help for the farm chores. That way she could spend more time with the little ones, teaching them to read and write."

Sarah's eyes went all dreamy. "Oh, wouldn't that be grand?"

He could see the wheels turning. "Think of all the good things that reward money could buy for the people you love."

"Oh, Marshal. If only I could."

"You can." He squeezed her hands and looked into her eyes. "*We* can. Together, we can make our way to town, where I'll deputize as many men as are needed to come back here and arrest that dangerous outlaw. And when you return, you can present your aunt with a bank draft that will forever change her life, and yours."

She was already shaking her head. "I could never leave without letting Aunt Molly know where I was. She'd be worried sick."

"You could leave her a note."

He saw the way she hesitated and decided to press. "Why don't you fetch my clothes and a slate and we'll figure out something that will put your aunt's mind at ease."

He watched Sarah walk away and leaned back. In the darkness his eyes gleamed like a cat's.

Women were all the same. Old or young, all they needed was a man to make them feel special. Feed them enough sugarcoated words, and they swallowed them down without question.

His aunt had been such a fool, she'd actually defended him, right up until the day she'd found him with her life's savings in his hand. Of course, if she'd waited just a few minutes longer to come home from town, she might still be alive. He hadn't wanted to kill her. But when she threatened to go to the sheriff, it was her life or his.

There were a whole lot of dead people who'd found out just how determined Eli Otto was to stay out of jail.

"YOU'RE SURE ABOUT this?" Sarah held the horse's reins while the man, using a pitchfork she'd brought from the barn as a cane, eased into the saddle.

He gritted his teeth against the pain, cursing the broken leg. It was the reason for all this plotting and planning. If he'd had two good legs, he'd kill this stupid little bitch right now, and then return to the house to kill all the others. By the time their bodies were discovered in this godforsaken wilderness, he could be halfway across the country, enjoying the good life with the bank's money. But there was a good chance the woman or the lawman would hear the first shots and overpower him. He wasn't about to get careless at this stage of the game. His life, his freedom, depended on playing this one very carefully.

The note had been an especially enjoyable little touch.

He had no doubt the lawman would trail him. Especially since he intended to leave a trail that was easy to follow.

The woman and kids were another matter. If he was as good a judge of character as he liked to think, he figured they'd be along sooner or later, and he could drop them with a couple of well-aimed shots. If they chose to stay here, he'd circle back and make sure all the witnesses were dead before making good his escape.

And all the while, he'd have this sweet little thing to entertain him.

"Your aunt will be proud of you." He took the reins and waited until Sarah pulled herself up behind him

It tickled him to note that she'd put on her Sunday dress, so that she'd look her best for the folks of Delight.

It had taken him nearly an hour to dress. He'd sent Sarah out to saddle the horse and fill the saddlebags with food. When she'd questioned him about it, he said it was just to see to her comfort until they reached Delight.

His pockets bulged with the bank's money. He'd insisted that it not be left behind, since it would be the proof he needed against the bank robber.

"You forgot this." Sarah held out the U.S. marshal's badge and saw the way his lips curved into a wide smile.

"Well, now." He pinned it on his lapel and gave a low rumble of laughter. "Doesn't that make this whole night just about perfect."

He flicked the reins and the horse started into a trot. Sarah's arms closed around his waist as the wind caught her hair and sent it streaming out behind her like a bright flag.

At the top of the hill he drew his mount to a halt and looked around, to get his bearings.

As they started forward Sarah said, "This isn't the way to Delight. You have to go across that stream and head east."

"Don't worry your pretty little head about a thing." He nudged the horse into a gallop to cut off her protest. Over his shoulder he shouted, "I know a shortcut."

"I NEVER TOLD you what a good cook you are." Hodge drew Molly close, loving the way she fit so perfectly against him.

She touched a finger to his thick dark eyebrow. "We spent the night together because you like my cooking?"

He wiggled his brows like a villain. "Yes, indeed, little lady. I do this with every good cook I meet."

She laughed and he thought how much he loved the sound of that throaty laughter. In fact, there were so many things he liked about her. The fact that this bold, obstinate female was actually shy with men. The fact that this hard-working farm woman was soft as an angel. The fact that she was smart and funny and so easy to talk with. When they hadn't been loving, they'd spent a great deal of the night just talking. It felt so good to have someone who was as good at listening as she was at making love.

He'd told her about his sister, and the hard-scrabble life he'd lived before becoming a lawman. She'd told him about her life in Ireland, and the death of her brother and his wife, and her decision to raise her nieces as her own, as well as the orphans, Charity and Flora.

"I bet they're a challenge."

"They are. Yes. But then, isn't everything that's worthwhile in this life?" She glanced at the window, seeing the first faint ribbons of dawn beginning to streak the sky. "I'd best get up."

She started to ease out of the bed.

Hodge drew her back. "Where do you think you're going?"

"It'll be morning soon. I'd best fetch your clothes."

"Stay awhile."

She laughed. "If I do, you know what will happen."

"Are you saying you're tired of me already?"

She looked at the big hand gripping her wrist, and then up into his laughing eyes, and prayed that all her feelings weren't there in her eyes for him to see.

This night had been such a special gift. And if it was possible, in the space of just these few hours, she'd completely lost her heart to him. She could no more deny him than she could deny a breath. "I suppose I could be tempted to stay a bit longer."

"That's my girl." Hodge eased her onto the bed and into his arms.

Within minutes they'd lost themselves in their newly discovered pleasure.

* * *

"You're an amazing woman, Molly O'Brien."

"I am?"

"Um-hmmm." He gave her a lingering look that had her cheeks flaming. "You're a young, beautiful woman, living alone in the wilderness, and raising four girls without benefit of a husband. To me, that's pretty amazing."

Beautiful woman.

Molly fell silent, allowing the compliment to play through her mind. She'd never had a man call her beautiful before. She'd never imagined how such a simple thing could affect her. There'd been no time to think about the way she looked to others. Always, there had only been the hard work, caring for all those who depended on her. But now, for just this one moment, she savored the glow that surrounded her at those simple words.

This had been such a special night. She hated that it had to end. But morning would be here all too soon.

"This time I'm really going." Molly pressed a kiss to Hodge's lips before slipping into her nightshift. She paused in the doorway. "I'll be back in a few minutes with your things."

"You'd better, or I'll come after you. And you wouldn't want a naked man walking across the field in daylight."

"Oh, I don't know. You're easy enough on the eyes."

"I'll look even better in my clothes."

"I wouldn't know. The last time I saw you in them, you and your clothes were so bloody, I could hardly bear to look."

She left him lying there in the early morning light, and

paused only long enough to retrieve her rifle in the parlor before hurrying to the kitchen, where she drew on her old, worn boots and tossed a shawl over her shoulders. Picking up the sheet she would use as a signal to Addison, she danced out the door and hurried to the barn, feeling light as a feather.

What a relief to finally know which of these men was the lawman and which the outlaw. Though she'd long felt the dour man in her bed was the marshal, she had no more doubts.

And all because he'd proven himself to be a man of honor.

Last night she'd had a few moments of sheer terror, convinced that her carelessness had brought her to the brink of destruction. If he'd forced her to submit, that wouldn't have been the worst of it. What had terrified Molly even more was the fear that once he'd finished with her, he would kill her and then her girls.

Her own life would mean nothing, if she placed those sweet children in danger.

But the danger was past now, and the future looked rosy. As soon as the girls were awake, they would all accompany Hodge and the outlaw to town. And their nightmare would be over.

She knotted an end of the sheet to the rope that hung from the pole and began pulling until the sheet flapped in the breeze. Then she turned away, confident that the old man would spot it soon.

As she shoved open the barn door and breathed in the familiar scents of earth and hay and dung, she marveled at what a difference a night made.

And what a night.

She could still hardly believe what she and Hodge had shared. How was it possible that this man had touched her heart in a way that no other man ever had? What was it about this hard-bitten man of the law that had attracted her?

There was his honor, of course. That had touched her more deeply than anything. And his offbeat sense of humor. She liked that in a man.

She climbed the ladder to the loft and ran a hand under the mound of hay. Puzzled, she rummaged farther, in search of the clothes, boots, rifles, and money she'd hidden there.

With a sense of relief she finally touched a boot, and then a second. A few moments later she came up with a pair of men's breeches and a coat, as well as a wide-brimmed hat.

But where were the weapons? The money? The rest of the clothes?

Frantic now, she began scooping mounds of hay, sifting through, then tossing it aside to sift through more.

As she climbed down the ladder and began racing toward the house, there was a feeling of absolute dread in the pit of Molly's stomach. Was it possible that the most glorious night of her life had just become her worst nightmare?

FOURTEEN

✦

"THEY'VE GONE." MOLLY thrust the slate into Hodge's hand even before he had time to sit up.

"What're you talking . . . ?" He stared at the neatly printed words.

Aunt Molly, don't worry about me. Gone to Delight with Marshal.

With a muttered oath he tossed aside the blanket and began drawing on the clothes she'd dumped unceremoniously on the bed.

He looked up. "My gun? My badge?"

"This is all that was left. Oh, Hodge." Molly buried her face in her hands. "This is all my fault. If I hadn't been in here with you, none of this would have happened."

He was suffering from the same guilt. If he hadn't given in to temptation, he'd have heard them. Hadn't he recognized how Eli Otto had been playing the girl? Hadn't he been listening these past few days, knowing that sooner or later that murdering bastard would find a way to use the kid's innocence? If he hadn't been busy with his own pleasures, he'd have been able to put an end to the outlaw's little game.

"We're equally guilty, Molly. But wallowing in guilt never fixed anything."

"She's just a child. An innocent, trusting little girl."

Hodge cursed the fact that there was no time to offer her the comfort she deserved. He wanted simply to hold her, to soothe her fears and ease her pain.

Instead he touched a hand to her arm. "I know. I know, Molly. It's just that her timing couldn't have been worse. Another few hours and . . ."

Seeing the bleak look in her eyes he quickly changed directions. "How many weapons do you have here?"

She looked up and gave a shuddering sigh. "My da's rifle. My brother's handgun. A few hunting knives."

"I need them. All of them." He bent to tug on his boots as Molly fled the room.

When she didn't return, he made his way slowly to the kitchen, to find the three little girls up and dressed and listening wide-eyed to Molly explaining what had happened.

Flora flicked a glance over at Hodge. "I told you he was the marshal."

"So you did." Molly nodded toward the pile of weapons on the kitchen table. "These are all I have."

"They'll do." Cursing his weakness he kept one hand on the back of the rough, wooden chair while stuffing the pistol into his holster. He lifted the rifle and balanced it in his palm, testing the weight of it. "Do you have any ammunition?"

"In the barn."

"I'll go with you. I need to saddle my horse. That is," he said as an afterthought, "if they didn't take it, too."

"They must have gone off together. There's only one horse missing." She indicated the slabs of bread and cheese on a platter, along with a pitcher of foaming milk. "You stay here and eat something to gather your strength. I'll bring your horse and the bullets."

"I can manage . . ." He was talking to thin air. She was already gone, and the children were staring at him with a mixture of curiosity and suspicion.

He dropped down onto the nearest chair and poured himself a glass of milk. It was cold from the cellar, and he downed it in one long swallow before reaching for a slice of bread and cheese.

He looked up. "Any of you care to join me?"

The three little girls took their places around the table and surprised him by joining hands and bowing their heads.

Delia, being the oldest now that Sarah was gone, led the prayer. "Bless this food, and please keep Sarah safe from that bad man."

With whispered amens, they bent to the food. But they did little more than nibble while they watched Hodge devour an entire plate of bread and cheese.

He was grateful when he heard the sound of a horse's hooves. But when he looked outside, he saw that his horse was tied to the back of a wagon.

159

He was out the door in a blaze of fury. "What do you think you're doing?"

Molly stepped down from the wagon. "What does it look like? We're going after Sarah."

"We?"

"The girls and I." She strode past him and began calling directions. "Delia, go to the cellar and fetch that sack of bread and milk and cheese I prepared for emergencies."

"Yes'm." The girl lifted the trap door and disappeared below.

"Charity, you'll fill the back of the wagon with as many quilts and feather pillows as you can carry."

"Yes'm."

"Flora." Molly turned to the youngest girl. "You'll run to the barn and wait for Addison. As soon as he arrives, bring him here."

"Yes'm."

As the children scattered, she was about to turn away until Hodge stopped her with a hand to her arm. "Woman, listen to me. I'm a federal marshal, seeing to official business. You can't expect me to allow my progress to be slowed by the four of you."

"Nor would I ask it of you. You can leave, Marshal"— she emphasized his title, which only served to fuel his anger more—"whenever you're ready to go. But you can't stop us from following."

When he opened his mouth to protest, she cut him off. "Sarah is my child. This happened because I allowed her to be placed in danger. Because I was more concerned with my own pleasure than her safety."

"Stop blaming—"

Her brogue thickened. "I'll not sit home and do nothing, when I've the strength to follow her trail and do what I can to save her. I'll go as far as I must. Do whatever it takes. And I'll not give up. Not while there's still a breath inside me."

He heard the pain in her voice and understood. And though he wished he could spare her, he needed to prepare her for the worst. With a hand on her arm he said, "Eli Otto is one of the most vicious killers in my memory, Molly. Despite your best intentions, you could already be too late to save Sarah."

He saw the way her color drained away. But to her credit she lifted her chin in that infuriating way he'd come to recognize. "Then heaven help him. For if he harms her"—Her lips quivered—"In any way, I'll not rest until he's found and made to pay for his crime."

"Molly, I wish I could . . ." He heard the door slam and turned to see an old man standing beside Flora.

The man's hair and beard were thick, long, tangled, and streaked with white. His brown face bore the ravages of time, as heavily wrinkled as aged leather.

When he saw Hodge, his eyes narrowed. "A lawman."

"How would you know that?" Hodge started toward him, hand outstretched. "Name's Hodge Egan. I'm not wearing my badge."

"Dealt with enough of your kind to know you, with or without the tin star."

Hodge lowered his hand and stopped in midstride. "I'm sorry to hear that you've come in contact with those who dishonor the badge. I hope I don't prove to be one of them."

The hostility between them was thick enough to cut.

While little Flora glanced from one man to the other in puzzlement, Molly stepped between them. "Thank you for coming, Addison. Sarah left in the night with an outlaw, believing he was the marshal. We're going after her."

"Don't fret over your farm. I'll tend things here." As she started herding the children out the door the old man added, "You raised a strong girl in Sarah. Strong as her aunt."

Molly turned and felt tears stinging her eyes. She blinked them away. "Oh, I fervently pray it's so,"

"Here." Addison thrust his rifle into her hands. "Use it wisely."

"Thank you."

As she and the girls made their way to the wagon, Hodge untied his horse and pulled himself into the saddle, hating the weakness that left him gasping for breath. Another few days and he'd have been good as new. It was another reason to resent the outlaw who'd made his life so complicated.

Nudging his mount forward, he called, "If you're determined to do this, Molly, you need to know that you're on your own. As a U.S. marshal, my first duty is to do everything I can to catch up with Eli Otto and arrest him, while seeing to it that his hostage is kept alive. I can't afford to waste time seeing to your safety, as well."

"I understand." And she did. Whatever they had shared had to be put aside. There would be no tender good-byes between them. No words meant to soothe or comfort. Now he was a man of the law, and she and her girls were nothing more than a distraction.

Molly handed him a sack.

"What this?"

Her words were clipped. "Basic necessities for the trail. Some food and water."

His were equally abrupt. "Thank you."

She helped the children into the back of the wagon before climbing to the hard seat.

By the time she'd flicked the reins, all that was left of Hodge Egan was a cloud of dust. She imagined that would be all she'd see of him until this odyssey played to its end.

HODGE FOLLOWED THE trail of the lone horse as it crossed a narrow section of stream before doubling back and starting toward the distant hills.

He wasn't surprised that the trail was leading away from town. He'd never for a moment entertained the thought that Eli would go anywhere near Delight.

Nor was he surprised at the ease with which he'd picked up the outlaw's trail.

Eli Otto wanted him to follow. He was using the girl as bait to get him as far away from civilization as possible, in the hope of eliminating them both and making a run for freedom. Which was another reason why Hodge had wanted Molly and the little ones as far away from this as possible. If Otto caught on to the fact that they were nearby, they'd suffer the same fate as Sarah.

"And me, if I'm not careful," he muttered aloud.

Cocky son of a bitch was counting on the fact that he hadn't fully recovered from his wounds.

"That makes two of us," Hodge said through gritted teeth. "At least I've got two good legs."

He knelt in the dirt and sniffed the pile of horse droppings that were already several hours old. Pulling himself wearily into the saddle, he glanced over his shoulder at the distant puff of dust drifting upward from Molly's horse and wagon. He hated leaving her on her own, but his main concern had to be Sarah.

The fact that he hadn't yet come across her body gave him hope that Eli Otto intended to keep her alive, for whatever reason. He could think of several, all of which made his skin crawl. Poor kid had to be scared out of her wits and horrified at the mess she'd gotten herself into.

That thought had him urging his horse into a gallop.

"TIME TO GO." Eli took a final drink from the banks of the stream before striding forward and hauling Sarah to her feet.

He'd dumped her unceremoniously at the edge of the water and left her to figure out how to quench her thirst.

Water cascaded from her wet hair and face as he dragged her upward. With her wrists and ankles bound, she stumbled and would have fallen if he hadn't steadied her with a punishing yank on her hair. She let out a cry and sank to the ground.

She looked up at him through her tears. "You got what

you wanted. You have the money, and the weapons, and your freedom. Why can't you just leave me here?"

"Because it's not enough." He gave her one of those smiles that she'd once considered so sweet. Now it sent ripples of terror snaking along her spine. "I want more."

"I don't understand."

"You don't think the marshal can sit idly by knowing you're with me, do you?"

"But he's wounded."

"That's not going to stop Hodge Egan. He has a reputation for always getting his man. And I'm counting on that."

"You want him to find you?"

"Us. I want him to find us. And while he's bargaining for your life, I'm going to enjoy ending his."

"Is that why I'm here?"

"That's why I'm letting you stay alive." He hauled her to her feet and cut the rope binding her ankles before lifting her onto the back of the horse. It was a struggle for him to climb into the saddle. Over his shoulder he wheezed out a breath. "You give me too much trouble, I have no problem shooting you. So keep your mouth shut, and maybe I'll let you live for another day."

As the horse jerked into a trot, Sarah clutched with bound hands to the back of Eli's coat to keep from falling.

She blinked at tears that burned the back of her throat and her eyelids. What had started off as a chance to be a hero to her family had quickly become a nightmare.

It didn't seem possible that she could have allowed herself to believe in this man.

All those sweet words. All those empty promises.

He'd gone from sweet charmer to frightening monster in the blink of an eye.

And she had no one to blame but herself.

FIFTEEN

———◆·◆·◆———

"AUNT MOLLY." DELIA tugged on her aunt's sleeve. "When are we going to stop? I'm tired. And Flora's already asleep."

Molly glanced over her shoulder at the figure in the back of the wagon, curled into a ball on top of the quilts.

"Am not." Flora sat up, rubbing her eyes. "But I'm hungry."

"We'll stop soon." Molly peered through the fading light, wishing she could see Hodge. They were into their third day on the trail. Except for a few glimpses of his dust, they'd had no contact. Another night would be upon them soon. Had he stopped to make camp? Or had he possibly come upon Eli Otto and Sarah?

Oh, she prayed it was so. She couldn't bear the thought of sweet Sarah with that outlaw. Each time the thought came into her mind, she had to struggle to push it aside and concentrate on the task at hand, otherwise she'd go half mad with worry. Each night, while the girls slept, she was tormented with thoughts about what that monster was doing to her.

"What's that?" Charity pointed to the left, and Molly turned in time to see a faint flicker of light.

"A campfire." Molly drew back on the reins, bringing their horse and wagon to a halt. As she climbed down she cradled Addison's rifle in the crook of her arm. "You girls know what you must do. You'll stay here while I check this out. At the first sound of gunfire, you turn the horse toward home. And you don't look back. Is that clear?"

"Yes'm." With Sarah gone, ten-year-old Delia had assumed the role of second in command. She gripped the reins and watched wide-eyed as Molly disappeared into the brush.

Minutes later the little girl gave an audible sigh of relief as Molly stepped closer.

She climbed up to the seat of the wagon. "It's safe to go on. It's the marshal's camp."

As their wagon rolled to a stop in a stand of trees, Hodge stepped out of the shadows, wearing a scowl. "It isn't safe to just come lumbering in without knowing who's waiting. That's a good way to get yourself shot."

"Mama Molly checked first." Flora hopped down from the back of the wagon and looked around. "Where've you been for so long? We haven't seen you in days."

Hodge ignored the scolding tone. Had it only been days? It felt like a year on the back of that horse. Every bone in his body ached.

Flora glanced around. "Where's your supper?"

"Don't need any." He'd polished off the food Molly

sent more than a day earlier. Annoyed with her questions, he set aside his rifle and assisted Charity and Delia
to the ground before turning to Molly, who was too quick
for him. Or perhaps, he thought, she was avoiding his
touch.

She glanced around at the stingy fire, the thin blanket
on the ground beside his saddle. "Well, doesn't this look
cozy."

"I'm trailing an outlaw, not planning a picnic."

"What's a picpic?" Flora asked.

"Picnic," Hodge corrected as he began unhitching
Molly's horse. "All it means is a blanket set in some pretty
spot, good food, and someone to share it."

"Can we have a picnic?" Flora turned to Molly.

"I believe we can." Anything to keep from the desperate worry that nagged at her mind.

She watched as Hodge led her horse to a nearby stream
before tethering it next to his mount. "Delia, get one of
those quilts from the back of the wagon. Charity, you can
fill a platter with meat and cheese and bread."

Flora was dancing around excitedly. "What can I do,
Mama Molly?"

Molly handed her a bucket. "You can fetch us some
clean water from the stream. But I think you'll need
Delia's help to haul it back here."

Within a short time the children were seated on the
quilt, devouring their meal and sipping fresh water, while
steam rose from a battered tin, filling the night air with
the wonderful aroma of bubbling coffee.

"This is a fine picnic, Mama Molly." Flora wiped her
mouth on the sleeve of her dress.

"I'm glad you enjoyed it. When you've had enough, you can wash up in the stream and get ready for bed."

"Yes'm." The three little girls carried their plates to the stream and were soon playing a game of tag along the shore.

Molly watched them a moment. "It's the first time I've heard them laugh since we left home." She sighed. "This is hard on them."

She filled two cups and handed one to Hodge. His mouth was watering before the first sip.

He drank long and deep before leaning his back against the trunk of a tree, both hands closed around the cup. He'd been telling himself that he could do without food, but the mere smell of coffee reminded him just how hungry he was feeling.

Molly set a plate of meat and cheese in front of him before settling down beside him with her own. "Any sign of Sarah?"

He gave a shake of his head. "They're still ahead of us on the trail."

"How can you be sure of that? What if they slipped away while we were headed in another direction?"

He turned to look at her. The worry over Sarah was taking its toll. Her dress was filthy. Her hair fell in damp tendrils around a face that looked as weary as he felt. And the fear was there in her eyes. A fear she couldn't hide.

"The same way Addison knew I was a lawman. I can smell an outlaw for miles."

"Do you think Sarah is . . . still with him?"

He nodded. "If she weren't, we'd have spotted her. A man on the run wouldn't take the time to bury his victim.

Beyond that, I think he wants to keep her alive to assure that I stay on his trail."

"He wants you to follow?"

Hodge drained his coffee and bent to his food. "When an outlaw doesn't go to the trouble of covering his tracks, I figure he's leaving a trail for a reason. Sarah's the bait. He hopes to catch me unaware along the trail, so he can eliminate the need to keep looking over his shoulder."

"Won't another lawman just take up the trail?"

Hodge polished off his meal. "Look around you, Molly. We're in the middle of nowhere. If Eli leaves us all dead, who's to say we'll ever be found? And even if we are, it's given him the time he needs to make good his escape and start a new life somewhere far away. With a lawman's badge, a stash of weapons, and a pocket full of money," he added ominously.

When Hodge pushed to his feet, Molly sipped her coffee and thought about what he'd just said.

It buoyed her to believe that Eli Otto would keep Sarah alive, at least until he had a chance to kill those who were trailing him. But how was poor Sarah holding up?

Her first impulse was to break camp and press on in the darkness, in the hope of spying the outlaw's campfire. But one look at her sleepy children now making their way toward the wagon, and the weariness etched in Hodge's face, and she knew that she would have to be patient. She'd fought this same battle each night, as she'd stopped along the trail. They needed to rest, to gather their strength for whatever was to come.

Molly got to her feet and began to clear up the remnants of their meal. Carrying the last of the dishes to the stream, she washed them, then did her best to wash the grime of the trail from herself, as well.

She hadn't brought nightclothes for herself and the girls. There'd been no time. They slept each night in their soiled clothes, and would until their journey ended.

She looked at the three little girls, hair damp and slick, shoes and stockings held in their hands. "I see that everybody washed up."

"Yes'm. The cold water felt good." Delia stifled a yawn.

The others nodded in agreement as they trailed Molly to the wagon.

"Then it's time for sleep."

The girls made no objection as Molly helped them climb into the back, among the quilts and pillows.

They joined hands and bowed their heads as Molly said softly, "Bless us this night, especially Sarah, and keep us all safe from harm."

"Especially Sarah," little Flora repeated solemnly.

Molly felt a band tighten around her heart and wondered that she could still breathe. She kissed each of the girls and watched as they drew close together for comfort, huddling beneath a single quilt. They were asleep before she'd climbed down from the wagon.

Hodge was standing in the shadows, sipping coffee. As she approached, he held out the cup. "This is the last of it. We'll share."

She took a sip before handing it back to him.

He tipped up his head, staring at the moon. "Haven't heard night prayers since I was a pup."

"You prayed?"

He shrugged. "Don't know if it was proper praying.

Hildy made up a few words, and we said them together. It mattered to her, so I did it to please her."

"Sometimes, that's reason enough." She glanced at his thin bedroll and saddle. "No sense sleeping on the ground when you can share the back of the wagon with us."

He glanced toward the sleeping children. "No offense, but if I were to snuggle in all those soft feathers and down, I might think I'd died and gone to heaven, and never wake up. And that could prove to be deadly for all of us. One of us has to keep watch."

She nodded. "I've barely slept since leaving home. Tonight we'll share the chore. I'll take the first watch."

He gave a firm shake of his head. "This is my job, Molly." Before she could protest, he touched a finger to her lips. Just a touch, but they both felt the rush of heat.

Molly's cheeks colored.

Hodge quickly lowered his hand. "You need to sleep. No telling what tomorrow might bring."

She started to turn away, then thought better of it and turned back to him. "Do you think Eli Otto is . . . hurting Sarah each night when they stop along the trail?"

Though she'd danced around the horror, Hodge knew exactly what she meant.

He chose his words carefully. "Otto's got to be feeling as tired and sore as we are. More so, because of that broken leg. I doubt he's in any shape to do more than tie her up and grab as much rest as he can before daylight."

"Oh, Hodge." She felt tears sting her eyes and blinked hard. "I hope you're right."

"Trust me, Molly." Though he hadn't meant to, he gathered her close.

She wrapped her arms around his waist and clung, grateful for his quiet strength. She hated giving in to any weakness in herself, but just for the moment, it felt so good to be held in his arms, hearing the strong, steady beat of his heart inside her own chest.

Against his throat she whispered, "I can't bear to let myself think of Sarah with that monster."

"Then don't think about it, Molly. Just let it go." He pressed his mouth to a tangle of hair at her temple and breathed her in. Then, because he was far more tempted than he cared to admit, he stepped back. "Go to sleep now."

"What about you? I'm sure you haven't slept since you left my farm."

"I need to be on the ground. Even if I should fall asleep, the vibration of a horse's hoofbeats will alert me to approaching danger."

"Would a warm quilt interfere with that?"

He gave her a heart-stopping grin. "Not likely. And I'd be grateful." The days were hot as a furnace; the nights surprisingly cold. And growing colder as they climbed toward the hills.

Molly handed him a quilt and watched as he wrapped it around his shoulders before settling down with his back against his saddle. He removed the pistol from its holster, and placed the rifle on the ground beside him.

"Good night, Hodge."

"'Night, Molly."

She turned away and climbed wearily into the wagon, lying beside the sleeping girls.

If she'd been stronger, she would have insisted on

sharing the night watch. But it would have just brought on another war of wills. Besides, it was comforting to finally sleep, knowing Hodge was keeping watch over them all. That was her last conscious thought before falling into a troubled sleep.

MOLLY LAY VERY still, lulled by the chirping of birds in the trees. Then she heard a sound that had her sitting up quickly. The crunch of booted feet.

She was out of the wagon, cradling her rifle and peering around until she saw Hodge striding toward her, buttoning his shirt. His hair was still wet from the stream, where he'd obviously enjoyed a quick bath.

He stopped and simply stared at her. Then he gave her one of those quick grins that had her heart doing somersaults.

" 'Morning, Molly."

"Hodge." She looked him up and down admiringly. "You seem to be feeling chipper."

"Must be that good food last night."

"Did you get any sleep?"

"Some." He gave a negligent shrug of his shoulders and finished tucking his shirt into the waistband of his pants before strapping on his holster. "Every time I checked on you and the girls, you were unconscious."

She glanced over her shoulder at the wagon. "They're still gone."

"They've put in some hard days." He saddled his horse before retrieving the rifle and shoving it into the boot. "Today won't be any easier."

"You're leaving?"

He nodded. "Eli will want to stay one step ahead of me. I intend to keep him on the run, so there's no time for him to catch his breath." He paused only long enough to tuck a stray curl behind her ear. He wanted desperately to kiss her, but knew he had no right.

He pulled himself into the saddle. "Let the girls sleep. And take time to eat. You'll be able to find me."

"How?"

He winked and wheeled his mount. "Until I catch that bastard, you'll see my dust."

He set out at a fast clip, without a backward glance.

It occurred to Hodge that seeing Molly O'Brien just waking in the morning, all mussed and heavy-lidded from sleep, was just about the prettiest sight he'd ever laid eyes on.

Not that it mattered. They couldn't possibly have a future together. Especially if he didn't catch Eli Otto in time to save Sarah. If the girl died, that knowledge would become a wall between them.

To keep from thinking about that, he reminded himself about the sort of woman he'd always preferred. One with soft hands and even softer lips. Long, satin dresses and perfumed hair. And when this thankless job was finished, he intended to spend the rest of his days surrounded by as many of them as he could afford.

Why didn't that thought cheer him as it always had in the past?

Molly, he thought. There was just something about her. Something sweet and fresh and untouched that tugged at his heart.

Probably because she reminded him of his long-dead sister.

Maybe it was a good thing he had an outlaw to catch. Otherwise, he might be tempted to linger in this miserable stretch of wilderness longer than was wise.

A sensible man knew better than to get tangled up with the kind of woman who was content to live out her life on a hard-scrabble farm, away from civilization, working herself into an early grave. No matter how tempting the female, it was all a trap, designed to steal his future and spoil all his carefully laid plans.

A sensible man knew when to cut and run.

He gave a soft laugh.

Hodge Egan had always prided himself on being the most sensible of them all.

SIXTEEN

❖◆❖

SARAH WAS DREAMING about home. She was asleep in her bed, under her grandmother's quilt. Even after all these years, she could smell her grandmother's lilacs. From the kitchen came the sound of Aunt Molly fixing breakfast.

She knew she should get up and lend a hand, but something was holding her back. Something dark and dangerous and evil. Something she wanted to push far from her mind. Instead of facing it, she turned away from it, choosing instead to linger a moment longer beneath the familiar quilt, and listen to the soothing, pleasant sounds of morning dancing through her head.

She was yanked abruptly from the dream to find Eli Otto hauling her roughly to her feet. Because her wrists and ankles had been bound tightly throughout the night, she'd lost all feeling in her fingers and toes. Her body betrayed her. She sank back down to the ground and looked up in a haze of confusion.

He swore and gave her a punishing shove with his foot toward the tethered horse. "You know what I want. Saddle that nag. Time to move on before that bastard Hodge Egan gets too close."

"My aunt Molly doesn't approve of swearing."

He let loose with a string of vicious oaths. "Before I'm through with you, you'll be doing a lot of things your aunt doesn't approve of. Now get."

Dazed, disoriented, Sarah crawled forward on her hands and knees. For a moment she simply stared at the saddle, too befuddled to figure out how she was supposed to do anything with it in this condition.

Eli pulled out a knife, freeing her wrists. When she couldn't regain her footing, he was forced to cut through the rope at her ankles as well.

Each day she seemed to be losing more strength. The long hours spent on the back of a horse, and the nights spent bound on the hard ground, with little or no food, were stealing her energy, making her weak in both body and mind.

She set about saddling the horse while her captor wolfed down bread and cheese that had been stowed in the saddlebags. When he made no offer to share, the girl realized that he had no intention of feeding her. She experienced a quick flash of anger.

"I'm hungry, too."

"Better'n being dead. Keep up that tone and you won't have to worry about anything." Eli continued eating.

Her anger soon turned to fear, for she knew that when she grew weak enough, she'd have no way of fighting back. Was that part of his plan, as well? Would he leave her to starve along the trail? The thought strengthened her resolve.

Without taking time to think, she tightened the cinch, looped the reins loosely around the saddle horn, and turned to him.

"I need to"—She nodded toward the water shimmering just beyond the line of trees—"Use the stream."

"Make it quick." Using a tree limb as a crutch, Eli got to his feet and began limping toward the horse.

Sarah's heart was pounding as she made her way to the water. This was the first time she'd been out of the outlaw's sight since the ordeal began, and she knew she had to take this chance to make her escape. There may never be another opportunity like this.

With no real plan in mind, she walked slowly into the wall of trees. Once she'd glanced over her shoulder to make certain she was out of sight of the outlaw, she picked up her skirts and began to run in the direction they'd come the previous day.

Her heart slamming against her ribs, she ran as fast as she could, ignoring the branches that snagged her hair and tore at her tender flesh. Blood soon oozed from half a dozen gashes to her arms and face, but she continued on. Her feet were still clumsy after all those hours of being bound. Several times she stumbled and had to pull herself up by the limb of a small tree before moving on.

She could hear a pounding nearby, but couldn't be certain if it was Eli's mount, or just her poor heart, hammering in her temples.

She felt a wave of despair when the thicket of trees

ended and she found herself in an open meadow, with nothing to hide her from view. Lungs straining, heart hammering, she continued running flat out.

Now she recognized the sound of hoofbeats drawing closer.

She veered to her right, hoping to make it to the safety of the river. A heavy object flew through the air, driving her to the ground with such force all the air was knocked from her lungs.

She was pinned beneath Eli's body. When she struggled to free herself, he scrambled to his knees, straddling her. His hand shot out, slapping her face so hard her head snapped to one side.

In mute shock Sarah looked up at him through a shower of stars.

"Thought you could run, did you?" His face was twisted into a mask of murderous rage. "Thought because I had only one good leg I couldn't beat a scrawny little female like you?"

Leaning heavily on the tree limb, he dragged her to her feet and toward the waiting horse. "Get up there."

"My boot." She looked around and realized that one of her boots was left lying in the dirt.

"Leave it." He twisted her arm viciously in an effort to force her to obey, and she realized she was no match for this brute's strength.

He pulled himself into the saddle and dragged her up behind him.

As they started away he gave a sneer. "We'll leave that boot for the marshal to find. Let him know he's on the right track."

"Why?" It was more a cry than a question.

"Wouldn't want him to lose his way." He gave a low rumble of laughter. "If we're lucky, I'll have him in my sights before the day is over. And then you and I can move slow and easy. Maybe I won't kill you after all. You got spirit. I like that in a female. Maybe, when this leg of mine is healed, I'll keep you around just to show you a real good time."

As they started off, Sarah hung her head, mourning her failed attempt at freedom.

"HODGE!" SEEING HIM kneeling alongside the trail, Molly felt her heart stop as she brought the wagon to a halt and leapt down. "What is it? What have you found?"

A pouring rain had turned the trail to a sea of mud. The temperature was dropping, driven by cold wind.

This was the first time Molly had seen Hodge since he'd left at dawn.

"Is it . . . ?" She couldn't bring herself to put into words the fear lodged in her heart. Thankfully, she could see no blood, no body along the trail.

He was frowning when he looked over at her. "This belong to Sarah?" He held up a pale blue ribbon.

"Oh, sweet heaven." She snatched it to her breast and closed her eyes on a wave of relief. "Yes, it's hers."

"And this?" He strode toward his horse and removed a boot from his saddlebag.

Molly gathered it close and felt her throat tighten. Just touching something of Sarah's had tears threatening. "Where did you find these?"

"The boot was back there, some distance from the trail."

"How could she have lost a boot?"

Hodge had done enough tracking in his life to know how to read the signs. It was obvious from the length of her strides that Sarah had tried to run. Obvious, too, from the horse's prints, that Eli had gone after her. The torn earth, the flattened grass, told him they'd struggled. In the end, Eli had won. The depth of the imprint of the horse's tracks told him there were still two riders. But all he said to Molly was, "Maybe she kicked it aside to mark the trail."

"Or maybe that horrible man is doing this to taunt us." Molly kept the items hugged close to her heart as she turned back to the wagon.

Hodge watched her walk away, hair wet and clinging to her neck, her gown plastered to her legs and backside, and felt a wave of sympathy for her. "I think you and the girls should stop and make camp."

"No." She gave a firm shake of her head. "I want to press on, Hodge. I need to stay on this monster's trail."

"Let me do that. I'll go ahead and see what I can find, then come back here and join you later."

"Don't say that unless you mean it. I'd never forgive you if you kept on going and left us behind."

He nodded in understanding. She needed to be there when they found Sarah. If they found her.

"I give you my word I'll come back for you when I can. But I can't promise it will be tonight. I need to get close enough to keep them in my sight."

"Won't the rain help you track them?"

He shrugged. "It might. Or it might wash away their tracks completely."

Molly glanced at the three little girls, and was forced to admit that this journey was wearing on all of them. They huddled in the back of the wagon, cold and shivering. If she were alone, there would be no stopping her. But she had to think about what was best for the little ones, as well.

"All right, Hodge. We'll follow the line of this stream for a bit, and then make camp before dark."

"Good. I'll do my best to join you." He wished he could hold her, just for a moment. Instead he pulled himself into the saddle and headed out at a fast clip.

SARAH CLUNG. DESPITE her bound wrists, to the back of Eli's jacket. The rain had begun in midmorning, and by late afternoon the temperature had dropped, leaving them not only soaked but thoroughly chilled.

They'd been climbing steadily for several hours now. Through heavy forest, across rushing streams, they continued to climb until even the rolling clouds in the darkening sky were shielded from their view. With each climb, the air grew colder.

On a wide outcropping of rock Eli reined in his horse. Without a word he slipped from the saddle, leaving Sarah to dismount on her own. She dropped to the mud and sat there, rubbing at her hands that had long ago lost all feeling.

After fumbling in the saddlebags, Eli began stuffing food into his mouth. He followed that with a long pull from the jug of water. His hunger abated, he quickly tied her ankles and checked the rope at her wrists.

Satisfied that she was thoroughly bound, he pulled himself into the saddle.

Sarah appeared startled. "You're leaving me here?"

"Nice to know I'll be missed." He gave a low rumble of laughter. "Don't worry. It won't be for long. I just have to take care of something. Then I'll be back."

"Wait." She heard his hiss of impatience and began speaking quickly, before he could leave. "Where are you going?"

"Wouldn't you like to know?" And then, because he couldn't help bragging, he added, "Been keeping an eye on our trail. The marshal isn't the only one tracking us."

"Who . . . ?" Sarah felt a moment of hope. Had the marshal found others to join him?

"I spotted a wagon back a piece. Stopped along the river. Looks like your busybody aunt and three little brats have decided to join our little party."

"Aunt Molly." Sarah closed her eyes.

"Maybe Marshal Egan has more on his mind than you. Or maybe he never had time to recover from the beating I gave him last time. Whatever the reason, our marshal's getting careless."

"I don't understand."

He angled his head. "From up here I can see for miles, despite the rain. Right now the marshal is stopped along the trail, maybe a mile or so ahead of your aunt. Probably cold and tired. So far he hasn't built a fire. Afraid it might be seen by someone bent on revenge." He chuckled at his own joke. "But I know where he is, all the same. Got eyes like a hawk. I figure by the time I get down there, he'll be fighting to stay awake. If I'm quiet enough, he won't even know what hit him. And when I'm through with him, I may as well pay a call on the helpless lambs in that wagon, too. Then it'll just be you and me." He patted his pocket. "And all this money."

He wheeled his mount and started back along the direction they'd just come, leaving Sarah lying in the dirt, sobbing great, wrenching tears that mingled with the rain to run in rivers down her cheeks.

MOLLY GATHERED THE three little girls underneath the wagon for shelter. Over the wet ground she'd spread evergreen branches, which she covered with the quilts and pillows. They ate their cold meal before snuggling in for the night.

While the little ones slept, Molly sat huddled under a quilt, listening to the sound of the rain battering the wagon.

The thought of Sarah, cold and wet and frightened, lay like a stone around her heart. She pressed both hands to her chest and forced herself to take deep breaths. It didn't help. Nothing did.

She'd thought, after the death of her parents and the sudden loss of her brother and his wife, that nothing would ever hurt her as much again. But she'd been wrong. This was worse. Far worse, and she wasn't certain her poor heart would survive it.

She wanted to be out there in the darkness, doing something. Anything. Instead she was sitting here, warm and snug in her blanket, while her child suffered.

Was Hodge closing in on them? Had he found something that had kept him from returning to them? Oh, she prayed it was so. But there was a nagging little thought that taunted the edges of her mind.

He was traveling on horseback, with almost no provisions. That was enough to wear down a healthy man, especially one accustomed to a life of comfort in the city. But Hodge had suffered nearly fatal wounds at the hands of Eli Otto. There'd been little time to heal. What if the pain of his wounds had dulled his mind, slowed his reflexes, stolen his edge? How long could he keep up this killing pace?

And there was another thought causing her a great deal of guilt. He'd told her bluntly that he hadn't wanted to be saddled with four females while doing his job. Hadn't he implied that she and the girls would be in his way?

Maybe he was right. So far, she and the girls had made no difference at all. They moved like slugs in their wagon, barely keeping pace with him. She'd run off without giving a single thought to what this might do to Delia and Charity and Flora. What right did she have to drag these children into the wilderness, to face any number of dangers? She'd said she was doing this for Sarah. But in truth, she'd come simply because she hadn't been able to stay behind. The thought of remaining at the farm, not knowing what was happening to Sarah, was impossible to imagine.

But what if she'd brought them all to death's door?

She couldn't think of that now. Wouldn't allow such thoughts to dim her hopes.

She was here. As were the children. And somehow, some way, they would find a way to bring Sarah home safely with them.

She shivered. Or die trying.

SEVENTEEN

———◆◆◆◆◆———

My fault.

All my fault.

The words played through Sarah's mind, dragging her down, down, until she was drowning in the very depths of despair. She was hog-tied like one of their heifers for slaughter, and she'd brought it on herself. What was worse, far worse, was the knowledge that so many would die this night because of her foolishness.

The marshal. The real one, and not the slimy liar who'd fed her all those pretty words, pretending that he cared for her. A smooth-talking outlaw who'd made her believe, for just a little while, that she would be a hero to her family. A good, decent man of the law would die this night, while doing his duty, because of her. But worse, much worse in her mind, was the thought of Aunt Molly and her little sisters dying because of her. Her own life meant nothing without them. After this night she wouldn't care if she lived or died. In fact, she'd rather be dead than have to live with what she'd done to all those she loved.

How often had she resented having to help care for three little girls, two of whom weren't even her own flesh and blood? She'd given Aunt Molly plenty of grief over that. But somewhere over time, both Charity and Flora had become as dear to her as her own sweet little sister, Delia. Oh, they were a handful. No doubt about it. They tested her patience a dozen times a day. But she would give anything, anything, to be able to see them one more time. To be able to tell them all how much they meant to her.

And Aunt Molly. How many times had she heard the tale of the hardship she and her parents had endured aboard the ship that brought them to America to join their only son and brother? Hadn't she seen the deep well of grief when Molly had buried her parents? But she'd carried on until, without warning, Daniel and his Kathleen were gone, as well. Sarah and her little sister, Delia, had been terrified of a life without their parents until their aunt had assured them that she would keep them together in the only home they'd ever known. Molly had fulfilled her promise at a terrible price. Sarah had heard the sneers, the whispers from the people in town about the foolish spinster who'd given up a normal life in order to raise somebody else's children. Added to that was the fact that an unmarried woman actually permitted an old hermit, a former slave, to live in the woods on her property. Not only did Aunt Molly permit such a thing, but she seemed to have a friendly relationship with him and allowed her children to do the same. Scandalous to most, but as normal, as natural as breathing to dear Aunt Molly.

There'd been a time when Sarah had felt embarrassed about her aunt's odd behavior. Now, thinking about Aunt Molly and her kindness not only to old Addison but to everyone she met made Sarah want to burst with pride. She may seem odd, but only because she refused to behave as others expected, and instead, did the right thing, regardless of the cost to her reputation in the community.

It was so unfair that someone so good and kind and unselfish would die this night without ever knowing how her niece felt about her.

In her mind, Sarah could hear her aunt's voice, in that wonderful brogue.

Fair? Life isn't always fair, Sarah. Or so it seems while we're living it. But since we never know what wonderful surprises our Maker has in store for us, we're called to live each day the best we know how. And then one day, when we look back, we'll realize that often our worst times were actually our best.

"Oh, Aunt Molly." Sarah's voice rang in the darkness. "It can't get any worse than this."

Steeped in despair, the girl allowed the tears to fall. And then, when they'd run their course, she thought again about the impossible things her aunt had tackled in her lifetime. Impossible for others. But somehow, Molly O'Brien had made them look easy.

What would Aunt Molly do now? Sarah wondered.

The answer came in an instant.

She would never give up. Not while there was still a breath in her.

Rolling in the mud to the edge of the outcropping of rock, Sarah began rocking back and forth, sawing the rough edge of the stone against the ropes that bound her wrists. Each movement tore her tender flesh until, bloody and raw, she cried out in pain and was forced to stop. She glanced down at the river of blood soaking the ground beneath her, and clamped her teeth against the pain. Nothing was going to stop her. She would break free, or die trying.

HODGE TOOK SHELTER from the rain under the boughs of an evergreen and huddled inside his soaked parka. He'd intended to return to Molly and the girls, but the continued rain changed his plans. He'd use the weather to his advantage. The sound of rain would mask the approach of a horse and rider. This was the perfect night to try to rescue the girl. He would stay here awhile, just long enough to give Eli and Sarah time to stop and make camp for the night. Then he intended to move ahead and try to use the element of surprise to his advantage.

He prided himself on knowing how an outlaw would think. If it hadn't been for Hildy's mother-hen instincts, and her incessant nagging, he could have just as easily become a man on the wrong side of the law. It hadn't been any noble idea of saving the world that caused him to wear the badge and wage war on thieves and murderers. It had begun simply as a way to earn a living. Once his sister died and he'd turned his back on farming, there'd been little opportunity for a half-grown kid to make his way in this world. But his early lessons on handling a gun and his fearlessness in facing down bullies made him the perfect choice for sheriff in the tiny town of Winding Creek, Wyoming. And when the brash young sheriff rid the town of one of the county's most notorious outlaws, his new-found fame brought him to the attention of the U.S. government. That, in turn, led him to the comfortable job of U.S. marshal, and a life of comparative ease in Chicago.

It had been an amazing journey from tough, small-town frontier sheriff to government official stationed in one of the finest cities in the land. He'd learned to enjoy the good life and all that came with it, especially the respect and ca-maraderie of men of wealth and privilege. Heady stuff in-deed for a man who'd started out life on a hard-scrabble patch of land, with little or no formal education.

He touched a hand to the spot where his badge ought to be and narrowed his eyes. He'd take great pleasure in getting it back from that bastard. It bothered him more than he cared to admit, that a thief and murderer was wearing the honored badge of a U.S. marshal. If allowed to get away, there was no telling how much misery Eli Otto could cause among good, law-abiding folks, while posing as a man of the law.

Hodge patted his chest pocket, wishing for a fine cigar. Hell, he wanted a nice, warm fire, too, but that's exactly what the outlaw would expect. No sense giving Otto a roadmap and compass to find him.

He pulled his hat down low over his face and decided to grab some rest. Soon enough he'd be back on the trail. He didn't intend to stop this time until he had what he'd come for. He hoped it would end with Sarah safe, though in his years on the job, he'd learned that there was no way to call the outcome of the game until the last card was played. As for the outlaw, Eli Otto, he didn't much give a care if he brought him back dead or alive. After killing a man of the law, Eli was as good as dead anyway. No judge would let him see the light of day until he was a very old man.

ELI HELD THE reins tightly, keeping the horse to a slow walk. The horse's hooves made little or no sound on the spongy ground. Not that he considered the rain a blessing. Because of it, his leg throbbed and burned like the fire of hell. He rubbed his hand over it, cursing softly. If not for this broken leg, he'd have been able to come in on foot. He'd have much preferred to sneak around the marshal's camp, find him, and slit his throat before he even had time to react. Instead, he'd have to make do on horseback. His plan was simple. Spot the place where the lawman had made camp and come in with guns blazing.

Hearing a sound in the darkness, he drew his mount to one side, using the thick underbrush as cover. Peering through the curtain of rain, he tensed and waited.

WHILE HIS HORSE picked its way up the hilly trail, Hodge half dozed in the saddle and dreamed of San Francisco. A city filled with ornate gentlemen's clubs, pretty women, and high-stakes poker. Life didn't get much better'n that. Hildy would probably turn over in her grave when she saw how he intended to spend the rest of his life. But he'd had his fill of this sorry lifestyle. From now on somebody else could chase desperate outlaws around gritty little towns that weren't even on the map, and across stretches of wilderness that even the savages didn't want. He'd earned the right to live in style, and he was, by God, going to grab it while he was still young enough to enjoy it.

Rain fell in sheets, obliterating everything except the trail directly in front of him. He hated the fact that he couldn't see into the brush on either side of him. If he were a man on the run, he'd use this as the perfect hiding place.

How far ahead was Eli? He might use the rain to put some miles between himself and those that followed, but Hodge was counting on the fact that the outlaw's broken leg would cause him to stop and rest.

He rubbed his shoulder and silently cursed the pain.

From somewhere nearby a horse nickered.

Hodge's head came up sharply and his hand went instinctively to the rifle in the boot of his saddle.

Before he could get it loose and take aim, a volley of gunfire shattered the night. Something hot pierced his thigh, and he fell from the saddle to sprawl on the ground. He was still clutching his rifle when a second volley sprayed into the mud around him, causing it to dance over him like crazed raindrops. One of the bullets hit his arm, and he felt the sudden rush of heat before his rifle slipped from his grasp.

Eli was on him in an instant, pinning him to the ground, while holding a pistol to his temple.

He heard the click of the trigger and felt the cold metal against his flesh.

And prepared to die.

* * *

MOLLY COULDN'T SLEEP. Earlier she'd huddled beside the girls, hoping the heat of her body would keep them warm and hoping the sound of their steady, even breathing would lull her to join them in dreams. It wasn't to be. She was too agitated, though she didn't know why.

She couldn't stop thinking about Sarah. During the day, the needs of the children and the discomfort of the trail kept her mind occupied. She was too busy to think. But here, with nothing but the rain to distract her, she found the fear almost paralyzing.

She was a woman accustomed to taking charge. Hadn't she always found a way to solve every problem that life handed her? But this was out of her control, and the feeling of helplessness was making her half mad with fear.

She remembered her grandmother, on their little farm in Ireland, regaling her with tales of her life as a new bride, forced to leave all that was familiar in her native Scotland to join her husband's family on their farm in Ireland. She'd been hardly older than Sarah was now. A child-woman, being forced to begin a new life far from all that she held dear. No family, no friends, except the strangers who were her husband's kin.

"How did you keep from being afraid?" Molly had asked the old woman.

"I prayed, lass."

"Did it help, Gram?"

"It did, aye. Of course"—The old woman's eyes twinkled as she added—"I'd been taught that ye must pray as though it all depends on the Maker, and then work as though it all depends on ye. Never forget that, lass."

Molly buried her face in her hands. "Please," she whispered. "Show me the way, for I'm feeling so lost. I'm not afraid of the hard work needed for the task, but I need some guidance."

The words trailed off at the roll of thunder echoing across the sky. She looked up. Despite the rain, there'd been no lightning.

Not thunder, she realized.

Gunfire!

"Oh, sweet heaven." She was on her feet, shouting to the children to wake, while she fumbled to hitch the horse to the wagon.

It seemed to take forever, her fingers stiff with fear and cold.

That done, she helped the little ones into the back of the wagon, urging them to hold on for dear life.

She pulled herself up to the hard seat, flicking the reins.

Within minutes they were racing into the darkness toward the unknown.

EIGHTEEN

———◆———

"WELL, NOW," ELI'S voice held a note of triumph. "Isn't this cozy? Just you and me, Marshal." He jammed a knee to Hodge's bloody thigh and laughed when he saw the pain that glazed his eyes. "You know how long I've waited for this?"

Hodge held his silence, further provoking the outlaw.

His smile turned into a look of fury. "You think you're so big and brave. But I haven't seen a man yet who didn't plead for his life when he knew the end was near." He moved the pistol down Hodge's cheek to his throat. Pressed the cold metal as hard as he could against his flesh, until the lawman sucked in a quick breath.

"I can make it fast and painless, or I can draw it out as long as I please. I know exactly how to kill a man and how to make him suffer. I've had a lot of practice." Eli bent close, peering into Hodge's eyes. "Let's see how much pain you can take, Marshal."

Hodge jerked his head up, catching Eli squarely on the nose. The gunman reared back, blind with pain, while a fountain of blood gushed down his chin.

Hodge used that moment to try to gain his footing.

"Oh, no! You're going to pay for that." Eli swung his hand in an arc, bringing the pistol down hard against the marshal's temple, snapping his head to one side, then the other.

Hodge blinked, struggling to see through the shower of stars that blurred his vision.

"Now I'll see just how brave you are, lawman. And to sweeten things, when I'm through with you, I'm going to pay a visit to that wagon that's been trailing you. And me and that female are going to have us some fun."

He saw the sudden narrowing of Hodge's eyes and gave a rumble of laughter. "Hit a nerve, did I? You think I didn't know what you two were doing in the next room? I ought to thank you. You made my escape twice as easy." He gave a sudden cackle of laughter. "Maybe, when I'm through with her, I'll have me some fun with all those brats, too, as well as their big sister. And when I'm done with all of them, I'm going to take my sweet time traveling across the country, just me and this shiny badge and all that bank money. Oh, I'm going to lead the good life while all those poor dumb citizens lick my boots, thinking I'm a high-and-mighty man of the law."

Hodge's silence deflated his bubble.

With a look of fury he took aim with his pistol. "Since you've got nothing to say, looks like I'm wasting my time talking."

"Bragging, you mean."

"Now you're trying to goad me into losing control. You'd like that, wouldn't you? But I'm too smart for you. So if you've got anything to say, say it now. It'll be the last word you'll ever speak, lawman."

As his finger began to squeeze the trigger, Hodge went very still, anticipating the explosion that would rip through him.

Directly behind the outlaw, something moved. A dark shadow loomed up, curtained by rain. Seeing it, Hodge tried to hold the gunman's focus.

"You won't get away with this, Eli."

"Who's going to stop me? You, lawman?"

A bloody arm swung out. An arm holding a tree limb like a club.

With a scream of pain Eli absorbed a blow and toppled to one side.

Sarah stood in the pouring rain, looking, despite the mud and blood, like an avenging angel.

"Watch out." Hodge's words of warning came too late as Eli roared up, fists swinging, and slammed Sarah against the trunk of a tree.

The girl fell to the ground and lay there like a wounded bird, moaning softly.

Though Hodge was badly wounded, the distraction had given him a moment to gather his strength for what was to come. He knew that unless he could overpower Eli, all would be lost. Not just his life, but all those innocents who were depending on him as well.

He got to his knees and felt the world spin. Shaking his head to clear it, he gained his footing just as Eli pulled himself up, using Sarah's discarded tree limb as a crutch.

"Lost your gun, I see." Hodge reared back with his fist, hoping to land a blow to the outlaw's chin.

Eli ducked. When he came up, he was holding a knife he'd fished from his boot. With a vicious swipe he laid open Hodge's arm from wrist to elbow. Blood flowed like a river, and Hodge felt his head swim.

He knew he was losing too much blood. Knew, too, that his body would soon fail him. He placed his hands on his knees and lowered his head, waiting for the weakness to pass. Unless he overpowered this outlaw quickly, he'd be too weak to finish the job.

"Now let's see if I can't open up your chest the same way. We'll find out if you really have a heart." As Eli brandished his knife and moved in for the kill, Hodge braced himself.

In an act of desperation he ducked, then brought his head up under the outlaw's jaw, and was rewarded by the sound of bone grinding on bone. He knew, by the pain in his head, that he'd managed to inflict a punishing blow to the outlaw.

The knife dropped from Eli's fingers as he closed both hands around his jaw. "You've broken it, you bastard. I'll kill you."

He dropped to the ground in search of his fallen pistol, and Hodge fell on top of him. Fists flew as they pummeled each other, each man desperate to gain the upper hand.

It seemed, in Hodge's mind, to be a replay of their earlier fight in Molly's field.

Eli's elbow connected with Hodge's jaw, sending him flat on his back. Using that moment, Eli fumbled about in the mud, hoping to find a weapon. For the space of a heartbeat he went still, then suddenly sat back on his haunches. On his face was a look of triumph.

In his hand was the pistol, aimed directly at Hodge's chest.

"Good-bye, Marshal. It would have been nice to keep you alive, so you could watch what I intend to do to the females. But I can't afford to keep you around. You're more trouble then you're worth."

They both looked up at a sound like thunder. Molly's wagon careened through the mud like an out-of-control train. It had barely come to a halt when Molly leapt to the ground, taking aim with Addison's rifle.

"Eli Otto," she shouted above the sound of the rain. "Unless you lower your pistol at once, I'll be forced to shoot you."

For a moment he merely stared at her. Then he threw back his head and gave a rumble of laughter. "Always the proper lady, aren't you? But you'd better be warned. By the time you squeeze off a shot, it'll be too late. Whether I'm dead or alive, I'll still have the satisfaction of killing this lawman who's been dogging my trail, making my life miserable."

Hodge saw the startled look in Molly's eyes, and the way she hesitated. This wasn't the reaction she'd expected from the outlaw.

Eli had seen it, too. With a smile of satisfaction he took aim. Before he could follow through, he gave a look of surprise when Sarah, lying in the mud, snagged the tree limb that was supporting him and gave a determined tug.

With a grunt Eli dropped to the ground. His shot went wild, missing Hodge and landing in the tree beside him.

Desperate now, Eli began fumbling around in the mud.

Molly ran closer, rifle at the ready, shouting to the children to take cover behind the wagon.

Instead of doing as they'd been ordered, they crowded around behind her.

With a little cry of triumph Eli wrapped an arm around Sarah, pressing the blade of his knife to her throat.

His voice was a harsh taunt. "Thought you were smart, didn't you, girl?" He turned to Molly with a snarl. "Woman, drop that rifle, or I kill the girl."

"No, Aunt Molly." Sarah's voice trembled with the tears that she couldn't hide. "He'll kill me anyway. Don't sacrifice your life for mine."

"Oh. That's so tender." Eli pressed the blade tighter, drawing a trickle of blood, causing Sarah to suck in a breath on the pain. "Did you hear what I said, woman?"

"Please. Don't hurt her." Molly tossed the rifle aside, while the little girls merely stared at her in astonishment. "Let her go. Take me instead."

"And why would I do that?"

"I'll clean your wounds and help you heal, as I did back at the house."

"Do you take me for a fool?" He gave a harsh laugh and tugged Sarah's head back sharply, all the while keeping the knife against her throat. "You're all going to die. Starting with this one."

Hodge struggled to his feet and stumbled closer, intent upon snatching Sarah from the grasp of this madman.

Seeing him, Eli pressed the blade harder, causing blood to stream from the girl's throat. "Don't try to be a hero."

Hodge stopped dead in his tracks. Beside him, the little girls began weeping.

"Please spare her life." Molly stepped closer. "Take me instead."

"Oh, I'll take you, all right. As soon as I've finished with her."

Intent upon taunting them with his savagery, Eli wasn't even aware of the tiny figure that stepped away from the others.

"I told Mama Molly you were a bad man." Flora picked up the biggest stone she could find and hurled it as hard as she could, catching Eli by surprise as it grazed his temple.

He was so startled, he actually loosened his hold on Sarah for a moment while he touched a hand to the bruise.

That was all the distraction Molly and Hodge needed. Racing forward Molly caught Sarah's arm and tugged her free.

Eli slashed at Hodge, who was able to step back, avoiding the blade. Before Eli could get to his feet, Delia and Charity followed Flora's lead and began pelting him with stones. Flora picked up the tree limb that Sarah had used earlier, and though it weighed nearly as much as she did, the little girl managed to bring it down hard against the outlaw's face.

The other two continued hurling stones at his face, his head, his neck, and his back until he was forced to cover himself with his hands.

When he looked up, Molly and Hodge were standing over him, their rifles aimed directly at his head.

"Your luck just ran out, Otto." Hodge's voice was a low growl of command. "My orders were to bring you back dead or alive. You'd be far less trouble dead."

Bloodied, exhausted, and too weak to face their combined strength, Eli had no choice but to lift his hands in surrender, and submit to being tied to a tree.

While the marshal bound him, the three little girls hurried to Sarah's side, where they gathered around her, weeping and shouting and hugging her as though to assure themselves that she was truly safe.

They were still huddled together, struggling to ease each other's tears when Molly joined them and drew Sarah into her fierce embrace.

"Oh, my darling. Are you all right?"

Sarah couldn't speak over the lump in her throat. At last she managed to whisper, "I'm fine, Aunt Molly."

"Truly? He didn't . . . ?" Molly tried again. "That monster didn't hurt you in any way?"

Sarah gave a firm shake of her head. "There was no time. He was determined to stay ahead of you and Marshal Egan."

"Praise heaven." Molly wiped the tears from her eyes and tenderly tied her sash around the girl's neck to stem the blood that flowed. Then she wrapped her in a quilt and left her in the loving care of the three little girls, who were hovering like mother hens.

She left them to hurry to Hodge's side.

He sat some distance from the outlaw, unmindful of the mud, still balancing his rifle across his knees.

Molly looked down at him. "How badly wounded are you?"

Despite the blood, he was wearing a silly grin. "Nothing fatal. I'll live."

"You're sure?" She dropped down beside him and touched a finger to the pulse at his throat.

"I'm sure. I'm just fine." He lifted a hand to her cheek. "And so are you, Molly O'Brien. It would take one damned fine woman to raise such fierce, independent little females."

Her voice wavered. "I'm so proud of them,"

"You should be. They were something to see," he muttered before passing out cold.

HODGE AWOKE IN a cocoon of warmth. The air was perfumed with the wonderful aroma of coffee and biscuits.

His eyes flicked open and he stared around in amazement. He was wrapped in layers of quilts, lying beside a blazing fire.

The sun was already high in the sky. The rain had fled; the grass around him was dry and fragrant with late summer clover.

With a feeling of dread he glanced across the space that separated him from the outlaw, and was rewarded with the sight of Eli Otto still tied to the tree, though he, too, was wrapped in a quilt. It would seem that even a monster who'd threatened every kind of horror would be treated with common courtesy by Molly and her girls.

From a distance came the sound of childish laughter. Hodge thought it the most amazing sound he'd ever heard. After so much bloodshed and violence, only innocent children could find something to laugh about.

A short time later Molly and the four girls came striding toward him. It was obvious they'd bathed in the stream. Their clothes were free of mud and blood. Their faces, their hair glistened with droplets of water.

Seeing him awake, Molly filled a tin cup with steaming coffee and carried it to his side. "Are you well enough to sit up?"

In reply he tossed aside the quilts, only to discover that he was once again naked beneath the covers. The only thing he wore were clean dressings on his thigh and arm. He gingerly touched a finger to the dressings, and found that, despite the aches, his wounds weren't nearly as painful as he'd anticipated.

He hastily pulled the edges of the coverings together and managed a glance toward the children as he sat up. "My clothes?"

"Clean and dry." She handed him the cup of coffee and called out to the girls, "Would you like to fetch the marshal's things?"

All four girls dashed away, racing to be the first to help the man who'd saved them. They returned minutes later carrying his pants and shirt, jacket and boots.

He noted that his clothes were as clean and sparkling as the day he'd bought them. The same couldn't be said for him.

He touched a hand to the growth of dark stubble on his cheeks and chin, and studied the mud and blood that stained his body. "I think I'd better make a quick trip to the stream."

"Can you make it alone, or do you need some help?" Molly held out her hands.

He felt his throat go dry at her offer. Then he saw the way the four girls were watching, and gave a quick shake of his head. "I guess I can manage."

With her help he got unsteadily to his feet and walked away, still holding the quilt around him for modesty.

After a hasty bath in the stream, he pulled on his pants and boots and returned to the camp, tucking his shirt into his waistband. As he reached a hand to his jacket, he saw the shiny badge pinned to the lapel.

For a moment he went very still, until he realized that Molly and the girls were watching him.

"Well." He ducked his head, struggling to swallow the lump in his throat while he made a great show of slipping his arms into the sleeves.

By the time he'd buttoned it, he had control of his emotions. "It's nice to have this back where it belongs."

"It looks right on you." Molly was gripping her hands tightly at her waist.

He saw something in her eyes, and wondered at the flood of emotions that would make her weep.

Molly blinked, and Hodge decided that maybe it had just been a look of pride in her eyes.

"I polished your boots," Flora said proudly.

Hodge was grateful for the distraction. He turned to her with a smile. "You did a fine job."

"I washed your shirt." Charity blushed clear to her toes. "It was all bloody."

"I bet you had to scrub hard to get it clean."

She nodded shyly. "I didn't mind the work."

"Sarah and I washed your pants and scrubbed all the blood from your jacket," Delia said. "And Aunt Molly used sand to polish your badge. She said it wouldn't do to return it to you with any blemishes."

"I thank you." He looked at Molly, so fresh-faced and pretty, then forced himself to turn away and glance at the girls. "All of you."

"Well." Molly saw the swelling of pride in her girls, then looked over at Hodge. "You'll be wanting something to eat."

"That would be nice. And then we'll head to town."

He caught the eager looks on the little girls' faces before Molly said, "It's already midday. You're not fully recovered from your wounds. Maybe we ought to wait until morning."

Flora's eyes turned stormy. "Why can't we leave now, Mama Molly? If the marshal is still hurting, we can sit up front with you, and he lie in the back of the wagon with the bad man."

Molly was about to argue, when Hodge intervened. "I like Flora's idea. Since we've all had time to rest, we'll start out as soon as I've had something to eat. We can stop along the trail whenever we feel the need." This would be safer. There were some strange feelings churning inside him. Feelings he didn't want to probe too deeply. He needed to be busy, to keep his mind off things that made him uncomfortable.

Molly shot him a considering look. "You're sure?"

He nodded. "The sooner we get to town, the sooner we can assure the authorities that Eli Otto is no longer a danger to the community. There are a lot of people who'll be eager to hear the news. Especially the widows and families of the people he's killed."

"And we can collect the reward." Flora's mouth curved into a wide smile.

"Reward?" Hodge arched a brow.

"A thousand dollars," the little girl said with an air of authority.

Hodge shrugged. "I wouldn't know anything about that."

"It said so." The little girl's hands went to her hips, ready to debate the issue.

"It said so where?" Hodge glanced from Flora to Molly and back again.

"On the poster Aunt Molly found with your things."

He accepted a plate of bread and cheese from Molly. "I don't recall reading about a reward, but then, I read so much about Eli Otto on my way to Wisconsin, I could have missed a few things. I guess we'll have to see about that when we get to Delight."

At his words, Flora's little face fell, and Molly had to catch her hand and lead her away to keep her from arguing the point further.

While Hodge polished off his meal, Molly and the girls began lining the back of the wagon with quilts and pillows. As soon as their supplies were loaded, Hodge tied the horses to the back of the wagon before dragging Eli to his feet. Using a tree limb as a crutch, the outlaw limped toward the wagon and was forced to submit to being hogtied in the back.

When all was ready, Molly and the girls rode up front, while Hodge reclined in back, a stack of pillows beneath his head, his rifle trained on his prisoner, and his mind in turmoil.

He had what he'd come for. What every U.S. marshal prayed for. A prisoner, taken without loss of life.

He ought to feel on top of the world. But something was happening here. Something that made him uneasy.

He was a man who'd spent a lifetime following a simple path, without complications. Not that Molly and her girls were complications. But over these past few days they'd begun to matter to him, and that wasn't a comfortable feeling.

He fell silent, determined to resolve whatever was troubling him before he arrived in Delight.

NINETEEN

———◆◆◆———

From his position in the back of the wagon, Hodge watched the way the three little girls hovered around Sarah, needing to be close to her, to touch her. They were so grateful to have her back with them, and trying desperately to draw her out.

"Weren't you scared?" Delia held tightly to her older sister's hand, as though afraid to let her go for even a moment, for fear she might vanish again.

"Uh-huh." Sarah hunched her shoulders.

Charity leaned over Delia to study the older girl's face. "If the bad man left you tied up, how did you get away?"

"Rubbed the rope against the edge of a rock until it tore loose." Sarah's voice was little more than a whisper. Each word seemed forced from between pinched lips.

"Is that how you cut your wrists?" Flora, sitting between Molly and Sarah, reached over to touch a finger to the girl's bandages.

"Uh-huh." Sarah flinched. Her head lowered until her hair swept down over her eyes.

"I thought that bad man was the one who cut you." Delia closed her hands over her sister's. "Did you really cut yourself? That was so brave."

Sarah couldn't find her voice. She merely turned her head, avoiding their eyes.

It occurred to Hodge that the catch in her voice could be the result of the painful cut to her throat. But he wasn't convinced. It sounded more like a guilty conscience.

Taking pity on her, he cleared his throat. "If that old seat is getting too hard up there, maybe you ladies would like to climb back here and sit on some comfortable quilts for a while, and I'll take the reins."

"What a grand idea. " Grateful to halt the little girls' questions, Molly picked up on his suggestion at once and slowed the horse to a halt. "Maybe, to pass the time, we could hold a spelling bee. I'll call out the words, and see who knows how to spell them."

Flora's competitive nature took over. "What does the winner get?"

Molly thought a moment. "An extra candy stick from Mr. Chalmers's mercantile when we get to town." She climbed down. "Is that reward enough?"

"Yes. Oh, yes." Amid shrieks of excitement, the three little girls scrambled over the seat to settle themselves in the back.

"How about you, Sarah?" Molly glanced toward the front, where the girl remained alone.

"I don't think so, Aunt Molly."

"All right." Molly watched as Hodge climbed stiffly

from the wagon and circled around to climb to the driver's seat. She knew he was sacrificing his comfort for the sake of Sarah's tender feelings and felt a welling of gratitude for his kindness.

Minutes later they were rolling along, with Molly calling out words and the three little girls struggling to spell them.

"Freedom," she called.

"F-R-E-D-A-M." Flora jumped in ahead of the others, eager to earn the right to an extra candy stick.

"There are two *e*'s, Flora. And an *o* instead of an *a*."

"Did I earn half a candy stick?" The little girl asked hopefully.

"I'm afraid not. How about this one. Safety."

It was Delia who spelled it correctly, earning her first point.

In front, Hodge kept the horse to an easy gait, while Sarah sat beside him, her back ramrod straight, eyes staring ahead and seeing nothing. The sash fluttering at her throat bore her bloodstains.

"You can be proud of yourself, Sarah." He kept his voice soft enough that the others couldn't hear.

"How can you say that?" She shot him a sideways glance before lowering her head. "This was all my fault. If I hadn't believed that outlaw's lies, none of this would have happened."

"Eli has had plenty of experience at lying. He was counting on using that experience against you. But when the chips were down, you didn't freeze or give up, even when it looked as though things would end badly."

"I didn't care about my own life. I thought he was going to kill all of you."

"He would have. But he didn't. Thanks to you. And also thanks to you, nobody got hurt."

"You did." She glanced at the linen strips that bound his arm from wrist to elbow.

"That's my job."

"And my job was to obey my aunt."

"You made a mistake. We've all done that. It's how we learn and grow."

"If that's so, it looks like I've got a heap of learning and growing to do." She sniffed back her tears and folded her arms across her chest, staring off into the distance.

"WE'RE STOPPING?" WHEN the wagon rolled to a halt, Molly looked up in surprise. She'd been so busy trying to keep the girls occupied with spelling and sums, she'd failed to notice that the sunlight had bled into evening shadows.

"Going to be dark soon." Hodge climbed down and began unhitching the horse. "We'll sleep here, then get a fresh start in the morning. Ought to reach Delight well before supper tomorrow."

While Molly and the girls climbed down and began setting about making camp, Hodge untied the horses from the back of the wagon and led all of them to a nearby stream. When they'd had their fill he tethered them in a stand of trees and hauled a bucket of water toward the campfire, where coffee bubbled and bread warmed over hot coals.

Hodge untied Eli's wrists long enough to permit him to feed himself. Then, assured that the prisoner's ropes were secure, he sat down wearily with his back against a tree trunk and accepted a plate of dried meat and cheese and bread from Molly.

"You have to be tired." She handed him a cup of steaming coffee.

"We're all tired. Tomorrow night we can sleep in real beds in town." He looked up. "Is there a hotel?"

She shook her head. "A boardinghouse. Martha Teasdale is a widow who keeps a really clean place, with fine feather beds and even finer food."

He managed a smile. "That thought ought to get us through another day." He nodded toward the little girls, chasing each other around the wagon. "It sounds as though they're pretty happy about going to town."

Molly flushed and dropped down beside him. "They don't get there nearly often enough. To them, Delight is next to heaven. So many people, so many activities. Barn dances. Swimming in the creek. Picking apples. Best of all there are children their age to do things with."

"It must get lonely so far from others."

She shrugged. "Sometimes. I don't think about it much. But I dearly love seeing the girls spending time with other children."

"My sister, Hildy, and I used to go to town once or twice a year. She hated it. I always loved it."

"Were you close to your sister?"

Hodge shrugged. "I didn't think so at the time. She was always bossing me around. I was the kid brother, and she was determined to see me walk the straight and narrow, whether I liked it or not."

"She sounds like a good woman."

Hodge smiled, and Molly thought how handsome he was when he let himself relax. "She was. Amazing to think how much responsibility she had to shoulder at such a young age. You'd have liked her. And I know she'd have approved of you."

"Really? How can you tell?"

"You're a good woman, Molly. A really good woman. If there'd been time for us to get to know each other better . . ." When he realized where this was heading, he let the words trail off. "Speaking of time"—He set aside his empty plate and wrapped his hands around the cup of coffee—"You'll want to spend a little of yours with Sarah. She's carrying a heavy load of guilt."

Molly wondered at the sudden band around her heart. For just a moment she'd thought he might be willing to rekindle the flame they'd lit on their one night together. Apparently it wasn't to be.

She swallowed back her disappointment. "I know. I'm hoping, when we get some time alone, I can get Sarah to talk to me. I just don't know what I can say to make her feel better."

He drank, then looked over at her. "You'll figure it out."

"I wish I could be as certain of that as you."

He held her look. A half smile tugged at the corner of his mouth. "I'm a gambling man, Molly. If life was a game of cards, I'd put all my money on you."

She watched as he got wearily to his feet and tossed aside the last of his coffee before walking over to check the bindings at Eli's feet and ankles.

Was there a reason why he'd made it clear to her that

he was a gambling man? Was this his way of telling her that he wanted no part of the dull, ordinary life on an isolated Wisconsin dairy farm?

Not that she'd actually believed for a moment that he would. They were, after all, little more than strangers. Their night together had been the result of loneliness and need and nothing more. He'd made it perfectly clear at the time that he could make no promises. She'd asked for none.

If her heart was breaking, just a little, she had no one to blame but herself.

Still, as she led the girls toward the wagon, and heard their evening prayers, she could barely hold a single thought. Her mind was awhirl with the possibilities.

She hardly knew Hodge Egan. He barely knew her. And yet, there were feelings in her heart for this man that she'd never felt for any other.

What if she let him go without ever telling him all that she was feeling?

And just what was it she was feeling? She knew all about love and commitment. Hadn't she committed herself to raising four little girls? But she knew nothing at all about men and women. And marriage. The very thought of it terrified her. She wasn't at all sure she could spend a lifetime with a man. Especially one she hardly knew.

She needed to talk to him about these strange feelings. What if he had them, too?

She glanced over, hoping that he might be waiting to talk to her. To her keen disappointment, he was already asleep across the fire from the prisoner, his rifle across his lap, his hat tipped low over his face.

Swallowing back her disappointment, Molly stretched out beside the children, knowing that she wouldn't be able to sleep at all this night.

From his vantage point beside the fire Hodge heard the children reciting their prayers in a singsong tone and bit back a grin.

He sincerely hoped that once the girls fell asleep, Molly might amble down to the stream. Maybe he'd follow her there, and they could find a few minutes alone.

He itched to hold her. To kiss her. Hell, he had an itch to do a whole lot more. He wanted to lie with her and feel the sweet press of that lithe young body on his.

He knew better than to play with fire, but this woman was like a fever in his blood. He wanted just one more chance to taste all that goodness, to savor all that pent-up passion.

"Little Miss Prissy got to you, didn't she?"

At the hiss of Eli's voice Hodge's head swiveled sharply. "Shut your mouth, Otto, or I'll shut it for you."

"What more can you do? Shoot me?" The outlaw gave a mirthless laugh. "I know you'd like to. But then there's that high and mighty code you live by." His look turned sly. "Except when it comes to the woman. Then you're just like all men, Egan. You're just like me. You take what you want, and to hell with honor."

"I said, shut your mouth."

Hodge had to struggle to bank the fury that rose up, threatening to choke him. To hide his emotions he pulled his hat low on his face and lowered his head.

Though he sat perfectly still, his mind was in turmoil. Eli's words had cut too close for comfort.

He'd known that Molly O'Brien wasn't like the women he sought in the gentlemen's clubs. Those women knew the rules of the game. They'd played it often enough to have no illusions.

Molly was an innocent. That fact had shocked him more than he cared to admit. And though he'd offered to leave her as he'd found her, the truth was, he'd already crossed a line, making it impossible for either of them to make a reasonable decision. And he'd accepted what she offered without giving a thought to what would happen to her when he was gone.

There was nothing to be done about it now. He had a job to do. He would see it to its conclusion. Molly had a life here, with a ready-made family that needed her. There was no hope for a future together.

From beneath the brim of his hat he glanced toward the wagon, to see Molly lying beside her girls, with her back to him. It was just as well. Even if she'd gone down to the stream, there was no way he would follow.

With a feeling of revulsion he knew that to do so would only prove Eli's words to be true. It galled him to think that he was, indeed, no better than the outlaw when it came to his treatment of Molly.

TWENTY

·—◆·◆·◆—·

As THEY ROLLED into the town of Delight, Molly thought about the last time she'd been here, picking up supplies. With all that had happened since then, it felt like a hundred years had passed. She found herself looking at her little brood of chicks through new eyes.

They'd grown. Changed. This event had changed all of them forever. Oh, their basic personalities hadn't altered. Sarah, though guilt-ridden, was still a sweet dreamer. Charity was still a shy little mouse. Delia still waited for a signal from her big sister before attempting anything new. And Flora was still impulsive and fearless. But their bond was obviously deeper, stronger, for having shared this fearsome adventure.

And what about me? Have I been changed by what's happened? Will it be apparent that Hodge was more than a wound to be tended? A body to be healed? Will anyone know, just by looking at us, that we shared something rare and intimate?

She wanted to believe that she didn't feel different. But it would be a lie. Her heart fluttered whenever he looked at her. She could feel her cheeks growing hot, her throat going dry, whenever he drew near. Her hands actually trembled whenever she so much as touched him in passing.

All her life she'd been cool and calm and sensible. And now, with this man, she was behaving like a foolish, lovesick girl. And there was no help for it. She simply loved him. And if he didn't return her affection, she knew her heart would be forever broken.

She cast a sideways glance at that stern, chiseled profile, and wondered if he had any idea that he had this effect on her.

"Molly! Molly O'Brien!" Martha Teasdale was just crossing to the mercantile when she looked up to see their wagon heading toward her. She peered with interest at the rugged man driving the wagon before returning her attention to Molly. "Whatever are you doing back in Delight so soon? And with such a fine-looking gentleman."

At a word from Molly, Hodge drew the horse to a halt. "Martha, this is Marshal Hodge Egan. Hodge, Martha Teasdale, owner of the boardinghouse just down the street."

Hodge tipped his hat. "Good day, Mrs. Teasdale."

Martha's cheeks turned a becoming shade of pink. "Marshal. How do you happen to be traveling with Molly?"

"It's a long story. I owe her my life."

Her hand went to her throat. "How . . . romantic. I do hope you'll be staying in our fine town for a while."

"I'm afraid not, ma'am. I have a prisoner to return to Madison to await trial. I'll be leaving as soon as I get word from the proper officials."

At his words, Molly felt her heart plummet. She'd thought, hoped, they would have some time together.

"Well, at least I can look forward to seeing you at supper." Martha turned her head to include Molly and the girls in her invitation. "All of you."

"Thank you, Martha. We'll come by shortly. If you have room," Molly added, "my girls and I will be staying the night."

"I always have room for you and your family, Molly. As soon as I pick up some supplies, I'll head back and make your rooms ready." She flicked a glance over the children's torn dresses, then turned to Molly. "Are you sure you wouldn't care to join me in a bit of shopping?"

Molly took one look at the children's travel-stained clothes, their wind-tossed hair, and realized how ragged they must look to others. They'd been wearing the same shabby garments for days.

She turned to Hodge. "Do you need us to fill out any documents?"

He gave a shake of his head. "That's my job."

"Would you mind dropping us here? You could bring the horse and wagon to the boardinghouse when you're finished at the jail."

"I don't mind a bit." He offered his hand and helped Molly down, while the three little girls tumbled from the back of the wagon, eager to see all the goodies in the store.

When Sarah hung back, Molly caught her hand. "Come with us, Sarah. You need a new dress and bonnet."

The girl hung her head. "You pick one for me, Aunt Molly. I'll just stay here."

Molly lowered her voice. "I know that right now you think everybody will be talking and staring. But nobody knows what we've been through. And nobody need know, unless you feel like telling them. For now, let's get what we need, and then go with Mrs. Teasdale to her boarding-house, where we can relax before facing the journey home."

"Can't we just go home now?"

Molly gave a gentle shake of her head. "I don't know about you, but I need a warm bath, clean clothes, and one of Martha Teasdale's fabulous meals. And best of all, I want to sleep in a soft bed tonight before facing another day in that wagon."

As she'd hoped, Sarah was persuaded to climb down. The older girl walked slowly behind the younger ones as they made their way to the mercantile.

Hodge waited until they disappeared inside before flicking the reins.

At the end of the main street he brought the horse and wagon to a halt in front of the jail and hauled Eli Otto from the back of the wagon.

Once his prisoner was behind bars, he had to shake off his fatigue to fill out the dozens of documents required and prepare the telegraph message to the authorities in the state capital, as well as Chicago, assuring them that he'd completed his assignment and had captured the dangerous criminal.

Police Chief Dan Marlow was an amiable fellow, with sandy hair, a red face, and a reddish mustache that drooped at the corners.

When Hodge asked to have a doctor check out Eli's wounds, he sent a deputy at once. A short time later the deputy arrived with the doctor in tow.

Dr. Woodrow Whitney, stick thin and more than six feet tall, introduced himself to Hodge.

"It isn't often we get a U.S. marshal in our little town."

Hodge smiled. "Your town looks like a big, bustling city after the time I've spent in the wilderness."

"I hear you got your man."

Hodge chuckled. "I did. But not without a lot of help from Miss Molly O'Brien and her girls."

The doctor's brow lifted. "You don't say?"

"It was Miss O'Brien who saved my life, as well as that of my prisoner, without knowing which of us she could trust. When she first came upon us in her field, we were more dead than alive."

The doctor cleared his throat and glanced at the police chief. "Our Miss O'Brien is a strong woman. There's no doubt about that. Even if she is a bit of a free spirit."

Hodge met his look. "I wouldn't be here if not for her. Now"—He turned—"You'd better take a look at the prisoner's leg."

The doctor held his little black bag at his side and waited while the cell door was unlocked. Once he was inside, the door was locked, and at Hodge's command, the deputy remained just outside the door, pistol at the ready.

The doctor's work took him more than an hour. When he finally stepped from the cell he glanced at the marshal. "If you'd like, I'll take a look at your wounds now."

"I'm fine."

Dr. Whitney smiled. "I'm sure you are, Marshal, but I'll just have a look anyway."

As Hodge rolled his sleeve and stuck out his arm, the doctor took his time examining the newest wound. "Looks like you got sliced up pretty good."

"The prisoner's knife."

"You're lucky he didn't have a gun."

"He did. Several, in fact."

The doctor looked up from the clean linen he was tying on Hodge's arm.

Hodge gave him a grim smile. "I told you I owe my life to Miss O'Brien and her girls. They're not just good at doctoring. They're pretty handy with weapons, too. They're as responsible for the return of this prisoner as I am."

Dr. Whitney glanced toward Chief Marlow. "I suppose none of us should be surprised. We've always known that Molly O'Brien is different from most folks."

When the doctor took his leave, Chief Marlow turned to Hodge. "Will you be staying at Mrs. Teasdale's boardinghouse?"

Hodge looked past him to where Eli Otto sat brooding behind bars. "I'd like that. But I'm thinking I'd better stay close to my prisoner. He's sly."

The chief shrugged. "Suit yourself. We have a room in back. Nothing more than a cot. You could still take your supper at the boardinghouse, or if you'd like, I could bring back a tray after I've had my supper."

Hodge nodded. "I'll take you up on that tray, Chief Marlow. Now." He glanced out the window. "I think I'll take myself over to the barbershop for a shave and a nice, hot bath."

"That's the place for it." Chief Marlow picked up his hat. "I'll leave my deputy here while I go over to the widow Teasdale's place. Your supper should be here in an hour or so."

"I'm much obliged." Hodge stepped out the door and sauntered over to the barbershop and bathhouse.

As he stepped inside he heard the low hum of masculine conversation and breathed in the rich aroma of cigars that permeated the air. He gave a deep sigh of pure pleasure. Now this had been worth waiting for.

MOLLY SURVEYED HER girls in their new gowns. "If you don't look as pretty as a row of flowers in the garden."

They giggled and turned to admire themselves in the looking glass.

Though Sarah hadn't been able to work up much enthusiasm, she allowed her aunt to brush her long red hair until it crackled.

Molly leaned over to kiss her niece's cheek. "In that yellow dress you look as fresh as a daisy."

"You look pretty, too, Aunt Molly."

At her words, Molly chuckled. "Pink wouldn't have been my first choice, but it was the only gown in Mr. Chalmers's mercantile that fit me."

Flora turned from the mirror. "I bet Marshal Egan will think you look pretty."

Molly's cheeks turned bright red. "Come on. Let's go downstairs and see if Martha Teasdale needs our help in the kitchen."

As she started down the steps behind her girls, Molly felt light as air. She couldn't wait to see Hodge's reaction to her new gown. It would be the first time he'd ever seen her all cleaned up, without smelling of cheese or cow dung.

She hoped he might be persuaded to offer her a compliment. If that should happen, perhaps later, when the girls had retired for the night, she would work up enough courage to talk to him about his plans for the future.

MOLLY AND THE girls sipped lemonade in the parlor, while several of the guests enjoyed a taste of Martha Teasdale's fine elderberry wine.

The talk was all about the capture of the infamous outlaw, Eli Otto.

Cyrus Keating, himself a banker, had plenty to say. He muttered an oath, then apologized to the women and children before saying, "I hope they hang that . . ." Again he apologized before adding, ". . . Outlaw."

"That'll be up to a judge." Dan Marlow stepped inside and accepted a glass of wine from Martha Teasdale, while acknowledging the others in the room.

"Chief Marlow." Molly stepped forward. "I thought the marshal would be with you."

"Sorry." He took a sip of his wine, wishing it was whiskey. "He said he'd rather sleep at the jail tonight, to keep an eye on his prisoner. He'll be taking him to Madison first thing in the morning."

Molly felt her hand bobble, and nearly spilled her lemonade before she hastily set the glass aside.

"Will he be joining us for supper?" Martha Teasdale asked.

The chief shook his head. "I promised to bring him a tray when I'm finished here."

Stricken, Molly stood perfectly still, clasping her hands tightly at her waist as she struggled to hold on to her emotions.

She'd known, of course, that the marshal had a job to do. He wasn't a man to take his responsibilities lightly. But he could have spent the night in comfort. Instead, he was sleeping in a room at the jail.

Was it responsibility, or the need to put some distance between them? The thought had her heart dropping to her toes.

"Molly? Are you coming?" At Martha's call, she looked up, only to find that the parlor was empty. The others had already moved on to the dining room.

"Yes. Of course." In a daze, she took her place at the table and helped pass platters and bowls and covered dishes.

Martha's suppers were famous for their variety. There was goose and roast beef smothered in rich gravy. There was a bowl of smooth-as-silk mashed potatoes, crusty bread still warm from the oven, garden peas, tiny carrots, and beets drizzled with butter. And for dessert, pound cake mounded with heavy cream.

Molly ate without tasting a thing. She seemed completely unaware of the conversation buzzing around her.

Across the table the banker was asking yet another question of the police chief.

"How many people has Eli Otto killed?"

"The marshal isn't sure of that. There's the bank clerk and bank president in Madison, of course, and the chief of police there. Apparently there are others. Eli Otto's aunt was found dead, her money missing, when he was just a boy. Some in their town believe it was his doing. The authorities will be looking into a string of murders across the country, to see if Eli can be recognized by anybody in those towns."

Molly looked thunderstruck. "So many. I suppose we're lucky to be alive."

"Not according to the marshal." The chief sat back and drained his cup of coffee. "He claims it's all because of you. You and your girls. He said if it hadn't been for all of you, he'd have died in your field." He turned to the others. "Marshal Egan said that by the time Molly and her children found him, he was more dead than alive. He claims that if it hadn't been for their care, he wouldn't have survived his wounds. And when they finally caught up with the outlaw, the marshal claims Molly and her girls were absolutely fearless." He touched a napkin to his mouth and said, "Mrs. Teasdale, that was just about the best meal I've ever tasted."

The woman beamed as she topped off his cup. She was as pleased by the gossip as by the compliment. For weeks to come, people would flock to her boardinghouse just to hear every tidbit of this exciting news. "Would you care for another slice of cake, Chief Marlow?"

"No, thanks. I'd better get back now. But I'd be happy to carry those trays to my deputy and Marshal Egan."

"No need. I'll see to them myself." Martha hurried to the kitchen, with her serving girls in tow, eager to get over to the jail. It wasn't often their town hosted such a handsome, rugged stranger.

The gentlemen were excusing themselves and heading for the parlor, where they would take a brandy before retiring.

As soon as she could escape, Molly led the way up the stairs, and though she was eager to flee to the privacy of her own room, she knew she needed to take the time to hear the children's prayers and kiss each of them good night.

Flora was untying her sash when she caught the look of pain in Molly's eyes. At once she crossed the room to tug on the woman's skirt. "What's wrong, Mama Molly?"

Molly sniffed, fighting tears. "Nothing, Flora."

The little girl put her hands on her hips and managed a stern look. "You taught us that lying was wrong."

Molly's eyes widened. For the space of a heartbeat she was speechless. Then, dropping to her knees, she met the little girl's direct stare. "You're right. I should never lie. I'm sad, Flora."

"Is it something I did?"

"Of course not." Molly gathered her close and could feel her breath hitch. Though she wasn't certain she could get through this, she had to try. "I'm sad because Marshal Egan is leaving in the morning."

"Isn't that what he's supposed to do?"

By now the other girls had stopped undressing and were forming a circle around Molly and Flora.

"It is. Yes. He's a man of the law, and it's his job to take his prisoner back for trial."

"Then why are you sad about it?"

Molly dragged in a breath. "Because . . ." She could feel her lower lip quivering and bit down hard.

"Mama Molly, are you crying?"

The little girl's earnest concern was the last straw. Molly turned away to hide the tears that welled up.

It was Sarah who suddenly understood. "You . . . have feelings for the marshal."

Flora looked from Sarah to Molly. "What kind of feelings?"

"She loves him, silly."

Three little girls gave simultaneous gasps.

Still, Flora needed to hear it from Molly's own lips. Touching a chubby hand to her cheek she stared intently into her eyes. "Is that true? Do you love the marshal?"

Molly couldn't seem to swallow the lump in her throat. All she could do was nod helplessly as the tears began filling her eyes while she blinked furiously.

At the sight of her tears, the children began patting her arms, her shoulders, her back, in the hope of offering comfort.

"Come on, Aunt Molly." Wanting to spare her aunt any further embarrassment, Sarah took her arm and led her out the door and across the hall to the pretty little room that had been made up for her.

Once in her own room, Molly dropped down on the bed while Sarah drew the covers over her.

"You rest now, Aunt Molly."

With her finger to her lips, Sarah pushed the others ahead of her and firmly closed the door.

Then they stood outside, listening.

Alone in her room, away from prying eyes, Molly did

something she'd never done in her life. She began to cry, softly at first, and then, as the storm was finally unleashed, great gulping sobs that were torn from her throat.

Hot, scalding tears flowed like a river down her cheeks, dampening the coverlet.

With her face buried in the pillow she wept until there were no tears left. Finally, exhausted from the torrent of emotions, she lay still as death, her mind emptied, her throat raw.

Her poor heart, she knew, would never be the same again. And though she was very good at tending others, she had no idea how to mend her own wounds.

TWENTY-ONE

———◆◈◆———

THE FOUR GIRLS gathered in their bedroom, their faces revealing their distress.

Sarah slumped down on the edge of one of the beds. "I've never seen Aunt Molly cry before."

"Me either." Confused and frightened, Delia caught her big sister's hand and clung.

"Should we have left her alone?" Charity was twisting the hem of her new dress around and around her finger.

"We had to." Sarah's brow furrowed. "You could see that she didn't want to cry in front of us."

"But what'll we do?" Charity's little face was turning red, a sure sign that she was about to cry, as well.

Sarah shrugged. "I don't see that there's anything we can do."

"Oh, yes, there is." Flora stood in the middle of the room, her hands balled into fists at her hips. "We can go over to the jail and tell the marshal that we know what he's done to Mama Molly."

"Flora!" Sarah was clearly shocked. "We couldn't."

"Why not?" Delia looked from her sister to Flora and back.

"Because"—Sarah chewed her bottom lip—"We can't meddle in grown-up affairs."

"Why can't we?" Flora could see that Sarah was hesitating, and as always, forged ahead fearlessly. "Mama Molly would meddle if one of us was hurting, wouldn't she?"

"Wouldn't she?" Delia repeated.

Sarah sighed. "I suppose she would."

"You see?" Flora was already heading toward the door.

"Where are you going?"

"To the jail. You coming?" Flora flounced out the door and down the stairs, without bothering to see if the others were following.

When they stepped outside, Sarah and Delia and Charity raced down the front steps and caught up with her along the path.

"What if Aunt Molly gets mad?" Sarah had to hurry her steps to keep up with the little girl who was now running in her haste to settle this matter.

"I'd rather see her mad than the way she looked when we left her."

Flora's words had the others straightening their spines as they raced through town, past the mercantile, past the dispensary, past the bath and barbershop, and straight to the end of the street, where they paused outside the jail.

Before the others could catch their breath Flora yanked open the door.

They saw the deputy seated at a desk. Just beyond him was a cell. Inside they could see the outlaw, Eli Otto, lying on a cot. The marshal was nowhere in sight.

"Can I help you?" the deputy called out.

"We came to talk to Marshal Hodge Egan."

The deputy grinned. "He's not here. Would you like to tell me what this is about? Or would you rather come back later?"

"Where is he?" Flora had appointed herself leader of the group.

"He's over at the bath and barbershop. But I wouldn't go there if I were . . ."

He found himself talking to air. The four girls had already spun away, slamming the door shut behind them.

They retraced their steps until they were standing in front of the barbershop.

"Wait, Flora. I don't think this is a good—" Sarah looked up as the door opened.

Samuel Schroeder stepped out alongside his father. Both father and son were sporting fresh haircuts.

"Well." Mr. Schroeder stopped to smile warmly at the girls. "We heard you folks were back in town. Your arrival with the marshal and his prisoner has caused quite a stir."

Samuel didn't speak, but merely stared at Sarah while his face turned beet red, all the way to the tips of his ears. Sarah, too, was blushing and couldn't seem to find her voice.

It fell to Flora to take charge. "Mr. Schroeder, we're looking for the marshal. Have you seen him?"

"I have indeed. A fine fellow, he is. But I wouldn't go in there if I were you young ladies. He's busy enjoying . . ."

His words trailed off as Flora flounced inside, followed by Delia and Charity. Sarah remained in the doorway, staring silently at Samuel, until his father dropped an arm around his shoulders and steered him toward their waiting wagon and team.

Over his shoulder Mr. Schroeder called, "I hope you folks will stop by our farm on your way home."

"I don't know if we . . . can." Sarah watched as Samuel followed his father's lead and climbed to the seat of the wagon.

It didn't matter what she said. They couldn't hear her. Besides, she reasoned, it hadn't been Samuel who had invited her; it had been his father, who was merely being polite.

As their wagon started away, Samuel turned and lifted a hand in salute. Sarah was so startled, she merely stared after them, her hands frozen by her sides. By the time she got her wits about her and waved back, Samuel had turned away and was staring straight ahead.

With a wave of self-revulsion, Sarah went in search of the others.

HODGE RECLINED IN a tub of steaming water, a cigar in one hand, a glass of fine whiskey in the other. After a haircut and shave, he was feeling almost human again.

One of the lads who worked in the bathhouse, Silas Rothwell, stopped by with another bucket of hot water.

As he emptied it, Hodge flipped him a coin. "See that you keep 'em coming, Silas."

"Yes, sir." Delighted, the boy pocketed the coin and

hurried away to heat more water over the stove.

Hodge drew deeply on the cigar and watched as a wreath of smoke curled over his head. He leaned back and closed his eyes.

This was heaven.

Everything that he'd had to endure on this miserable assignment had been worth it, just so he could enjoy this moment. Being forced to leave the comfort of Chicago to track that miserable Eli Otto; having to survive in the wilderness, without any of the luxuries he'd come to expect, was all behind him now.

It was hard to believe that scant weeks ago he'd been more dead than alive. Now, here he was, his wounds healing nicely according to Doc Whitney, and his assignment successfully completed.

Now that he'd had the luxury of time to mull his future, he realized that it was time to accept some cold, hard facts. He was sick and tired of enforcing the law. He'd earned the right to retire and spend the rest of his life doing as he pleased. The telegram accepting his resignation, and promising a fat bonus, had sealed his fate.

"You can't come in here!" At the sound of the lad's cry of alarm, Hodge's eyes snapped open.

Walking toward him were Flora, Delia, and Charity. Running to catch up with them was Sarah, whose face was nearly as red as her hair.

"Marshal." Silas hurried forward. "I tried to tell them they couldn't . . ."

Hodge lifted a hand. "It's all right, Silas." He turned to the girls. "Well, don't you look pretty. Mr. Chalmers must have been happy to see you bringing him so much business. In those new dresses you look like a garden of pretty flowers."

Delia and Charity covered their mouths and giggled. Sarah stared hard at the toe of her new boots, acutely aware of the fact that she was in a man's bathhouse.

Flora's dark eyes flashed fire. "Is that what you told Mama Molly? That she looked like a pretty bird?"

Hodge almost swallowed his cigar. Choking, he set it on the side of the tub and shot her a look guaranteed to freeze the blood of the most hardened outlaw. "Why don't you tell me what this visit is about?"

"It's about what you did to Mama Molly."

"What I . . . ?" Did they know what had transpired that night? It didn't seem like something Molly would have confided to little girls. Maybe they were guessing. Or fishing. Hell, they were only kids. But then, he didn't know much about what kids knew these days.

His whiskey was forgotten now. He sat up, sending sudsy water sloshing over the edge of the tub.

He took no notice of the puddles of water as he growled, "I suggest you say what you came here to say. All of it."

"Did you tell Mama Molly that she was beautiful?"

"Flora!" Sarah was scandalized at her boldness.

Hodge was merely puzzled. "Of course I did. It's the truth. She is beautiful."

"And did you tell her you loved her?"

He shrugged. "Why do you care?"

"Because Chief Marlow told us at supper that you're leaving in the morning for Madison."

"That's right. I'm a U.S. marshal. I have a job to do. And I intend to do it."

"When your job is done, will you be coming back here to marry Mama Molly?"

"Marry"—He gritted his teeth—"That's an impertinent question."

Flora lifted her head the way he'd often seen Molly lift hers when she'd been challenged. "I don't know what impertent means."

"Impertinent. Bold. Like you, Flora."

Instead of backing down, she repeated her question. "Will you be coming back here to marry Mama Molly?"

Hodge could feel himself beginning to sweat, and blamed it on the hot water. It was true that he'd given it some thought. Hell, a lot of thought. And had discounted it as nothing more than pure foolishness. How could he expect to make a life for himself with Molly O'Brien? She lived a simple life as a farmer. It was the very life he'd been eager to leave behind all those years ago. He simply wasn't cut out to be a farmer. Besides, people married because they could be a helpmate to one another. How could he possibly hope to help that independent female? She could work circles around most folks he knew. The only thing he knew how to do was handle weapons and cards, neither of which would help Molly or her brood.

Four pairs of eyes were watching him closely. Four little girls didn't move. Didn't even seem to breathe.

"Okay. Fair enough. I can see that it's time for some honesty, no matter how tough the question or the answer."

He deliberately kept his tone level. "When my job is done, I plan on going to San Francisco."

"Why?" Sarah blurted out.

Hodge heard the pain in that single word, and decided to be brutal, as well as honest. "For years I've been planning on spending the rest of my life in San Francisco. I've earned the right to do as I please. And now, by God, I intend to do it."

"What about Mama Molly?" Flora demanded.

"You wanted the truth. Here it is." Hodge's voice lowered to a whisper. "The truth is, I'm not the marrying kind. I wouldn't be any good at it. And I'm certainly not cut out to be a farmer. The only thing I'm good at is handling a gun. And winning at cards and dice. I'd just be one more mouth for Molly to feed. And after a while, with my vile temper, and the fact that I'd want to be as much in charge as your aunt, she'd want me gone. All of you would. And that's the plain truth."

Delia and Charity started to cry.

Annoyed, Hodge signaled to Silas, who hurried over to dump another bucket of hot water into the tub.

Without a word Sarah grabbed hold of Delia's and Charity's hands and dragged them toward the door.

Flora refused to follow. Instead she stood her ground, staring at the marshal with those big, dark, wise old eyes.

Hodge looked over. "You got something left to say?"

"Mama Molly loves you."

He took a direct blow to the heart. "Did she tell you that, Flora?"

The little girl shook her head.

"Then how could you possibly know how she feels about me?"

"Because she was crying over you."

Another blow that had Hodge's jaw dropping before he recovered and clenched his teeth to keep from saying a word.

Flora's hands fisted on her hips. "I was wrong about you. That mean old outlaw isn't the only bad man. You're not a good man. Not when you hurt Mama Molly after all she did for you."

She turned on her heels and stormed out of the bathhouse, leaving Hodge to stare after her.

He took a puff on his cigar, but it tasted like ash. He sipped his whiskey, but it had gone flat.

He leaned back and closed his eyes, determined to enjoy his bath. But all he could see was Molly, keeping the girls busy and entertained day after day, while seeing to the million and one things necessary to their well-being. Molly, giving up the safety and comfort of her home to scour the countryside in search of Sarah. Molly standing up to Eli Otto without a care for her own safety.

Molly, weeping.

It was the one thing he couldn't bear to imagine. It just didn't fit the image he had of that fiery, independent female who could do anything she set her mind to.

In truth, he'd allowed himself a brief fantasy about making a life with Molly O'Brien and her girls. He'd almost convinced himself that it could happen. But that was pure selfishness on his part. She was beautiful, unmarried, and the kind of woman a man dreamed about on long, lonely nights. She had a successful farm, a growing family, and a satisfying life. What did he have to offer such a woman?

Other than his skill with a gun, he had no talents to speak of. The only thing his presence in Molly's life would do was create more work for her. She had enough of that already.

If he really cared for her . . . He clenched a fist as he mulled the word he found so difficult to even acknowledge. Love. Such an awesome word. An even more awesome feeling. But if he truly *loved* Molly, then he would do what was best for her, no matter what the cost to him.

He stood up, the water sheeting down his body, and reached for a towel. Somehow, this whole celebration had gone just as flat as his whiskey.

TWENTY-TWO

———❖———

"TIME TO GET up, girls." Molly forced herself to put one foot in front of the other, moving from bed to bed, laying out their clothes. "I told Martha Teasdale that we'd have breakfast here before heading out. Old Clement is already hitching our horse. He'll be bringing the wagon around shortly."

"Mama Molly?" Flora saw the way Sarah's head came up sharply, as if to remind her of their pact. Before going to sleep, the four girls had agreed not to tell Molly about their visit with the marshal. It wasn't lying, Sarah had insisted. It was the right thing to do, if they wanted to avoid causing her any more pain.

"Yes, Flora?"

"Nothing." The little girl used that moment to study Molly's weary, red-rimmed eyes before dropping to the floor to struggle into her new cotton stockings.

"Aunt Molly?" Sarah gathered her courage. "Will we be stopping at the Schroeder farm on the way home?"

Molly sighed. "I don't think so. I'd just like to get home."

"Yes'm." Sarah couldn't decide if she was happy or sad about her aunt's decision. On the one hand, Samuel had waved good-bye. But on the other hand, maybe he was just being polite and would have waved good-bye to anyone. Besides, the Schroeder family might want to talk about their adventure with the outlaw, and Sarah was certainly not ready to discuss it with anyone, especially in front of Samuel. Not when she was weighed down with all this guilt.

When the four girls were dressed, they followed Molly down the stairs to the dining room, where several guests and townspeople were already gathered for another of Martha Teasdale's fine meals.

There were coddled eggs and thick slices of ham. There were flapjacks and syrup, and freshly baked bread with some of Annabelle Whitney's strawberry preserves. There were gallons of foamy milk and mugs of steaming coffee. And through it all, Molly was forced to make pleasant conversation.

If anyone noticed her weariness, they were quick to blame it on her recent adventure in the wilderness. Facing danger at the hands of a hardened outlaw was enough to give anyone a few sleepless nights.

"I believe I hear Clement with your wagon, Molly."

At Martha's words, Molly and the girls shoved away from the table. They were heading along the hallway when Martha, stepping onto the front porch, called, "Will you look at that? It appears the marshal is coming to pay a call."

Everyone hurried from the dining room and began congregating on the porch and steps.

Molly felt her heartbeat begin racing. Her palms were sweating. He'd come to his senses. He was coming to tell her he loved her. He wanted a future with her. He would be back when he'd delivered his prisoner.

With a spring in her step she hurried outside and waited beside her wagon, watching as the rig, with Hodge and a deputy seated up front, Eli in shackles in back, rolled to a stop.

Hodge stepped down and glanced at the children, who were eyeing him with equal parts of curiosity and hostility. Then he turned to Molly.

Why did she have to look so pretty in that new pink gown? Why did her hair have to billow down around her face and shoulders like a bridal veil? Why did he want, desperately, to kiss every one of those freckles parading across her nose?

Conscious of the people who were watching and listening, he doffed his hat and used his most formal tone. " 'Morning, Miss O'Brien."

"Marshal." She was clutching her hands together at her waist so tightly the knuckles were white from the effort.

"I brought you some good news."

Molly was vaguely aware of the children smiling and whispering among themselves. Did they know something she didn't? "Good news?"

"That's right." He reached into his pocket and withdrew a telegram. "I wired the authorities with the news of what you had done, and they agreed that you had earned the reward that had been offered for the capture of Eli Otto. A sum of one thousand dollars will be sent to the bank here in Delight and credited to your account."

"The reward?" She felt an odd sort of buzzing in her brain. She was suddenly dizzy and light-headed, as though, if she but moved from this spot, her legs would fail her and she would foolishly drop to the ground. It was a supreme effort to remain standing. "That's your good news?"

He handed her the document, and their fingers brushed. Even though Hodge had prepared himself for this, he felt the rush of heat all the way to his toes and pulled his hand back as though burned.

"You should be proud. You have the gratitude of your government for all that you did." He lowered his voice. "And you have my gratitude, as well. You saved my life, not once but twice, and for that I will be forever in your debt."

She swallowed hard. And then, because there were so many watching and listening, she found the strength she could always count on in times of need. "I don't want your gratitude, Marshal." Her voice was cool. Controlled. Haughty as an ice princess. "You owe me nothing."

He hated that so many had gathered to watch them. There was no possible way he could inject anything personal into their conversation. Not that he wanted to. This was business. Official business. Still, the thought of holding her, for just a moment, had him swaying toward her.

Of course, if he were to hold her, for even a heartbeat, he'd have to kiss her. And if he should kiss her even once, he'd never be able to let her go.

"Whether you want it or not, you have it. My gratitude, and that of my superiors. You and your girls showed amazing courage under fire. Thank you."

Because there was nothing more to say, and because he couldn't bear another moment of her glacial stare and stony silence, he turned away and climbed to the seat of the rig. With a tip of his hat he saluted the crowd smartly, and flicked the reins. The team leaned into the harness and the rig rolled ahead.

"Oh my." Martha Teasdale hurried forward to lay a hand on Molly's arm. "That man is so handsome and rugged, I could almost faint."

"Try to control yourself, Martha." Molly was grateful that her voice didn't tremble and reveal her true emotions. Nobody standing nearby could see what this had cost her.

"You're the only woman I know who wouldn't be thrilled to spend time in that man's company. No wonder you've never married. Not that there hasn't been ample opportunity." The widow sighed while Molly gritted her teeth. "And a thousand dollars. Think of all you can buy with that reward money."

"I'm sure I'll think of a few things we need." Molly tucked the telegram into her waistband and signaled to the girls. "Come along now. It's time to head home."

She helped the little ones into the back of the wagon before climbing to the hard wooden seat and picking up the reins. Sarah surprised her by choosing to sit up front beside her.

Molly managed a tight smile. "Thank you for your hospitality, Martha. We're grateful."

"You know you're always welcome here, Molly. Please come back soon. There's a new farmer moved into the old Hoskin's farm. I hear he's looking for a wife. Next time you're in town, I'll have him to supper."

"You might want to keep him for yourself." Molly flicked the reins and they rolled through town before heading across the hills toward home.

Theirs was a solemn, subdued group. There was no singing. No sums to tally, no words to spell. The little girls in back, sensing their aunt's mood, talked quietly among themselves or dozed amid the quilts and pillows.

When she was certain the girls were asleep in the back of the wagon, Sarah glanced over at her aunt. "Aunt Molly?"

"Yes, Sarah?" Molly kept her gaze averted, staring straight ahead, bravely fighting the ache around her heart.

She would not cry again, she told herself. Not ever. Especially over a man who didn't even care enough about her feelings to spare her the time of day.

She had foolishly believed that he'd come to his senses and would ask her to wait for him. She would have waited a lifetime, if he'd asked. Instead, he'd only been interested in making some sort of grand gesture for the whole town to witness. A reward. Scant weeks ago she'd have thought a thousand dollars a princely sum. Now it paled in comparison to what she'd really set her sights on.

"I'm sorry, Aunt Molly."

Molly's head came up as she dragged herself back from her reverie. "For what?"

"For everything. I've made such a mess of things. If I hadn't believed that outlaw's lies, none of this would have happened. He"—Sarah sniffed back tears—"Called me a woman. Nobody had ever called me that before. And he said I was pretty. A pretty little milkmaid. And I believed him. And because of that, I betrayed you. All of you. For a pack of mean, petty lies."

"Now you listen to me." Molly slowed the horse to a walk and dropped her arm around Sarah's shoulders, drawing her close. "Why wouldn't you believe it when he said you were pretty? You are. As for calling you a woman, it's easy to see that you're growing into one. You're a beautiful young woman, Sarah. Why shouldn't you believe the truth?"

"You're just saying that to make me feel better."

Molly lifted the girl's face to meet her eyes. "No, luv. I'm telling you this because it's the truth. You are truly lovely. And some day the right man will come along and appreciate not only your beauty, but your goodness."

The girl continued to shake her head in disbelief, unwilling to listen to her aunt's words meant to comfort.

Molly took a deep breath, and realized that she needed to say more. "As for believing that outlaw, I'm just as guilty."

"You?"

Molly nodded. "I allowed myself to believe all the marshal's sweet lies."

The girl drew back. "Don't say that, Aunt Molly."

"It's the truth. When he told me I was pretty, I wanted to believe him. And even when he tried to do the right thing by me, I wouldn't listen. I wanted to let myself be sweet-talked. While you were being tricked by a slick young outlaw, I was being tricked, too. By my own foolish heart. So you see? I'm old enough to know better. And still, I made such a mess of things. A fine, grand mess."

"But the marshal is a good man, Aunt Molly. He didn't lie to you, did he?"

"No, luv. He never lied. Nor did he make me any promises. I was the foolish one, hoping that he would be so dazzled by my beauty, he would want to make a future here with me. With us. It was a pretty dream, but a silly one. I'm no dazzling beauty. And my life is hardly the stuff of men's dreams."

"You're beautiful to me, Aunt Molly."

"And you to me, luv." She kissed Sarah's brow. "We'll talk no more about blame or guilt. We've both made mistakes, and we'll learn from them."

Sarah took a deep, shuddering breath. "Will I ever feel good about myself?"

"You will. We both will. In time."

On a sigh Sarah said, "I'll never trust a man again. Not ever."

"Don't say that, luv. Don't even think it. There are plenty of good men in the world. They shouldn't bear the blame for the few who chose to be otherwise." She took a deep breath. "For now, we'll go home, thankful that we're all safe."

"But what about your broken heart, Aunt Molly?"

Molly flicked the reins, urging the horse into a trot. "Hearts mend. I've always found that there's nothing like hard work to take your mind off your troubles."

Oh, she prayed it was so. But she knew it would take a heap of hard, physical work to put Hodge Egan out of her mind, not to mention getting him out of her heart.

If she could, she would just lie down and weep and wail and wallow in misery. But there were four girls who needed her. Four girls who were watching her and learning how to live. And though she resented the work that loomed in her future, she was grateful for it, as well. It would, she knew, be the key to surviving this all-consuming pain around her heart. A pain caused not by Hodge Egan, but by her own foolishness. Hodge had never been anything but honest with her. She'd been the one to take his honesty and spin it into some silly fantasy.

Now she must pay the price.

TWENTY-THREE

"WE'VE FINISHED CLEANING the henhouse, Aunt Molly." Sarah herded the girls up the porch where they plunged their arms into a bucket of water and soaped thoroughly before drying and stepping inside.

"And just in time." Molly indicated the table, set with a platter of roast beef and cheese and hard-boiled eggs.

The kitchen was perfumed with the scent of freshly baked bread. Molly placed a slice on each of their plates, lavishly spread with apple butter, and filled four glasses with milk.

As Molly turned to the door Sarah called, "Aren't you going to have breakfast with us?"

"I'm not hungry, luv. I think I'll just head out to the barn and start my chores."

Flora stared at the closed door. "Mama Molly never eats anymore."

Sarah sighed. She'd noticed the same thing. In the

weeks since their return from town, her aunt worked from sunup to sundown. But when the others were asleep, Sarah often heard the sound of footsteps leading out to the summer porch, where she would find her aunt watching the moon, or perhaps the sunrise.

The first thing they'd done when they returned from town was to strip away all traces of the two men who had once occupied the porch and her aunt's bedroom. The pallets were gone, as well as the table that held medical supplies. The porch had been swept, and then scrubbed with hot, sudsy water until the wood gleamed. In the bedroom, Molly had stripped the bedding and hung it in the sunshine to bleach. She'd done the same with the rug on the floor, before scrubbing every inch of the bedroom floor. It had seemed, to Sarah, that her aunt was determined to erase even the faintest scent that might remind her of the man who'd been there.

But had she erased him from her heart?

As far as Sarah could see, there had been no trace of tears. Even when she came upon her aunt at sunrise, sitting on the porch, tea in hand, her eyes had been dry and bright. Perhaps a little too bright. But at least they were dry.

Sarah was determined to follow her aunt's lead. Though she still regretted, with every ounce of her being, the fact that she'd allowed herself to be misled, the pain had begun to fade. She could think of Eli Otto now as the cunning, sly killer he was, and hope that she would never forget the most important lesson he'd taught her. Even good looks and charm could hide an evil heart. What mattered most in a person was the goodness of his heart.

Sarah was certain that her aunt's open, honest heart was still shattered. But she was surviving, one day at a time.

Sarah was determined to do the same.

"After lunch, I think we should go to the barn and give Aunt Molly a hand."

"She'll be mucking stalls." Delia shuddered at the thought.

"All the more reason she'll appreciate our help." Sarah sipped her milk. "And then we'll tackle the garden. We need to pick the last of the vegetables before autumn comes. Aunt Molly will be wanting to store as much food as possible in the cellar before the first frost."

"I'll help," Flora said firmly.

"So will I." Charity drained her glass.

"All right." Delia was determined not to be left behind.

"Good." Sarah began gathering up the dishes. "Let's get started."

MOLLY HAD EXCHANGED her dress for the britches and shirt that she reserved for the tough farm chores. On her feet were dung-covered boots. On her head, a wide-brimmed hat to shield her fair skin from the sun. Not that it helped all that much. The freckles that paraded across her nose seemed even more pronounced in late summer.

She moved through the cow barn, forking dung and wet straw into the wagon. Later she would hitch the horse to the wagon and spread this manure over the fields that she was planning to plant next spring.

She welcomed the slow, tedious chore. While her hands stayed busy, she could let her mind work its way over knotty issues.

Ever since she'd shared her sorrow with Sarah, the two seemed to have formed an even closer bond. Sarah had begun showing a maturity that hadn't been apparent just weeks earlier. She'd taken over some of the most unpleasant chores without being asked. She had truly become a second mother to the younger girls, helping them with their lessons, sharing their chores without a word of protest. In return, the younger ones had changed, as well. Not only did they offer help without complaining, but they'd actually begun to show an interest in the process of cheese-making. If they kept it up, they could more than double the amount of cheese they produced next year.

Molly wanted to experiment with other cheeses. Not just the cheddar, which brought compliments from all her neighbors, but some of the soft cheeses as well. Already her neighbors called it O'Brien's Farm Cheese. The thought of it had her smiling. Someday, all of Wisconsin would know that name. Maybe the entire country would be buying her cheese.

She leaned on the pitchfork and stared off into space. Would Hodge see it in San Francisco one day, and think of her?

Annoyed that he had once again crept into her thoughts, she gave a vicious swipe with her pitchfork, hurling dung into the cart. He wasn't worth thinking about.

By now he would be in some fancy gentlemen's club, drinking whiskey, smoking cigars, and gambling away his money. Well, let him. It wasn't any of her concern.

And if he told other women they were pretty, and took them to his bed . . .

She felt a shaft of pain around her heart and closed her eyes to dispel the thought.

What Hodge Egan did with his life was none of her business.

She took another vicious swipe.

"Careful, Aunt Molly."

She turned to find the four girls wearing boots and holding rakes and pitchforks. They had tied on pinafores over their dresses.

"You don't need to help. This is much too hard."

"We want to." Sarah motioned to the three younger girls and they fanned out, circling the cart and fighting to lift the straw and dung.

Molly watched them, struggling under the heavy load, and felt some of the sadness lift from her heart. They were so dear. And as transparent as glass. Whatever revulsion they felt about shoveling cow dung, they were willing to put it aside out of love for her. How could she not love them even more in return?

Sarah kept her head down as she worked. "We thought we'd finish picking the last of the garden after we're through here. I know you're worried about storing everything in the cellar before the first frost."

"I am, yes. The nights have been growing cooler. One of these mornings . . ."

She looked up at the sound of a horse's hooves. "Now who could that . . . ?"

They heard the crunch of footsteps, and saw a shadow fill the doorway of the barn. With the sunlight streaming in from behind, all they could see was a dark silhouette. But even that was enough to have them gasping in recognition.

"Hodge." It was the only word Molly spoke, before her throat went dry and her voice died.

The children gaped as, without a word, he continued standing there, his gaze fixed on Molly with fierce concentration.

At last Molly found her voice. "Have you forgotten something, Marshal?"

"I'm no longer a man of the law. I'm just plain Hodge Egan now."

"So you've retired as you planned." She was relieved to note that her tone was pure ice. Now if only she could command it to remain that way. "Why are you here?"

His voice sounded raw and weary. "I didn't want to come. I couldn't stay away. God knows I tried." His gaze was fixed on Molly with a kind of hunger that had her shivering. Though he hadn't touched her, she could feel him in every part of her body.

"After depositing my prisoner, I resigned my position and went back to Chicago to say good-bye to old friends. I actually boarded a train for San Francisco. Within two days I was so miserable, I got off the train at St. Louis and took another train back to Milwaukee, where I bought a horse and headed here."

"It seems you've burned a lot of bridges." Molly fought to keep her tone civil, though her legs were actually trembling. "Where will you go now?"

"There's no place I want to be except here."

She shook her head and took a step back. "That's not

possible. I have my reputation to think of, and that of my children."

He lifted a hand to stop her protest. "You misunderstand. I don't mean to just live here, Molly. I came here to ask you to marry me."

Seeing the electrifying looks passing among the girls, Molly's voice grew even colder. "Look around you, Hodge. You're on a simple farm in Wisconsin now. This is certainly no gentleman's club in San Francisco. No life of luxury. We work this farm from sunup to sundown. We make a decent living, but there's no money left over for games of chance."

His voice was deep with passion. "I've spent a lifetime playing games. Now I know that what I truly want is to be part of this family. I haven't been a farmer since I was young, but I still know how to work a farm. And if you'll have me, I'll even learn to make cheese."

Flora piped up, "But you said you weren't cut out to be a farmer and make cheese."

Molly turned to the little girl. "When did he say this?"

"That night we went to see him at the barbershop."

"You what?" Molly glanced around at the others, who hung their heads.

As always, it was Flora who plunged ahead. "You were crying, and we wanted to help."

Molly's tone was sharp as she looked at Hodge. "What did they tell you?"

"They pointed out the truth. That despite all my protests, I loved you." He stepped closer. "And they said you love me."

She took another step backward. "They're children. They can't possibly know—"

He held up a hand to stop her. "They're your children. And that makes them smart and independent and brutally honest."

She started to smile. "I could almost believe you mean that as a compliment."

"I do." He cleared his throat. "Molly, I've had a lot of time to think about what I wanted to tell you. I hope you'll hear me out."

When she didn't protest, he took her silence for permission. "You know what it's like to have a dream. It's hard to give up on it. But something strange happened to me. After meeting you, I realized that everything I'd been planning for my future was just pure foolishness. When I turned my back on my childhood farm, I never thought I'd want to return. And now, I can't imagine my life anywhere else. This is where I want to spend the rest of my days. Here. With you. That is, if you'll have me."

He dropped to one knee and caught her hand in his. "Molly, you'd make me the happiest man in the world if you could put away the things I did to hurt you and agree to marry me."

She'd steeled herself against ever hearing those words. But now that they'd been spoken, she needed to be certain. She couldn't trust the way her heart was behaving. She snatched her hand away. "I'll remind you that I come with responsibilities. Four of them, to be exact. These girls are my children, as surely as if I'd given them life. Any man who takes me, takes them on, as well."

"I'd like that. I'm not sure I'll be any good at being a father, but I'd like to try."

She saw the wide grins on the girls' faces, and cautioned, "Four busy children leave little time for privacy."

He winked. "I'm sure we'll find a way. It didn't stop us before."

Molly wondered at the way her poor heart was racing. It was a wonder it didn't fly clear out of her chest.

Still, she needed to be sensible. She wasn't in this alone.

She turned to the girls. "This can't be my decision alone. It affects all of us. I'd like to know what you think about making Hodge part of our family."

Charity giggled. "I've always thought it would be fun to have a papa."

Delia blushed. "All the girls in Delight have daddies. Why shouldn't we?"

Sarah studied her aunt's eyes and, seeing the light that had come into them, after so many nights of darkness, slowly nodded. "I guess I wouldn't mind."

It was Flora who would have the last word. "You'll be our papa? A real papa? And we'll be a family? A real family?"

Hodge gave a solemn nod. "That's my hope."

"Will we call you Papa Hodge?"

He wondered at the strange tingle around his heart at those words. "I'd like that."

"There's just one thing." The little girl wasn't finished with him yet. "You have to promise you'll never ever make Mama Molly cry."

Hodge could feel the beginnings of a grin touch the

corners of his mouth. "I give you my word, Flora, that I'll do my best to keep that promise every day of my life."

The four girls turned to Molly, who was shaking her head in wonder. It didn't seem possible that the dream she'd cherished, the dream that had been dashed to bits, was whole again, as was her poor, shattered heart. And all because of this brash, tough, horrible, wonderful man, who had touched her heart in a way that no other man ever had.

She met Hodge's eyes. "Well then, I guess it's settled. If my girls are willing to take you, how can I refuse?"

"Do you mean it?" Hodge stepped closer, still afraid to touch her. Once he did, there would be no stopping him.

"I do." She leaned toward him, then seemed to realize that she had an audience.

Flora looked from Hodge to Molly. "Are you going to kiss now?"

Hodge winked. "That's my plan."

Sarah began herding the girls from the barn. "We'll get started on picking the garden clean."

Flora planted herself squarely in front of Molly and Hodge. "I'm not going. I want to stay and—"

Her protest turned into a yelp when Sarah picked her up and carried her from the barn.

When the door was closed behind them, Hodge took Molly's hand. "All the way here I was so afraid."

"Of what?" She could feel the warmth of his hand slowly begin to melt the ice that had formed around her heart.

"Of you. I was afraid you wouldn't be able to forgive

me for the way I carelessly hurt you. Molly, you're the dearest, sweetest woman I've ever known. I close my eyes and see your beautiful face, and think about all the hateful things I—"

"Hush now." Molly touched a hand to his cheek. Just a touch, but he could feel the heat rush through his veins. "We won't think about the past. We'll look ahead to the future."

At last, Hodge realized that he really had a future. Here. With this beautiful woman and the girls she'd made her family.

"It's been so long, Molly, since I held you. Loved you. Let me love you now."

She tried to draw back. "I'm filthy. I smell of barn and manure and . . ."

"Molly O'Brien, even in britches, mucking stalls, you're the most beautiful woman I've ever known. You're all I've thought of on this long, lonely ride. And I don't want to wait another minute." He gathered her into his arms and kissed her long and slow and deep until they were both trembling with need.

She lifted her face to stare into his eyes. "Do you know how long I've waited to hear you say that?"

Against her mouth he whispered, "I promise to tell you every day of our lives together."

They came together in a firestorm of passion that had them both dragging air into their lungs.

Hodge lifted his head to run soft, wet kisses over her cheek, her brow, her forehead. "There's so much more I want to tell—"

She stopped him with a finger to his lips. "There's no need. Just show me, Hodge."

And then there were no words as they showed each other, in the way lovers have from the beginning of time, all the desperate feelings they were finally free to express.

EPILOGUE

———◆◆◆———

"GETTING BUTTERFLIES, LAWMAN?" Old Addison stepped from the woods, keeping one hand behind his back.

Hodge turned from the long wooden table he'd hauled behind the barn to hold the jug of whiskey and the box of fine cigars he'd brought from town for the men who would be attending the wedding.

"Not a chance. I'm sure Molly is having second thoughts about taking on another mouth to feed, but the only way she's going to get out of marrying me is by running away from home."

The old man chuckled. "I doubt she'd get too far before you'd catch her."

"You've got that right." Hodge poured a tumbler of whiskey and handed it to Addison, then poured one for himself as well.

The two men sipped. It was clear that the former slave

had managed to put aside his dislike for this particular man of the law. In the weeks since Hodge had returned, the two had formed an easy friendship.

Hodge glanced up. "I appreciate your help with the barn roof."

"Glad to help." The old man nodded toward the little dormer room tucked under the eaves. "Especially now that you've added a place for me to sleep when the winter snows start."

Hodge grinned. "I thought you might like to be high and dry come winter. What's that you're hiding behind your back?"

"Flowers for Miss Molly."

"Why didn't you say so?" Hodge turned toward the house. "Come on."

The two men started across the yard.

Halfway to the house they were met by Flora, dressed in a brand-new pale yellow gown. Her dark eyes were as big as saucers. "Papa Hodge, wait'll you see Mama Molly."

"Is she dressed already?"

"Uh-huh. And she let all of us help her. I got to tie her sash."

"Not too tight, I hope." Hodge winked, and the little girl's eyes danced with laughter. It was clear that she shared his wicked sense of humor.

The little girl raced ahead and slammed into the kitchen. "Mama Molly! Addison's here. Come see what he brought you."

Molly walked down the hall toward the kitchen. When she stepped through the doorway, the old man smiled, a wide, toothless grin. "Oh, now, Miss Molly, don't you look pretty."

"Thank you, Addison."

Behind him, Hodge went very still at the sight of her. She wore her hair long and loose, tumbling down her back in a cascade of curls the way he loved it. Her gown was a spill of white lace that fell to her ankles. It had a high neckline and long, tapered sleeves. She looked, he thought, like an angel, and he was reminded of the first time he'd seen her. His angel of mercy.

Was that when he'd first lost his heart?

It occurred to him that he'd been foolish to fight these feelings. They were bigger than life. Deeper than death. She was, quite simply, his destiny.

Molly saw the look on his face and felt her heart trip over itself. He had only to look at her and she grew as weak and fluttery as a newborn calf. Would it always be this way?

"These are for you." Addison thrust an armload of wild roses into Molly's hands.

"Oh, Addison, they're lovely." She buried her face in the flowers and inhaled their perfume.

Hodge lifted his tumbler. "You'll be the first to toast my beautiful bride."

"It would be my pleasure." Addison lifted his glass. "Here's to a long and happy life together."

"I'm looking forward to it." Molly smiled at the two of them. "As soon as everyone's here, Reverend Dowd will perform the ceremony out in the yard. Will you stay, Addison?"

He gave a shake of his head. "Too many people. I'll

watch from the edge of the forest. This is enough ceremony for me."

Delia and Charity came dashing across the yard that separated the barn from the house, where they'd been watching from the hayloft. "They're coming! We can see half a dozen or more wagons heading this way."

At her announcement Addison drained his tumbler and set it aside. As he turned to leave Hodge pressed a cigar into his hands.

The old man tucked it into his pocket with a grin. "Well, now, I'll enjoy this later if you don't mind."

Long before the first of the wagons began pulling up in the yard, he had melted into the woods.

The Wisconsin countryside was ablaze with autumn color. Trees of deepest red and orange and purple were reflected in the placid waters of the lakes and streams. The ground was carpeted with lush color. The days were golden; the nights had turned crisp. And on this special day, the sunshine was almost blinding.

It looked as though the entire town of Delight had made the journey to the O'Brien farm to witness the marriage of spinster Molly O'Brien to the ruggedly handsome former U.S. marshal Hodge Egan.

As each family emerged, the women began laying out an assortment of food for the potluck supper. Hodge had butchered a calf, and it was roasting over a pit. Makeshift tables of long planks held an assortment of Molly's finest cheeses, as well as fancy potatoes, garden vegetables, breads, and cakes and pretty desserts. Annabelle Whitney had brought her famous strawberry preserves. Carleton Chalmers had brought a supply of exotic canned goods from his mercantile, considered quite a delicacy by these simple farm women. Martha Teasdale had outdone herself, with a whole ham, deviled eggs, and her famous biscuits.

Molly had been sewing for weeks to make the new dresses that each of her girls were wearing. Flora was in buttercup yellow that set off her dark eyes and wild, gypsy curls. Charity had chosen sky blue, to her match her eyes. Delia wore softest spring green. And Sarah, as her aunt's maid of honor, was wearing pale, shimmering lilac.

While the women sat in the sunlit yard and shared gossip and waited for the ceremony to begin, the men joined Hodge behind the barn for a smoke and a drink.

Reverend Dowd, wearing his stiff black Sunday suit, arrived with his wife and daughters. Molly's girls were delighted to share the company of girls their own age, and were soon engaged in a game of hide-and-seek among the trees.

When the Schroeder wagon rolled into the yard, Sarah watched from beneath lowered lashes as Samuel climbed down. He'd grown muscular from his farm chores, and was now almost as tall as his father. When he caught Sarah staring, he blushed and looked away quickly, and Sarah did the same.

The banker Cyrus Keating arrived with his wife and little boys, and they were soon followed by Police Chief Dan Marlow and his deputy.

Behind the barn Carleton Chalmers accepted a tumbler of whiskey from Hodge. "You've snagged yourself a fine woman."

Hodge smiled. "I'm a lucky man."

Cyrus joined them and leaned close to accept a light

for his cigar. He emitted a wreath of smoke before saying, "Some thought she was wrong to take on so many orphans. Especially those that weren't kin. But she's done a fine job making a home here."

"At least you know you'll never go hungry." Chief Marlow joined their circle. "Your woman makes the finest cheese in Wisconsin."

Your woman.

Hodge found himself standing very still, while the conversation swirled around him.

Had there ever been two more beautiful words?

He set aside his whiskey and started away.

From behind he could hear the jumble of voices.

"Now where do you suppose Hodge is off to?"

The police chief's voice held a hint of humor. "I'm betting he just got cold feet."

"Not a chance." Cyrus Keating chuckled. "That might be true for some men, but I got a look at his face. I'd say he just wants to get his woman alone before all those old hens take over the celebration."

Hodge walked past the rest of the men without even seeing them. He pushed his way through the crowds of children, past the women exchanging gossip, and made his way to the parlor, where Molly was seated on the sofa, talking quietly to her girls, who sat in a circle around her.

They looked up in surprise.

Sarah started to bar his way. "Aunt Molly said you'd stay with the men until it was time for the vows."

"I need to be here."

"But . . ."

"It's all right, Sarah." Molly stood and crossed to him. "Have you changed your mind, Hodge?"

"Is that what you think?" He kept his hands at his sides, afraid to touch her. If he did, he was afraid he might just pick her up and carry her away to some private place, away from all the noise, the fuss, the crowds.

"Then why do you need to be here?"

"I had to see you." His gaze moved over her, from the tumble of fiery hair, to those wide, trusting eyes; from the long column of white lace to the tips of her brand-new high-top shoes peeking beneath the hem.

He knew his voice trembled, but he forced himself to say what was in his heart. "Do you know how beautiful you are, Molly? How very special you are?"

She reached a hand to his cheek. "Why don't you tell me?"

He closed his hand over hers. "When my sister, Hildy, died, I figured I'd spend the rest of my life alone. I didn't know how to belong to anyone but myself. That's why I nurtured that foolish dream of living the life of a gambler in San Francisco. It was better to reach for something I knew I could have, than to try for something so far above me." He kept his eyes steady on hers. "You're the best thing, the very best, that's ever happened to me. I'm not much of a farmer, but I'll make you the best damned husband anyone's ever seen. And though I don't know much about females, I'll be the best father I can be to our girls. Molly, I give you my word—"

She placed a finger on his lips to stop him. "Do you know what you just said?"

"I give you my word . . ."

She shook her head. "You said our girls. Ours. They're no longer just mine, but ours. And that means the world to me."

Martha Teasdale popped her head in the door and called, "The preacher's waiting."

Molly stood on tiptoe to brush a kiss over Hodge's lips. "It's time for our girls to see their parents get married. Unless you've had a change of heart."

"Not on your life." He drew her close and kissed her long and slow and deep. "I wouldn't miss this for the world."

They stood, arms around each other, before turning to include the four who had gathered around them, beaming with delight.

"You heard your papa," Molly said with a laugh. "It's time for some promises."

Flora tugged on Hodge's pant leg. "Do we have to make a promise, too?"

"I don't see why not." He picked her up, so that her eyes were level with his. "After all, we're in this together."

Charity was clinging tightly to Molly's skirt. "I don't want to have to speak in front of all those people."

"Then you don't have to." Molly caught the little girl's hand.

Afraid to be left out, Delia stepped between Molly and Hodge and caught both their hands.

"What about Sarah?" Flora asked.

Molly brushed a kiss over Sarah's cheek. "You're the oldest, so you'll lead the way."

With a look of pride Sarah walked down the steps and out into the bright sunlight, with the rest of her family following. With the entire town of Delight watching, Molly and Hodge, with their daughters like pretty flowers around them, spoke their vows in clear tones.

Afterward, they walked among their friends and neighbors, accepting congratulations while they ate and drank.

Someone struck up a fiddle, and someone else had a mouth organ, and soon all were on their feet, dancing.

Hodge danced with Sarah and Delia, with Charity and Flora, much to the delight of the crowd. He shared a square dance with Martha Teasdale, and a step dance with Annabelle Whitney. And finally, when he took Molly into his arms and began to dance, the crowd stepped back to give them some room.

"Hello, Mrs. Egan." He dipped his head to brush a kiss over her cheek and felt the way his blood heated. "I've waited a lifetime for you."

"Me, too." Molly dimpled, and noticed how perfectly she fit into the circle of his embrace.

"Did you notice Sarah?"

At his question, Molly glanced over to see Sarah and Samuel Schroeder dancing.

Though they kept a respectable distance between them, and looked a bit awkward, there was a flush on their cheeks and a look in their eyes that was unmistakable.

"Young love." Molly sighed. "It's a very special thing."

"So is old love." Hodge was watching her in that way that had her heartbeat racing like a runaway wagon. "Do you think we could hurry our guests back to town?"

"Hodge."

"Sorry." He nuzzled her cheek. "But I can't wait to get you alone." He glanced toward the barn. "I have an idea."

Seeing the direction of his glance she began laughing. "I just bet you do."

"Our special hideaway. Up in the loft. One hour. Whether our guests are gone or not. By then, they'll have enough whiskey in them that they won't even miss us."

"Hodge Egan, you're incorrigible."

"That's what you love about me."

"It's true." As they kept time to the music, Molly's laughter rang on the evening air.

She couldn't wait to spend the rest of her life with this man. It had been such a long journey from her little farm in Ireland to this wilderness in Wisconsin. From aunt to mother. From lonely spinster to wife. But every step of the journey had been preparing her for this. And she was certain, as her grandma had always told her, that the best was yet to come.

Turn the page for a preview of the
next historical romance from
Maureen McKade

A REASON TO BELIEVE

Coming soon from Berkley Sensation!

WITH SUPPER ON the stove and Madeline taking a nap, Dulcie went out to the porch to clean the vegetables she'd taken from the garden earlier. She paused to watch Forrester washing up by the well, using the dented tin basin, soap, and threadbare towel that she'd put there for his use. With her floppy hat shading her eyes, she glanced over to see that he'd finished replacing the corral poles and had chopped the old ones into firewood. Impressed again by his labor, she managed a slight smile when he looked over at her.

Taking a seat at the top of the porch steps, she tried to ignore him, but could see his movements at the edge of her vision. Picking up a carrot, she trimmed it and tossed the greens into a tub. She'd only done a few carrots when she felt more than saw him approaching. Her fingers tightened on the knife handle.

"Mrs. McDaniel," he said by way of greeting.

Steeling herself, she met his steady blue eyes. "Mr. Forrester. I see you've finished for the day."

"I figured it was too late to start something new. Hope you don't mind."

How could she mind? She had never expected him to be such a hard worker, given his pay. She shook her head. "As long as the work gets done."

Dulcie kept her focus on the carrots as she continued to lop off the tops, but the strength of his perusal sat heavy on her.

"Got another knife?" he suddenly asked.

She jerked her head up. "What?"

"If you have another knife, I can give you a hand."

She thought of the dull, worthless knives in the cabin and shook her head. "I don't need any help."

He shrugged. "I don't mind. I'm not used to being idle."

It struck her that someone like him shouldn't have any problem finding a paying job, rather than working for only room and board. However, she shied away from that thought, unwilling to look too closely lest she lose the badly needed help.

She shrugged. "Suit yourself. If you're bent on doing something, you can snap the ends off the beans."

He grinned. "I haven't done that in years."

She snagged the large kettle that she'd put the beans in and handed it to him. He took it and lowered himself to a step, setting the kettle on the ground.

From her position above him, Dulcie could see his long fingers pick up a bean and snap one end off, then the other, tossing the ends into the tub with the carrot tops.

"Looks like you haven't lost your touch," she commented.

"The orphanage used to have a huge garden. All of us kids had to take care of it." He kept his head turned to his task so Dulcie couldn't see his expression, only the top of his damp hair. "If one of us didn't do our share, we couldn't eat. It didn't take many missed meals to get us to work."

Intrigued in spite of herself, Dulcie asked, "How many children were in the orphanage?"

A shrug of his broad shoulders. "Numbers changed, but usually anywhere from twenty to thirty."

"Did many get adopted?"

"Some. Mostly bigger kids who could do the work on a farm or ranch."

"What about you?"

He grinned boyishly. "I was a skinny one. Those who came looking for a boy said I was too small, wouldn't be able to pull my weight."

Dulcie stopped cutting in midmotion and studied his broad shoulders, wide, strong hands, and the muscles that flexed beneath his tanned forearms. She couldn't imagine him as skinny or small. "These people who came to adopt didn't want children to love?"

Forrester chuckled, but it wasn't a pretty sound. "Maybe a few of them did, but mostly they just wanted cheap labor. At least I was spared that."

Dulcie continued her work, but her mind sifted through what Forrester had said and, more importantly, hadn't said. Her memory flashed back to the sad orphan girl. "How old were you when you got put in the orphanage?"

Forrester paused, his motions stilled. "Six. I had two older brothers. Creede was sixteen so he didn't have to go there. Slater was eleven."

His voice was even, almost flat, but Dulcie had the impression his control was hard-earned. "At least you had Slater," she said.

"Not for long. Someone took him away a few months after we got there." He resumed his task and snapped off the ends of a handful of beans before speaking again. "I haven't seen either of my brothers in nearly twenty-five years."

Dulcie gasped, unable to imagine having family but not knowing where they were or even if they were still alive. In spite of her father's drunkenness, he'd been family. "I'm sorry, Mr. Forrester."

He glanced at her over his shoulder. "Call me Rye. And no need for you to be sorry, ma'am. It was a long time ago, and I've made my own way."

Ill at ease and uncertain what to say, Dulcie finished lopping off the carrot tops. "I can give you a hand with those beans."

Forrester—Rye—set the pan on a step where they could both reach. As they worked, the quiet snaps blended with birdsong and the far-off barking of a dog. Occasionally, a hawk's haunting cry echoed down from the hot blue sky.

"So what about you?" Rye asked. "You live here all your life?"

"Most of it," Dulcie replied, uncomfortable talking about herself.

"When did your ma die?"

"Pa said about a couple of years ago." Fresh anguish

squeezed her lungs, bringing a lump to her throat, which she cleared with a cough. "I wasn't here."

"Were you with your husband?"

Dulcie's defenses, which had lowered, slammed back into place. "Yes."

"I didn't mean to pry, ma'am." Obviously he'd picked up on her renewed guardedness. "I just figured since you said you were a widow."

She relaxed only slightly. Too accustomed to men wanting but one thing from a woman, she had to watch her words. "He was in the army. Died about five months back."

"So you came back here."

It wasn't a question, but she nodded. She kept her focus on her hands as she worked, afraid if she caught his eye, he'd ask more questions. Questions like how had her husband died and what kind of man had he been and how she'd made the journey back home.

Time lengthened and Dulcie finally breathed a sigh of relief when it appeared he wasn't going to continue his interrogation. He might be merely curious, but she couldn't take that risk. Her failures were her own, not things to be held up in the light of day to gain pity or charity. Or to be used against her.

"I'll check on supper. Could you get rid of the greens?" she asked.

Rye nodded. "I'll give them to the livestock, then wash the carrots and beans."

"Thank you." She rose and dusted off the seat of her breeches, then hurried into the house. The potatoes were boiling, as were the peas and corn. All she had left to do was fry the salt pork and slice the bread.

She got Madeline up so the girl had time to wake and wash up before eating. Twenty minutes later the meal was ready and Dulcie had settled Madeline at the table. Before she joined her daughter, she carried Rye's meal out to him.

Rye had swept the porch and only the two pans of washed carrots and beans remained.

"Thanks for taking care of those," she said stiffly.

"It wasn't any hardship, ma'am." He accepted the tray from her. "Smells good."

"Salt pork," she stated with a shrug. "It's all we have for meat."

"Did your father hunt?"

"He used to, but not since Madeline and I came."

"What about you?"

She shook her head. "I never learned, and even if I had, I wouldn't have trusted Pa to stay sober long enough to watch Madeline."

"If you can spare me, I'll go out tomorrow morning and see what I can find," Rye said.

She'd hoped he might offer, but she was unable to bend her pride to give him her gratitude even though guilt twinged her conscience. "As long as you aren't gone all day."

"Yes, ma'am."

She couldn't tell if he was mocking her or not.

"Done eating, Ma," Madeline shouted.

Saved by her daughter's call, Dulcie fled back into the cabin.

That night, after the dishes were washed and Madeline was asleep, Dulcie settled in the old rocking chair, a tin cup in her hand. Silence filled the darkness and with it came the familiar emptiness.

Memories filled the void, chilling her with their mocking accusations. She lifted the cup to her lips and welcomed the whiskey's heat that burned her throat and belly, and dulled the voices for a little while.

PREDAWN FOUND RYE riding away from Mrs. McDaniel's place. His mare, unaccustomed to days of inactivity, tugged at the reins and Rye let the horse gallop down the road. He closed his eyes to fully appreciate the cool morning breeze against his face. After three months of endless days where there had been only dank, stale air, Rye had sworn he'd never again take anything as simple as a morning ride for granted.

It was good to be away from the woman and her daughter, if only for a few hours. It was tough keeping up his pretense of not knowing Mrs. McDaniel's husband. The lie of omission grated on his conscience, but he was convinced he'd done the right thing in keeping the truth from her. The proud woman wouldn't have accepted his help otherwise.

Two hours later, he had two rabbits skinned and tucked into the flour sack tied to his saddle horn. He'd spotted signs of deer, but never had a decent shot. With his money and supplies low, Rye didn't want to waste even one rifle cartridge.

As he headed back to the cabin, his horse suddenly shied and Rye, lulled by the morning's warmth and peacefulness, was nearly unseated. Regaining control, he patted the mare's neck and glanced around to see what had spooked her. A flash of color not twenty feet away caught his attention.

"Who's out there?" he yelled.

Leaves rustled and a group of finches rose up not far away, startled by something. Unwilling to let go of the mystery, Rye dismounted and looped Smoke's reins about a nearby branch. He ducked under branches and pushed through spiny brush.

"Who's out here?"

Even as he called out, Rye cursed himself for being ten kinds of a fool. If it was someone who had nothing to hide, he would've answered him. If the stranger didn't want to be found, Rye was probably going to be shot for his trouble or, at the very least, have his horse stolen.

Hoping he hadn't gotten smart too late, Rye retraced his steps back to his mare. He spotted a figure standing by Smoke and drew his revolver. As he neared the opening, he realized the person was very small or very young. Or both. Then he recognized the too short and oft-mended overalls. He stuck his revolver back in his holster and strode through the brush, not bothering to mask his approach.

"What're you doing out here, Collie?" he asked.

The boy who worked at the bathhouse shrugged as he continued to stroke the mare. "I'm out here a lot. I heard the shots. Looks like you was hunting."

Rye had to take a moment to process the boy's seemingly unrelated statements. "I wanted some fresh meat."

"You mean you and the widow?"

Rye pressed his hat back off his forehead and crossed his arms. "So how do you know I'm working for her?"

"I seen ya."

Mrs. McDaniel's farm was three miles from town. "Why have you been out there?"

Another indolent shrug. "Nothin' else to do. Ain't many folks that use the bathhouse."

"What about school?"

He wrinkled his nose. "Don't like it."

"What about the family you're staying with? Don't they worry about you?"

"Why?" Collie seemed genuinely curious. "It ain't like the Gearsons is my real folks. They only took me in 'cause they said it was their Christian duty."

Rye considered the boy's words. He'd known people like the Gearsons and oftentimes their Christian duty included working the adopted children like slaves under the guise of teaching them a work ethic. He fought down a wave of anger. "Do they give you chores to do?"

"Nah."

Startled, Rye tried to see past Collie's indifference. "None?"

"The other kids do 'em. I'm just underfoot."

The way Collie said "underfoot" made Rye suspect the Gearsons used the term a lot around the orphan. "So they don't miss you when you're gone?"

"Hard enough to keep track o' their own."

Rye eyed the boy's skinny frame. "They feed you?"

Collie turned his back to Rye and rubbed the horse's nose. "Yeah."

Something told him the kid wasn't being entirely truthful, but he didn't want to push him too hard. "Want a ride back to town?"

Collie spun around, his eyes wide. "Sure, mister."

"The name's Rye, remember?"

"Sure, Mr. Rye."

Smiling, Rye mounted his mare. He leaned down to grab Collie's wrist and hauled him up to sit on the horse's rump behind him. "Hold on to me."

Collie wrapped his thin arms around him, and Rye tapped Smoke's sides.

"You ever ridden before?" Rye asked the boy.

"My pa used to let me sit in front of him."

Collie's wistful tone stirred Rye's own memories. "When did your folks die?"

" 'Bout a year ago."

"Do you have any brothers or sisters?"

"I had a little brother, but he got sick and died when he was a baby."

So Collie was alone.

"How many children do the Gearsons have?"

"Seven."

Rye was surprised a couple with that many of their own would offer to care for an orphan. "You like them?"

He felt Collie's shrug. If Collie spent so much time roaming around alone, it was doubtful he did much with the Gearson children.

"Mrs. Gearson was Ma's friend. She said she was obla . . . obla—"

"Obligated?" Rye guessed.

"Yeah. Obligated to take care of me. Mr. Gearson didn't want to." Collie tightened his hold around Rye's waist. "At least he don't hit me."

And for a young boy alone that was probably the best

he could do. Rye patted the boy's arm. "You mind stopping at Mrs. McDaniel's place before we go into town?"

Collie stiffened. "Don't want to."

"But you said you've been there already. This way you can meet the widow and her little girl."

"No!" Collie released Rye and wiggled backward off the horse, dropping to the ground.

Rye halted Smoke and turned to see the boy climbing to his feet, his eyes wide. "Why'd you do that?"

Collie merely shook his head, his shaggy hair falling across his eyes. He shoved the strands back and, without a word, turned and fled.

"Collie," Rye shouted. "Come back here. Collie!"

Only the sound of crashing brush answered him. Rye was worried about the boy, but he knew that if Collie didn't want to be found, Rye wouldn't stand a chance of locating him.

Why was he frightened of Mrs. McDaniel?

The answer was plain to see. Collie probably feared her for the same reason the townsfolk shunned her. She was the daughter of a supposed murderer.

Enter the rich world of *historical romance* with Berkley Books.

Lynn Kurland

Patricia Potter

Betina Krahn

Jodi Thomas

Anne Gracie

Love is timeless.
penguin.com